DEVIL ON MY TRAIL

DANIEL DIFRANCO

an encyclopedia over waves of bourbon and Philly sewage before you know it. And you will lap it up. And you will like it. *Devil On My Trail* takes you on an otherworldly vision quest, possessing you with a rhythm that teaches you how to serve the song and own the stage all at once."

–Claire Hopple, author of *Echo Chamber*

Dedicated to Ellie Miller,
for whom I would sell my soul

DEVIL ON MY TRAIL

PRESENT: KUNG FU NECKTIE, PHILADELPHIA: I FOUND THE SIMPLE LIFE AIN'T SO SIMPLE

My hand slipped when Mary or Margaret or whatever her name was winked at me. I was onstage finishing the final song of my band's set when I played the secret chord. The same one Jimi Hendrix knew. The same one Robert Johnson found. The one Keith Richards' ghost showed me years ago. I swore I'd never play it, but since he showed me, it was always lying there, a sore tooth waiting to be tongued.

Nothing happened just then. It didn't work that way from the little I understood. Lots of guys play the secret chord by mistake without knowing it. But I knew it—desire lie in my heart—and that's all that mattered. A force surged through me, a bell tolling once. Something bad was going to happen.

The audience cheered, and the hot smell of bourbon and cigarettes hit my nose. The rattle of chains. Keith Richards was beside me.

"Jesus Christ," I said.

"Not by a longshot," Keith said. "I told you not to play the bloody thing."

I waved to the audience, thanked them. They wanted an encore.

I turned my head to Keith. "Why'd you show me the fucker to begin with?" I whispered.

Keith Richards shrugged. "Let's call it a momentary lapse of reason." He reached over and twisted my guitar's G string back in tune.

My drummer clicked off our encore number. Keith snapped his fingers and did a jig off to the side of the stage. Then he disappeared.

He's been doing that ever since I was fourteen.

2. EIGHT YEARS AGO: AWAKE, SHAKE DREAMS FROM YOUR HAIR

Marc sat on the edge of his bed with a beat-up guitar, a student model Fender Stratocaster his uncle gave him for his 13th birthday last year. The week his parents died. Marc played the shit out of that guitar. The frets were worn down and the top two strings buzzed past the ninth fret. The volume knob had long disappeared, and the guitar barely kept in tune.

Marc ran some scales to warm-up, but quickly got bored and started riffing on a blues lick his teacher showed him. The strings were dirty and dead—muted steel fighting for sustain. He cranked the amp to compensate and began playing "Start Me Up." A string broke mid-riff, and he got on his knees and pressed the guitar into the face of his amplifier creating a loop of feedback à la Kurt Cobain.

"Marc!" his aunt yelled up the stairs, but she might as well have been screaming into a vacuum.

His door burst open. "Marc!"

His aunt in her bathrobe, bags under her eyes, stood in the doorway. He stopped. The guitar squawked a death screech as he turned the amp off.

"It's 8:30 in the fucking morning," she said. "What's the matter with you?"

Marc shrugged and set his guitar down. "It wasn't that loud," he mumbled.

"We talked about this. No guitar before 11 on the weekends."

"Sorry," he mumbled again.

His aunt left the room, slamming the door. She wasn't a bad person, but Marc could never shake the feeling that he was a guest in her house—hedging on being an unwanted one.

Marc grabbed his phone and earbuds off his dresser and flopped down on his bed. He put on *Exile on Main St.* and looked at the poster of The Rolling Stones at Altamont his uncle gave him with the guitar. *It was chaos. Danger. Rock and roll and free love gone too far. The man isn't the only one out to fuck you given the chance. Don't give anyone the chance*—his uncle warned him during that first week after the accident, the gifts and words his clumsy way of trying to comfort Marc. And that's as far as that conversation and consolation went. Still, it was a welcome diversion. Marc had never played electric guitar before. His studies from age six to thirteen had been classical. Etudes, scale studies. Repertoire for the concerts at the local conservatory. He had his eyes on Curtis in Center City. But after his parents died, the classical guitar went in the closet. He enjoyed the raw power and vibration and noise and freedom the electric guitar gave him though he couldn't articulate why.

Marc reached under his bed and pulled out an old shoebox he used to keep trinkets— guitar picks, a note from a girl he liked, a spork he drew a face on and called "Sporkman," a picture of his parents from their trip to The Wizarding World of Harry Potter, a wad of money— his total savings. He counted. 623 dollars. Same as last night. The most money he'd ever seen. He spent the odd bit here and there on movies or bus fare, but he excised most expenses to save for a new guitar. His friends made fun of him and said he was probably the first person to carry around a reusable water bottle in the name of rock and roll.

Today he would go to the local guitar shop and buy a new guitar. He'd dreamt of this since he saw an all-white Strat in the shop window last year—the same kind Hendrix played at Woodstock.

He closed his eyes and rocked his head as "Rip This Joint" started. The up-tempo blues number catapulted itself into his ears. Piano jangling along the galloping guitar—Jagger's vocals tearing the seam off the top.

"That one'll keep ya on yer toes," a voice said, creeping under the earbuds from somewhere outside.

Marc bolted upright, his headphones yanked out of his ears, money flying through the air like feathers, the contents of the box spilling to the ground.

He looked around the room.

"Over here, sonny," the voice said again.

Marc turned around and Keith Richards was lying on his bed, just beside him. Marc jumped up and crashed into his dresser.

"What the shit…what…shit?" Marc gasped. He peed his pants just the tiniest bit.

Keith Richards lit a cigarette and tucked the lighter away in his pocket.

"It's all right," Keith said. "It's all right." His voice was charcoal—vocal cords vibrating against each other like dried out chains in a smokehouse.

"What…how…," Marc managed, again. "Wh…"

"Relax," Keith said and sat up and swung his legs over the other side of the bed. He stood up and went over to Marc's guitar. He picked it up. Examined it. "This won't do, eh?" He looked at Marc. He flicked his cigarette and the ashes fell to the carpet, and then he put the cigarette between his teeth. Keith played a lick on the guitar. "She did the job, though." Keith held the guitar out to Marc. "Show me what you got, kid."

Marc fainted.

***

When Marc came to, he was lying on the floor on top of his money and scattered items from the shoebox. He saw a little pile of ashes next to his guitar. He sat up, quick, and looked around the room. Keith Richards was gone. Marc rubbed his eyes and checked under the bed. On the other side. The closet. He was alone. He picked up his money and smeared the ashes into the carpet with his sneaker. He checked the time on his phone. It was 11:02. The music shop was open. He changed his underwear and shoved his money into his front pants pocket.

On the way to the shop, he convinced himself he had dreamt Keith Richards in his room. Not enough sleep he told himself. A hallucination. Made it up. Just to be safe, he checked the news. 2009. Keith Richards was still alive. Couldn't have been a ghost. Still, the ashes.

He tried not to think about it and put on a Them Crooked Vultures album.

***

The music shop, Coval's, was run by an old man—Coval himself. He'd owned the place since time immemorial. The old man always had the stump of a cigar in his mouth. Sometimes he'd light it up mid-lesson.

Marc's aunt and uncle kept him in lessons, and once they realized it was cheaper than a babysitter, they booked him Monday through Friday. Marc went to the shop after school, and his uncle would pick him up late, usually when the shop closed, really milking the shop's generosity and compassion towards Marc. He could just hang out there and practice or do his homework or whatever as long as he wasn't getting into trouble.

Marc switched from studying classical guitar that summer his parents died and waded into rock and jazz. All unchartered terrain for him. He receded into guitar and music. It was his cocoon—security blanket. A new way forward.

Marc pushed the door open and was greeted by the familiar scent of wood, cigar smoke, and dust. A little bell tied to the handle rattled.

"A minute," Old Man Coval yelled from the back room. It was the same every time. The old man would take his sweet ass time getting out to the front. Marc leaned against the counter and admired the white Strat—a used reissue of the one Jimi Hendrix played. Someone had put a bunch of stickers on it, and the body was scratched up, but for half the price of a new one, Marc was willing to forgive the blemishes.

Marc smelled smoke. Then bourbon—a smell and taste he wouldn't soon forget after sneaking two big swallows recently when his aunt and uncle went out for the evening. He thought he'd be like the rock legends he'd read about and get all boozed up and play his guitar. He ended up getting sweaty and throwing up.

The sound of the door rattling.

Marc looked over. It was closed.

He looked towards the back room where he expected to see Old Man Coval emerge. Keith Richards was standing in the doorway smoking a cigarette. He winked at Marc. Marc's heart stopped, and as soon as it did, the old man walked through the doorway, through Keith Richards, and into the showroom.

"What's a matter?" Old Man Coval asked. "You all right, Marky?"

Marc swallowed hard. "Uh, yeah, fine. I'm fine."

"Want to see her again?" Coval motioned towards the case.

Marc nodded.

He looked at Keith Richards. Then back at Coval. "I want to buy her."

"That one's shite," Keith Richards said.

The old man went to the case and took down the guitar. He handed it to Marc. "There you go," he said.

"Don't buy that one," Keith Richards growled. "Cheap knock-off." He went over to a case behind the counter and stuck his hand through the glass and fiddled around with some price tags.

"Tell him you want this one," Keith said and pointed towards the case.

Marc wiped the bead of sweat that formed on his brow.

"Go, on. Tell him," Keith said again.

"Actually, uh," Marc stammered, "can I try that one over there?"

Marc pointed towards the case where Keith Richards was standing.

"A Telecaster?" the old man asked. "Hmph. Thought you were a Strat-man." He moved slowly around to the case. "Which one?"

"The blonde," Keith Richards said.

"The blonde," Marc said.

The old man laughed to himself. "More of a redhead man myself, but different strokes." Coval took out the butterscotch blonde Telecaster. "Just came in yesterday. Almost didn't take it, but the fella looked like he could use the money." He looked at the price tag. "That doesn't seem right," he said more to himself than Marc.

Keith Richards took a drag of his cigarette and blew it in Old Man Coval's face.

"But, I guess that's what it says," Coval said, dazed.

"Give him your money," Keith Richards said.

Marc handed over the money to Old Man Coval.

"She's a banger," Keith said.

"She comes with a case," Old Man Coval said.

"She always comes with a case," Keith Richards said and laughed to himself, guttural.

Old Man Coval took Marc's money and counted it. He gave him back $312 and then sauntered off to the back of the shop.

Keith Richards hopped on the counter and sat with his legs crossed. "She's the one."

"Are you a ghost? Keith Richards isn't dead," Marc said.

"Everybody's got a ghost, kid. Don't need to be dead to have a ghost. Shit, some say I've been dead since '68. Might be more ghost than man by now anyway." Keith Richards flicked his cigarette on the ground. "Or, you're bonkers and making me up. You know, there was two loony bins in the town I grew up in. It's possible you're a figment of *my* imagination." He laughed a low, uncontrolled laugh—a garbage disposal full of bones. "Use the rest of that scratch to get a tuner pedal and some good cables. And lots of picks." Then he disappeared.

Old Man Coval brought out a beat-up hard-shell case and lay it on the counter. "This is the one," he said. "Congratulations. She's your responsibility now."

3. PRESENT: BACK AT KUNG FU NECKTIE: BEFORE THE MORNING COMES

After our set, I went out onto the floor to score a beer before the bar closed. Everyone was going to the after-party, and I told them I'd catch up with them later. The venue stocked the green room with Coors Banquet stubby bottles, which was way better than the cans of Hamm's we usually got, but the opening acts ripped through those while we played. The girl who winked at me, who was supposed to interview me for a local rock zine, was sitting on a stool, head down into her phone. I'd seen her around the clubs the past few months and we began recognizing each other. She had a killer smile and a laugh that floored me. There weren't too many black girls that hung out in the rock clubs, and the first few times I nodded or said hi were probably more to make me comfortable with trying to make her feel comfortable. Social politics aside, I found myself looking for her.

"Thanks for coming out," I said.

Nothing like starting a conversation with the default line you say to people you have nothing to say to. A thing you had already said a few hours prior before your set.

She turned to me. "I had to."

"Oh."

She rolled her eyes. "I'm fucking with you. I mean, I did have to, but I'm glad I did. You guys were awesome."

"Thanks," I said. And I don't know if it's because I was rattled from playing the secret chord, or from having a pretty girl say they liked my music, which is sort of like saying they liked me, but I added. "You too."

"What?"

"Sorry. That was a reflex."

"A premature appreciator. I'll have to keep that in mind."

"Funny."

"Soooo… your band. You. Let's talk."

I ordered a beer and pulled up a stool next to her. The bartender said he'd let us know when it was time to go. That he still had some cleaning and restocking to do. He took the drawer and went upstairs.

I was in the middle of telling Maybelline—her fucking name was Maybelline. Just like the Chuck Berry song. How did I forget that? I was in the middle of telling Maybelline how the band formed when a crack like a whip on a steel drum shot through the place and the stage began to crumble into the ground.

Smoke rose from the stage. The drums slid forward, and cymbals crashed against the amps that fell over and inward. The lighting system sparked blues and reds and greens. A vortex opened and the floorboards craned upward at the edges and all the gear and wires were sucked into the spiraling center.

"What the fuck!" Maybelline said as dust and rubble rolled across the floor towards us. We stood up, both at the same time, the bar stools jettisoned out from under us. And all in one beat, rattles, bourbon, cigarette smoke. "You better get out of here, kid," Keith Richards said, appearing beside me. "I'll take care of this." Keith Richards had a guitar with him. He'd never come to me with a guitar before.

I grabbed Maybelline's hand, or she grabbed mine, I can't remember, and we ran. I looked back and saw the image of a body floating out of the smoke. We made it out of the building through the back and into an alley. We kept moving away from the place and stopped at the end of the block.

"What the hell was that?" Maybelline asked, out of breath. "A gas explosion?"

She was already pulling her phone out of her pocket and dialing.

"I don't think that was a gas explosion," I said.

"It was something bad."

"My guitar," I said. "I left it in there. I have to go back."

Maybelline lowered the phone away from her mouth. "Are you fucking serious? It's not worth it." And then back into the phone, "Uh, there was a gas explosion…"

I sprinted back down the alley and threw open the door to the venue. I didn't smell gas. I made my way to the front of the house where the stage was.

And still was. Everything intact.

My guitar leaning against the bar right where we were sitting. Safe. The stools tucked up against each other. The bartender coming back into the room carrying a case of beer. Keith Richards sitting on the bar, his legs dangling, a cigarette in his right hand.

"That was a close one, bub," he said and laughed his short, low throated laugh. Sirens in the distance. "You should beat it."

I picked up my guitar and hurried back to Maybelline.

"You're ok. Thank God. That was fucking stupid," she said and hit me.

"Let's go," I said.

"The police are almost here."

"It'd be better if we aren't around when the police are. I'll explain."

We walked a few blocks to an all-night diner. It had rained earlier in the evening and the street was streaked with lights, green and red and white from the store signs. Christmas in August. I tried to explain to Maybelline that everything was fine, but I wasn't sure how to do that without giving up the ghost, so to speak.

At the diner I ordered a coffee. Maybelline ordered toast.

"Maybe we had a mass hallucination," I said.

"Two people can't have a mass hallucination. I know what I saw."

I thought that I could just leave. *Ok, the stage collapsed. Fine. Goodnight.* She'd find out later that it didn't and maybe forget about it, or maybe it'd haunt her, or maybe she'd think she just had one too many drinks. At least I'd be done with it, with her. Thing was I didn't want to be done with her. Didn't want to gaslight her either. And goddamnit, as stupid as it was, she smelled really nice.

"Ok," I said. "What I'm going to tell you is going to sound really fucking crazy."

"Try me," she said.

I took a deep breath. "I'm friends with Keith Richards." I couldn't believe I just told her that. I never told anyone. Not even my oldest friend and drummer, Bollocks. My closest friend. My brother by everything but blood. I wasn't sure if it was because I felt like I had a connection with Maybelline—that sometimes it's easier to tell a stranger your secrets. Maybe it was just dumb dude hormones. I didn't want to kiss Bollocks.

She stopped mid crunch on her toast. "That's *sooo* crazy. I'm pen pals with Bono. What are the odds?"

"I'm serious."

"Me too," she said, and smirked.

"There's more," I said. "Do you believe in ghosts or spirits?"

"Um. I don't know. Sort of, I guess?" She picked up her toast.

A fist against the window outside our booth pounded against the glass and I jumped, spilling my coffee. A flash of a mohawk through the reflection. Fucking Bollocks. He banged again and gave me the finger, the chains on his leather jacket rattling against the glass.

"Isn't that your drummer?" Maybelline asked.

"Yep."

He told everyone he was called Bollocks because The Sex Pistols were his favorite band, but the truth is I started calling him that after he got stuck climbing a fence in the eighth grade and had to have surgery. We joked that whenever he got laid (not that either of us were) he'd have to tell the girls to "never mind the bollocks."

He came into the diner and plopped down in the booth next to me.

"Dude, the club is crawling with the fuzz," he said. "I left my phone charger in the green room." He reached across the table and took a piece of Maybelline's toast and shoved it in his mouth. "There were firetrucks and ambulances," he said, crumbs shooting out of his mouth. "They wouldn't let me in. The barman was outside. Fucking baffled. Said someone called in a gas explosion."

"Everything's fine?" Maybelline asked.

"'Prank call' dude said." Bollocks shrugged. "I snuck in the back all stealthy like Gollum into Mordor." He smiled, toast toothed and crumb lipped, and held up a white phone charger.

4. TWENTY-THREE MINUTES PRIOR IN THE VENUE: NO MORE RED DOORS

A figure rose out of the smoking rubble of the stage. The silhouette of a man, a woman, a horned beast revolving.

Keith Richards approached the stage. "He's not ready yet," he said and played a lick on his guitar, a double stop on the 2nd and 3rd strings. Bent those fuckers up a whole step and a half.

"It isn't your decision," the figure said. "He called me."

"That was my fault," Keith said.

"We made a deal."

The form reached out to Keith, a hand, a claw. Keith Richards played an old Spanish tune, embellished it, made it his own— crawled his way up the neck to answer the phrase an octave higher. The figure recoiled and shrunk back.

"I need more time," Keith said, wrangling the notes out of his guitar like he was wrestling a snake.

"Time is not on your side," the figure said with the slightest hint of a laugh, and then vanished. The room back to normal. Sirens outside.

5. THE AFTER-PARTY AT BOLLOCKS' PLACE: WE WALK RIGHT THROUGH THE DOOR

Maybelline, Bollocks, and I went around to the after-party. Bollocks' loft on the top floor of a building he rented for next to nothing because two expressways and their respective off-ramps converged on the corner. We walked in and Bollocks put his arm around me and grabbed a bottle of beer from some guy near the door and took a swig from it and handed it to me.

"Hear ye, hear ye! Marcus Andronicus has arrived," he yelled to the room.

A few people looked over, but it was an otherwise unremarkable entrance. I ducked out from under Bollocks' arm.

"Dude, can I stash this in your room since we have practice tomorrow?" I said and lifted my guitar case.

"Of course," he said and took the case from me. He looked at Maybelline. "I'll leave you two alone," he said and raised his eyebrows twice and fast.

"I'll catch up with you," I said.

"You'll never catch me. I'm the gingerbread man," he said. He punched me in the arm and darted away to the other side of the apartment.

I set the bottle he gave me on the floor. I noticed the guy whose bottle it was glaring at me. One of his eyes was all black. I shrugged and put my hands up. The guy was stone, and he kind of creeped me out. "What year is your guitar? Where'd you get it?" he said, barely audible.

"What?"

"He's a fucking nut," Maybelline said pulling me away from the black eyed stone dude.

"Uh, yeah." I said, realizing she was talking about Bollocks. "Helluva drummer, though. Drink?"

"Shit yeah," she said.

The bathtub was filled with ice and cans of beer. We cracked two open and knocked them together.

"Cheers," I said.

"Cheers," she said. "So… the fucking stage."

"Let's go someplace and talk."

"We were someplace. We are someplace."

I took a long drink on my beer. I sighed.

"This is going to sound batshit," I said and looked around the room to make sure no one could overhear me. I leaned in towards Maybelline. "I think I invoked the Devil."

Maybelline stopped drinking her beer and made a *you've-got-to-be-fucking-kidding-me-if-you-expect-me-to-believe-that* face.

"I told you it was going to sound batshit," I said.

"The Devil? Like Lucifer? The I go by many names Al Pacino guy?"

"I think so."

"What does the Devil want to do with you?"

"I played the secret chord by accident when you winked at me. That's like the bat signal for the Devil. Well, for a musician anyway."

She had half a smile on her face. "The secret chord?"
"Yeah."

"The Devil?"

"Look, you saw what happened to the stage yourself."

"That magically didn't happen?"

"I think the word is supernatural. It's not really magic."

She shook her head.

"I'm not crazy," I said.

"I don't believe you," she said. "But, I don't not believe you either."

"That's a start."

"So, hypothetically, what does the Devil want with you? A white boy guitar player from Philly in a rock band?"

"Probably my soul." I felt ridiculous hearing myself say that. "I know it sounds insane. But that's his deal. Your soul for greatness. It started with Robert Johnson..."

"Jesus Christ. That's a myth invented by Son House," Maybelline said, cutting me off.

"You like Son House?"

"Not really, but what? A girl can't know about the blues?"

"I didn't say anything."

"Just because all the blues dads think Johnson is theirs, doesn't mean other people can't know shit."

"Who?"

"You know. Middle-aged guys who buy expensive gear, cover classic rock songs, and generally play hot licks to each other's drunk wives. Blues dads can usually be spotted by the circle-ness of their beards and how their eyes always drift below the collar," she said.

"Holy ghost of Christmas Yet to Come..."

Maybelline laughed. She hit my arm. Left her hand there for a second. "Okay. The Devil." Her hand dropped from my arm. "No offense, you're awesome—your band is awesome, but breaking through regionally doesn't exactly put you on the verge of greatness."

"Well, I didn't make a deal with the Devil. He likes to tease it out. First hit is free kinda thing," I said. "You think it's why we just headlined a sold-out show on a Thursday, and you're writing about us?"

Maybelline shook her head. "I don't know. A sold-out show and a write-up in a blog isn't much of a tease, is it?"

"Yeah. I guess you're right."

"Hey!" Bollocks yelled as he came crashing towards us. "Dude! Look," he said, barely stopping as he shoved his phone towards my face. I didn't have time to read the whole message. I caught a glimpse. XPN. Fest. Mainstage.

"We're on the fuckin' mainstage this weekend," he said. "Dawes dropped off the bill. John from the station wants us on before Beck at XPoNential! Before motherfucking Beck! Dude, let's bring back 'Devil's Haircut'!"

***

Bollocks went on about the gig and what songs we should play for a killer set. Maybelline finished her beer and when she was done said we should meet up the next day to finish the interview.

"Do you want me to walk you home?" I offered.

"Walk?" she said. "That's why there's Uber now. One more blockade against old-fashioned chivalric advances. You'll have to do better."

"Tomorrow?" I said.

"Hand," she said. I put out my hand and she wrote on it.

"Isn't writing old-fashioned?"

She didn't say anything and closed my hand, smiled, and left. I watched her walk away, and I felt like a schoolboy, my chest pounding a fuzzy counterpoint to the butterflies in my stomach.

I opened my hand and looked at her name and number. She dotted the 'i' in her name with a heart. Devil or not, it was a pretty good evening.

6. THERE AIN'T NO MIDNIGHT TRAIN

I left the party not much later and hopped on the El to take me across town. The train was pulling up and I didn't have my card handy, so I jumped the turnstile and darted inside the doors. I tried to play it cool, but it didn't matter since there was no one around to care either way. The car was about a half an hour too early to be the drunk train, and too late for the addicts to be nodded out across the seats. I took up a seat in the back of the train and closed my eyes.

"I think it's time we have a talk," Keith Richards said to me.

I opened my eyes. "You think? What the hell was that back there?"

"You know I made a deal with the Devil, and he's been on my trail for years. Ever since you called me. He can smell fresh meat."

"I thought you were being hyperbolic," I said. "And what's with this 'since I called you' shit? You showed up out of nowhere."

"Kid, you were knocking. It was in your bones. The records, the riffs, the posters, the dreams. You didn't know it, but you were calling. A branch blowin' against a window doesn't know it, but sometimes it gets blown too hard and the glass shatters." He took a drag off his cigarette. "You shattered the glass, bub."

The train screeched to a halt at the next stop. A lady in scrubs got in my car.

"Ok, so what?" I said to Keith.

The lady looked over at me.

"Sorry," I said to her. "I was talking to someone else."

She looked back down to her newspaper and put in her headphones.

"The problem is," Keith said, "you was asking to be chosen."

"To be haunted?"

"Ah, did more than haunt, now. Come on, kid, you know that."

There was a sadness in his eyes that I hadn't seen before. He was right though. He was like an older Uncle. Much older. Still, I was pissed at him.

"You showed me that fucking chord, and now the first time I play it, years later, the goddamn stage collapses and the Devil comes out of it. Yeah, I'd say you did a bit more." I was near yelling and the lady turned towards me again. I motioned that I was sorry again, but she stood up and went into the next car.

"Should've never shown you it. Thing is, I didn't know you then and thought, 'big deal. Save myself, pay what I owe and call it a life. One bluesman to the next.' But now I know it ain't as easy as all that. Nothing is with that bastard."

"What does he want?"

"My soul," Keith Richards took a drag off his cigarette. "And now yours."

"But I didn't make a deal."

"You were marked."

"By the Devil?"

Keith Richards flicked his cigarette. Ashes falling toward the sticky gray blue floor. He looked away. He exhaled the smoke from his ghost lungs. "Not exactly."

***

For the rest of the ride home and the 12-block walk after the train, Keith pleaded with me, explaining himself.

"I'm sorry, Marc," he said over and over—it becoming his mantra in between each layer of his confession.

Turns out that part of the deal he made with the Devil was to find another soul if he wanted to save himself. I gave him the cold shoulder after he pretty much told me he pegged me for the Devil so he could save his own ass. He rambled on, listing a bunch of famous people that got wrapped up with the Devil as if that would make it ok that he did too. As much as I tried to block him out, I was interested in the list.

Johnson, Jimi, Janis, Jobs.

Morrison, Monroe, Mozart.

Phoenix, Pac, The Big Bopper.

Colonel Sanders.

It was surprising how many people sold their souls for greatness. All the pressure that comes with it. It was too much, and with the Devil on their back it was amazing they lasted as long as they did.

I suppose in an attempt to win my favor with humor, he went on about lots of others you'd have thought for certain sold their souls—how else could it be explained? Turns out most were simply tragic cases of the culture at the moment, no Devil needed. Conan O'Brien tried to sell his soul but was turned away at the crossroads because he didn't have one to sell. He told me Kenny G made a deal, but Bolton did not.

"He's actually an angel," Keith said.

"Right," I said unlocking my door.

"I told you I'm gonna fix this. I've gotten out of plenty of jams. No reason I can't wiggle us out of this," Keith said, then mumbled, more to himself, "though, admittedly, this is a bit stickier than getting busted or kicking dope."

Keith made me a cup of herbal tea and put on my favorite work by Beethoven.

"Here you go, Marc," he said softly. I took the cup without saying anything.

He hummed along to the late string quartet. "Me mum used to play this for me." He stared off. "Listen," he said. "I readily confess that at first I didn't really give a shit and was just trying to protect my guitar. But that lasted for all of a minute. We've been mates for years now."

He sat down next to me. Lit a cigarette. "You know my story. You know about my past and the tragedies that have come my way. After meeting you I felt like I was given a second chance."

"At saving yourself?"

"No," he said into his hand holding the cigarette before taking a reticent drag. He exhaled. "My boys."

The air around us grew static.

"I should have been there for them more. I can't change the past, but I knew I could do right by you."

Keith had a son, Marlon, who was still alive. His upbringing was rough. Nomadic. I shifted on the couch and my arm got zapped where it met the upholstery. Keith used his thumb to wipe his cheek when he took another drag. I never saw a ghost or soul or whatever he was cry before, but fuck. This dude lived a charmed life and sold me down the river and he's the one crying?

"Keith…" I began. Then it struck me. Tara. Tara who died at 3 months old. Keith wasn't there at all. He was on the road. Played a gig in Paris the night he found out. That death had haunted him long before he met me.

"I'm gonna get you out of this, Marc," Keith said. "I'm not leaving you until I do."

I took a deep breath. Motherfucker. Besides Bollocks, he was the only constant in my life. Always looking over my shoulder. I put down my cup of tea. "I know," I said. And I did.

"Let's talk more tomorrow," I said. "We'll figure this out."

"Aye," he said. "Sweet dreams." He disappeared.

He's never bothered me when I was sleeping. I'll give him credit for that. He might be there when I wake up, but he always let me sleep and never showed up during my more private moments, alone or otherwise.

7. INTERLUDE: JUNE 13, 1964 – THE ROLLING STONES' FIRST US TOUR: BEAST OF BURDEN

The Stones were basically a glorified blues cover band. They had a gritty prowess for sure—they were a very good band, there's no denying that. But, they couldn't write a song worth shit. Truth is, their first hit, "I Wanna Be Your Man," was written by Lennon and McCartney. Jagger and Richards' first attempts at songwriting were modest, almost impotent numbers, if they weren't flat out saccharine garbage.

They had managed to turn out a ballad, "As Tears Go By," which was currently charting in the UK as the first single from the young Marianne Faithfull. But that only came to fruition after being locked in a kitchen by their manager until they had a song. That's not a sustainable model for songwriting.

They were halfway through the tour on their way to Detroit after playing Omaha. The shows were going well, but in his heart Keith Richards knew they had to start writing their own songs. They hadn't done bad for themselves, a bunch of white boys from England bringing the blues back to America. They hadn't done bad at all. But it couldn't last. The shelf-life of a popstar was 2 to 3 years max. Music had been Keith's life—his calling. If he intended on keeping it that way, he had to create instead of copy. This became apparent when they booked two days at Chess Studios in Chicago a few days earlier. Muddy Waters—*fucking Muddy Waters*—one of his heroes, the real deal, was doing maintenance and performing the duties of a roadie for the bands recording that day. If Muddy couldn't hack it on music alone, what chance did Keith have?

The Stones recorded fourteen tracks in two days. It wasn't shit, but it wasn't authentic either. Just more proof of how good of a blues cover band they were. Something was missing. A spark, originality. It rattled Keith. He felt a strange surge. Some magic left over from being in the same studio where great blues players laid their tracks. The thing with magic is that it doesn't last. He had to use it soon. It's all about timing—about capitalizing on the moment.

They left Omaha immediately after playing. Keith was unsettled for the whole gig—distant while they ripped through their set and dashed off the stage before the girls tore them to shreds. Mick had asked him what was wrong.

"Preoccupied," Keith said.

He was more than preoccupied. Consumed would be the more apt state of mind. It was the 13th. The Mississippi wasn't far. It was almost midnight.

They'd make Detroit by morning and check-in to a hotel to rest and conduct a radio interview before the show. Keith studied a map at a road stop earlier in the day. He convinced Ian Stewart, their factotum—road manager, driver, recording and live keyboard player, roadie, fellow jazz and blues aficionado, friend—to swing below Davenport to get close to the Mississippi on US 61. They wouldn't make the crossroads this trip, but they could ride the famed highway for a short while and pull over towards the great river that would eventually flow south, pulled down by gravity and inertia, towards Clarksdale, where the Devil supposedly came calling at midnight to those who looked for him.

They pulled over where the highway dipped under the city and rode close to the river. Charlie Watts and Bill Wyman were sleeping in the back seat. Brian Jones was nodding off and woke up only to pull a swig from a bottle of moonshine he had picked up somewhere. Mick Jagger was reading and smoking a cigarette.

"What're we stopping for?" Mick Jagger asked.

"Gotta piss," Keith Richards said.

Keith opened the door and stepped out onto the highway. He felt almost electric when his feet touched the ground. A pulse shot through his body. This was the circuit the bluesman traveled. Up and down the country, playing the juke joints. Shacking with a kind-hearted woman in each town. Robert Johnson. John Lee Hooker. Howlin' Wolf. All of them. How many times had each of them looked out into this very river and sang their blues?

The night was dark. It was 3 days past the new moon and only a sliver hung in the sky, barely illuminating the short walk over the grassy bank to the edge of the river. It was not a particularly hot day that day, and the air was still. The faint scent of the river, fresh and stale, turning over drifted towards Keith. He made his way to the edge of the Mississippi and unzipped. He pissed in the river and watched the arc twinkle in the dim moonlight and disappear in the calm waters.

"Hey," Mick yelled to Keith, running over towards him. "Is that the Mississippi?"

"Yeah," Keith said.

"Fucking right," Mick said and unzipped.

They stood there, the two of them pissing into the river. There's something primal about the act—something more than primal about doing it into a moving river as great as the Mississippi. It's giving a part of yourself back from where you came—looking up into the sky and feeling small yet connected to the universe. Keith thought it could be a metaphor for something, the journey he was on, but he knew why he was there, and it was almost midnight.

Mick zipped up. "Well, let's get to it."

"I'll catch up in a minute," Keith said. "I sprained my ankle on stage tonight."

"You're getting old." Mick laughed. "What a drag, mate."

Mick jogged back to the van. Keith checked his watch. Midnight. Nothing happened.

He walked along the bank of the river a few yards. He shook his head.

He let out a sigh.

"Fuck it," he said and turned around towards the van.

A breeze kicked up off the river and the tree branches rustled and the water lapped against the rocks behind him.

Keith felt the presence of something behind him. Someone lurking. He put his hand on the pistol sticking out of his waistband. The pistol he picked up in Texas. He turned around.

"You'll find no satisfaction from using that," a voice said.

Keith squinted. A figure moved towards him from under the tree, from out of the water. He couldn't tell. Then the man was there. Waxy and illumed. Shifting.

Keith kept his hand on the pistol, gripped tighter.

The figure laughed a short, slow laugh. "If it will make you feel safe. But, I bring no harm."

"Who are you?"

"You know who I am." The figure appraised Keith. Slowly. "You can already play. So, what is it?"

Keith looked into the eyes of the figure.

The horn honked from the van.

"Keith," Ian Stewart yelled over. "Let's go, mate."

Keith looked over at the van and waved weakly. He turned back towards the figure. Nothing but open river and sky.

8. PRESENT: FIDDLES IN THE DARK

In the morning, the first vague wisps of memory crept in as I opened my eyes and yawned. I looked at my hand. Maybelline. It all came back.

"Morning, kid," Keith Richards said, sitting on the windowsill, the light falling around him like he was the second coming, resurrected.

The kettle whistled and I turned off the stove. I ripped open a pack of instant coffee and dumped it into a mug. I almost convinced myself it was good after the economics of instant were proven.

"A mug of Earl Grey'll do ya better. Dash of milk," Keith said from across my small studio apartment. I looked over at him, and he looked gray, slightly translucent. Usually he was solid, but I figured it was the light playing with my eyes.

I drank my coffee. "I like this," I lied.

"I've been thinking," Keith said and hopped off the windowsill and came in the tiled area that designated the kitchen. "I can fix this."

"How?" I asked. "Do we go to the crossroads and battle the Devil for a shiny gold fiddle or some stupid shit like that?"

"Yes," Keith said. Stone cold. "Hopefully it'll be me saving the two of us. But it might have to be you on your own if it comes down to it."

"You're fucking kidding me. I was joking about that."

"It's a way out of this," Keith said. "I'm not a shredman, and neither are you. How could we possibly beat him?"

"Come on, kid. It's never how many or fast the notes are. You know that. It's gotta be the *right* notes, at the *right* time."

"This is crazy."

"Not any more than talking to me, is it?"

He had a point. I had long ago accepted that Keith Richards was real—my spirit guide or Patronus. That I wasn't just making him up. Where was I supposed to draw the line? If I accepted that he was real, why should battling the Devil for my soul and sanity be any different?

"Ok," I said. "What do I have to do to get him off our back?"

I didn't mean to say "our"—maybe I did—Keith noticed and made a sad, happy smile. The kind of sympathetic smile you make at a funeral. He put his hand on my shoulder. I didn't feel it there. In fact, I wasn't entirely sure how he could interact with the natural world. He once told me that *Ghost* almost had it right, but he couldn't explain it. Some shit he could do with great concentration, other stuff was at will.

"First I think I should come clean about my guitar," Keith Richards said.

"Your guitar?"

"Well, yours now. Mine before," he took out a cigarette and lit it. "Micawber."

"Micawber?" I damn near dropped my coffee cup.

"Aye."

"The '53 Telecaster?"

"That's the one."

"I thought the human Keith Richards has it."

"I ain't human?" Keith said. "Be kind, baby." He took a drag. "The guitar, tough bird to cage that one. Ever since she was nicked at Nellcôte in '71 during the Exile sessions she's been in and out my possession."

"You mean to tell me that I've been playing one of the most famous guitars in history for the past 8 years?"

"Yes."

"The one Eric Clapton gave you for your 27th birthday?"

"Why do you think he did that?" Keith Richards chuckled a smokey grunt.

"You're kidding."

"Poor bastard didn't know I'd already made the deal years before." Keith Richards took a drag. "Facts are he would've been better off keeping the thing for himself. Didn't know that at the time, but he could've wielded it had he needed."

"Can't he still? Can't you just get Eric Clapton to battle the Devil for us? For all of us?"

Keith Richards shook his head. "Sorry, kid. Ol' Beelzebub would never go for that. Eric'll have to reckon on his own when the time comes. And the way he's going lately, he'll have a lot to reckon for."

"Ok," I sighed and shook my head. "The guitar. What can we do with it? Just play a song?"

"She's got magical properties. Bring her out."

"I left her at Bollocks' place. We have practice later."

Keith Richards furrowed his brow. "Right," he said. Wrinkles deepened within the wrinkles. "Hmph," he grunted.

"What?"

"Nothing," he said and stubbed out his cigarette in the sink. "I hope."

***

I left the apartment and made my way to the subway to get over to Bollocks' place. It was almost noon, which was still pretty early by gigging standards. Bollocks wasn't answering his phone, but I figured he had it on silent, or he never got it charged with the party going on. Though, that didn't seem like him. He was always charge conscious and would freak out if his phone dipped below 70 percent. I tried giving him a call one last time before the train went underground. No answer. The train entered a tunnel and began its quick descent underground—graffiti decorated walls flashed past like looking through a fucked-up zoetrope.

My phone buzzed. A phone call. A local number I didn't recognize but seemed familiar. I answered.

"Marc!" a girl's voice said.

"Maybelline?" I looked at my hand.

The phone cut out. Then back in. Then out.

"Hello?"

Choppy words and then nothing. The train screeched to a halt and the lights inside the car flickered and went dark. Outside, the tunnel was lit every ten yards or so with a cloudy, piss yellow lamp.

The other passengers groaned and asked each other what happened. Everyone turned on the flashlights on their phones. The train lit up—a bunch of fireflies trapped in a car-jar in the swamps of underground Philly transport. People complained and tried to make calls or check the internet, but we were in a dead zone. The conductor came over the speaker. Static voiced nonsense. He could have said anything and it wouldn't have mattered. It just added to the melee of confused and annoyed hot passengers. *What did he say?* As if by asking enough times an answer would emerge.

A sense of panic crept in me. I whispered, "Keith? What's going on?"

Nothing. He wasn't like a dog that came calling, but I'd been able to summon him before—usually when I couldn't figure out a guitar lick or didn't know the answer on a test in high school. He was good in that regard. I once tried to use him to swindle people out of money while pretending I was a mind reader. After he admonished me about choosing the right path and that he wasn't going to be used as a fucking parlor trick.

I whispered again. Nothing. I checked my phone—still no service.

The panic burrowed deeper. Bollocks not answering his phone. Maybelline finding my number and calling me—the urgency in her voice. Keith not showing up.

A couple of skater kids were fucking around with the emergency exit window, but then realized it led directly to a wall. Nowhere to go.

One of the doors, if it was open, led to a service corridor that one of the skaters said would take us to the pedestrian concourse. That he used it before when tagging walls.

They went to work shoving their skateboards in between the doors to pry them open. I went to help with the doors. A big muscly sonuvabitch with dread locks came over and gave us a hand. "Man, I've got an interview. Already gonna be late 'cause of SEPTA and their stupid shit." He slipped his fingers and hands in between the doors and gripped them. The muscles on his arms flexed taut. The Jaws of Life manifest. "You know where you're headed?" he said to the skateboard kids.

"For the most part," one of them said. "Just head up, and eventually it's all good."

"Where's your interview?" I asked, trying to be polite and make small talk since we were basically standing on each other.

"The Opera House," the dude with dreads said.

"Like for the stage crew or something?" one of the kids said.

"Man," Dreads said, letting the doors relax for a second. "What, you think I can't sing?"

The skateboard kid's face went pale. "Shit dude. I didn't mean that. I just thought…"

"That a brother can't get down with Verdi?"

"No, I…"

Dreads laughed. He re-gripped the doors. "Security. But if you don't fuck with Puccini, you're missing out."

We all pulled, Dreads doing most of the work, and the closing mechanism unlatched and the doors opened. The skateboard kids jumped off the train and up into the corridor, their lights bopping up and down. The muscular guy looked at me and shrugged.

"Fuck it," he said and hopped off the train across to the grimy platform.

People were looking over, contemplating following, some urging caution about the train moving—getting caught mid-jump. A murmur of excitement pulsed through the train.

An old lady tapped me on the shoulder.

"Help me down?" she asked, holding out her hand.

"You sure?"

She grabbed my hand and made for the gap between the car and corridor. I tightened my grip and took her by the elbow. I looked towards the skateboard kids and guy, just a few yards away.

Yeah man. Fuck it, I thought and hopped off into the darkness as well. The old lady and I caught up with the group. Our motley crew assembled, we set off into the darkness.

I felt a chill on my back and I swear I heard my name whispered from down the long corridors we walked past. I didn't dare try to call for Keith again with the old lady by my side. No reason to make her think she was with a crazy amid all of this. The kids were getting away from us—I guess their eyes adjusted to the darkness quicker than mine, or their leader was guided by instinct. They were moving faster than I could with the lady, but I wasn't going to leave her. I could see them up ahead. They turned a corner. And then I lost them. A yard or two away there was a fork in the tunnel, and I couldn't see them in either direction.

"Shit," I said. "Hello," I yelled, and was met with the slap back echo of my own voice.

The old lady squeezed my hand. She looked around. "Thanks for sticking with me."

I was briefly annoyed, but then got that shit under control. I was doing the right thing, and the chances of us getting stuck down here and dying were very slim. *Just head up,* the kid said. When you're underground there aren't many choices if you want out.

"It's ok. We'll get out of here just fine." I said more for myself than her. I needed to find out what was going on with Bollocks and Maybelline. And Christ, even Keith Richards. I couldn't believe I was actually worried about him. It was the first time since I'd known him that I felt something more than a sense of wonder and excitement and privilege—after the initial days and weeks of being freaked the fuck out.

We stood there, the two of us, the old lady and me, looking around into the darkness faintly lit by my cellphone flashlight and the small, weak floodlights above.

"What are you thinking?" the old lady said, her hand squirming lightly like nervous worms.

We could just head back, I thought. We hadn't gone too far, and I didn't think it'd be too hard to retrace our steps and wait on the train and just say fuck it to all of this. Bollocks would turn up— he always did—and shit, I didn't even really know Maybelline. I'm sure she was fine. Probably still rattled from last night and she wasn't really implicated in any of this, so…

I looked back the path towards the train. Where it *should* be if it was still there.

I sighed. Even if it was, there was no guarantee it wouldn't just sit there for hours. I've heard stories of immobile trains too many times to count.

I heard my name again, from the left. Or behind. It was tough to tell—the acoustics down there left a lot of room for guesswork. It's probably what the Stones had to deal with when they recorded *Exile* in the basement of Keith Richards' mansion in Nellcôte. No time to think about that. Up ahead seemed to rise on an incline. The right looked like the left.

My name again. From the right? Straight ahead? *Goddamnit,* I thought. A train rattled past on the other side of a wall not far off. The walls shook thunder and screeched endless stressed track.

I took a deep breath.

"Ok," I said. "Let's go. Let's get out of here."

We set off straight.

We walked the incline and found what we hoped would be salvation: an old, rusty ladder. I went first and then leaned back over to help the old lady. The walls were covered with graffiti and the stink of piss sweated out of every pore. We climbed and the sound of passing trains was replaced with feet and wheels over tile above. And then my fucking phone slipped out of my sweaty hand. It bounced against the rungs and then the wall, the LED spiraling and flashing like the taillight of an airplane descending into mist.

"Goddamnit," I said. I couldn't go back. The old lady was behind me. I'd have to go back after.

We reached a landing the size of a small cubicle guarded by a chain and a sign telling people not to trespass. I reached back and grabbed the old lady's hand and pulled her up. Past the chain was a door, light pushing out from around its seams. We emerged into the harsh light of the pedestrian concourse under City Hall.

A few yards away, on the other side of the concourse, kids on skateboards zipped away. The phlum-phlack of their wheels swooshing over cracks echoed and diminished.

The old lady gripped my elbow. "Thank you," she said. I nodded and wiped my forehead with the bottom of my t-shirt. I turned back through the door and began the dark descent in search of my phone.

***

I reached the bottom quicker than I thought I would. Warm, moist concrete slapped the bottom of my right foot when I was expecting another rung. My eyes adjusted enough to know that unless my phone was face down, light up, it'd be a while before I'd find it.

I resisted the urge to get down on my hands and knees and feel around. That was an Olympic sized pool of gross I wasn't yet ready to wade into. Instead, I carefully rubbed the toe of my shoe along the ground. I had barely made a half arc when I caught a glimpse of a light bouncing down the corridor to my right. Then it disappeared. Came back. Disappeared. Came back.

"Hey," I yelled. "That's my phone." The sound echoed and ricocheted against the cavernous walls. I felt a little silly yelling at…actually, I wasn't sure what I was yelling at. A rat? Racoon? Some other sewer creature existing in the filthy underbelly of Philly's public transport which was built over a century ago on top of who knows what caves and tributaries that had existed since the continents split? The light stopped. I moved towards it, and it started again. "Hey," I yelled once more and doubled my pace, doing more of a careful shuffle than a run so I didn't trip and fall over into a puddle of subway grog.

I got close enough to see that it was definitely a person with my phone. Or at least I hoped it was a person—a subway creature that big, well, I wasn't prepared to come face to face with one of those. But then, was I really prepared to confront whoever was hovering around down here? I had to be. I didn't know a single phone number by heart, and all my photos were on there. I quickened my pace and followed the light until I was within arm's reach of the form.

I put my hand on his shoulder, and he turned around and hissed at me. The motherfucker hissed at me. Then pushed me and darted through a slim opening between the tiled walls. I followed him into the darkness and then the bottom dropped out from under me like I just stepped into an open trap door. My ass finally made contact and I slid and slid. My sneakers squeaked against the sides of the chute and I fought to grab something, anything, on the sides, but it was useless. I was ejected into a room and landed on my feet, but was thrown forward by the inertia from what must've been a mile long slide.

I was in an open space strung up with Christmas lights, patio lights, wall sconces, single bulbs, lamps—floor and table. There was shit everywhere twinkling and glowing like a dragon's lair. Chairs, books, dishes, rugs on the floor and walls, statues, knick-knacks. An upright piano and bass. Horns and fiddles. My palms were dirty and rubbed raw from the fall into this underground bazaar. My ass cheeks hurt.

I looked back up into the crevice I Santa Claused through. An old ventilation shaft? There was no way I'd be able to climb back up that way. It was about ten feet off the ground and too steep. I scanned the room for a way out.

I walked the perimeter running my hands on the walls looking for an exit through the rugs. There was a guitar in the corner. It looked like an old Kay archtop. The kind you'd buy at a department store or something back in the '50s and '60s. A thick chill seemed to rise from the floor.

Marc…

"Who's there?" I said and turned around.

Marc…

The voice was behind me. I shot back around and the fucking guitar was floating right in front of my face. The crack of a train overhead shook the room and the lights faltered. My head clouded with visions of electricity. Intangible power. I was gliding across a stage with my guitar in an old honky-tonk deep in the south. There were thousands of voices. My fingertips surged.

A hand on my shoulder pulling me around. I was back in the underground lair face to face with a long-haired, bearded dude in a sleeveless CBGB's t-shirt. My phone in his left hand.

"What are you doing?" he said. This motherfucker was questioning me. He took my phone, made me chase him, lured me into his underground hideout, and was questioning me. For a brief second, I thought I should sock him.

"I just want my phone," I said mildly, punking out. The initial adrenaline had worn off and nervousness bloomed in my bowels. "I dropped it back there, so…"

"Please," he said, his left eye twitching, "put that guitar down."

I looked down, and sure as shit I was holding the guitar. I don't even remember picking it up. "Oh, sorry. I…," I said. I put the guitar down carefully, leaning it back against the wall. The air-pressure must've messed with me or something.

He tossed my phone on a couch and then sat down on said couch and pulled a sandwich out from his pocket and began eating it, nibbling it like a rat. I stood there watching him for a minute, trying to figure out how to get my phone back and have him show me the way out. He was kind of twitchy all over. His eyes darted from place to place. His movements were jerky.

He ignored me while he ate. I stood there feeling really dumb and considered just taking my phone and getting out of there. He must've come in from somewhere. Figure it out, just head up. Try not to get smashed by a train. I took a few steps over to my phone. The screen was fucked. I picked up the phone and it worked, thank god. I turned the flashlight off. No new messages—no service either. A gust of hot, stale air came into the room. I noticed the edge of a wall rug flap slightly. Salvation.

"So," I said slowly, "I'm just gonna go." I backed up slowly towards where I thought the exit was.

"Wrong way," he said, still sitting on the couch. "The 11:57 will get you before you take three steps."

"Didn't you just come in from there," I said, hoping for him to show his hand.

He stared at me like *you think I don't fucking know where I just came from?* The room was in a perpetual hazy twilight. A gust of air blew the rug harder—the thunder whoosh of a train.

"Woulda made a pancake outta you," he said. "Sit."

I breathed in and out deeply through my nose, slowly, closed and opened my eyes.

"Where," I said flatly.

He stood and grabbed a small stool from a pile of piles and set it down at my feet. He was more nimble and agile than I presumed. I could see the sinews of his muscles running up and down his arms. Maybe he could have kicked my ass.

"You're a musician?" he asked me.

"Uh, yeah."

"Play me something you wrote. If I like it, I'll show you out."

"Play you something? Come on, man. Just show me out." The rumble of another train—I couldn't tell where it was coming from. This room existed in some eye of a storm, some calm, greasy and electric center of a spider's web. I'd need him.

He dug into another pile of stuff and pulled out an old acoustic that had no branding or decals anywhere that I could see. I strummed a chord, tuned the strings. He was sitting on the edge of the couch, maybe two feet from me. It was the first time I got a good look at his face hidden behind long hair and a beard.

"Holy shit," I said on impulse. "Johnny Newman? The Sevilles?"

He grunted an affirmation.

"Holy shit," I said again. The Sevilles were a legendary punk band from Philly who were huge in the late '70s and early '80s. Like mega huge. They were the counter to all the hair bands and electro pop of the day. The anti-Hall and Oates from Philly. Where Daryl went smooth, Johnny went hard. Cobain cited them as a major influence. Hell, everyone did. They came up during the same time as The Ramones, Circle Jerks, Buzzcocks. They took the Melvins under their wing early on. Then grunge hit. The Sevilles broke up and Johnny Newman disappeared. Mid-tour. There was no press release or anything. A zine circulated on South Street. People said Johnny was handing it out in front of Zipperhead. It was pages and pages of "our time was our time and time marches to new blood only" over and over and over. It was rumored he was living in South America or on an island with Jim Morrison and Biggie. Others said he had a massive dong and moved to L.A. to be a stunt cock.

"Dude," I said, "'Pennikillin.' 'Bill's Trill.' Fuck. 'Weenie Blues' changed my life."

"Thank you," he said. Humble as shit. I was not expecting that.

"Do you need help?" I asked. "So many people would line up to hear you again."

"I'm doing fine." He shrugged.

"Why are you living here?"

"I like it." He leveled his eyes at me. "No one bothers me."

I cleared my throat nervously. "But…"

"Son," he said. "This is about you. Play. Play me the last thing you wrote."

I reached in my pocket for a pick and chunked out a punky blues number that bordered on pop. There was a rhythmic element missing since I was playing solo—I mimicked it as best I could, tapping on the body of the guitar and letting the guttural raking against the muted guitar strings imitate the snare. I whistled the synth part that Bollocks played in between verses.

"Son," he said when I was done. "Not bad. But do better."

I began playing a different song. He stopped me. "Did I ask you to play a different song?"

"No."

"I said 'do better.' Now, do better."

I played it again. Really doubling down on the percussive element. I tapped my foot loud as well. He was silent the whole performance.

"So your version of doing better was to turn into a wind-up monkey?" he said.

"I…"

"Try one more time. Breathe. Play the song, not the guitar."

Fact is, he was right. I was trying to do Bollocks' part when I was playing solo. I knew better. Keith had taught me this lesson. I guess sometimes you just need to get lost in the subway and fail in front of one of your heroes who everyone thought was dead or missing for some lessons to settle.

Marc…

"Did you hear that?" I asked. It must have been him. "How'd you know my name?"

I turned towards the Kay guitar I saw when I first arrived.

"It does that sometimes," he said.

"Does what?"

"Go on. Play her," he said and nodded to the Kay guitar. "No one's been able to crack that one since I've been here."

"What do you mean?" I was already setting down the guitar he gave me and picking up the archtop.

It vibrated in my hands. *What the fuck* I whispered to myself. Then clickety-clack. The unmistakable sound of a pick dropped into the hollows of a guitar.

"You get one shot," he said.

It's tough getting a pick through a regular sound hole of an acoustic guitar. This one had two f-holes. Virtually impossible to shake a pick out of those. Without thinking or intent, as if guided by unseen hands, I held the guitar parallel to the ground and in one quick movement flipped it over like a pig on a spit. The soft impact of the pick against my shoe.

"Incredible," Johnny Newman said.

I picked up the pick, teardrop shaped, barely worn or used it seemed. It felt heavier than it should. I bent it and it wouldn't give, super hard and definitely not made of plastic. It was sinking into my fingertips, settling into a groove it perfectly fit.

I looked at Johnny. I thought I could see a smile under the wilderness of his face.

"Incredible," he said again. "Play."

I didn't think. I just played. Nothing fancy. The chords and the melody laid bare coming down from the tower of song. When I was finished, he just sat there. Staring at me.

"So…" I began.

"What's your name?"

"Marc."

"Well, Marc. Let's get you out of here."

"But what was that all about?" I held the pick out. "I felt…"

He stood and closed my hand over the pick.

"It's yours now," he said looking me in the eyes, holding my closed hand with both of his. "That's all I can say."

He pulled a cloth from his back pocket. "Sorry, Marc. This is gonna have to go over your eyes. Can't be found if that's cool."

"But…"

"Marc." He put his hand on my shoulder. "Please respect my solitude."

I nodded. "Ok." I sort of understood what he meant. With the exception of Bollocks and Keith Richards, I've been living a life of solitude since I was eleven. I didn't seek out solitude—it had found me early on. Still, I could understand why he would want to be left alone. He put the blindfold on me and led us out and away from his space underground.

We trudged along. He ducked my head for me and held me against the walls when necessary. At last we stopped walking.

"End of the line, Marc," he said. "Remember. No matter how serious or silly it is, you must always serve the song. Nothing else. There's going to be a time when that means the most. When it means life or death. Understand?"

"Yes."

"Say you understand."

"I understand. Life or death. Got it."

He gripped me by the shoulders and squeezed.

"Thank you Johnny Newman of The Sevilles," I said. I couldn't see him and my ears were covered as well, but I swear I heard him laugh. I stood there, still for a few moments.

"Johnny?" I said. Nothing. I took the blindfold off. Before me was a thin vertical ray splitting a pair of doors in half. I turned around—darkness. Nothing more.

I pushed the doors and they opened to a stairwell that I recognized. I'd been under City Hall. Deep under it. People were coming up and down the steps, more than one of them annoyed that some asshole was taking up half the steps with a door. I closed the door behind me, heard it latch.

The light from the sun glared down the stairwell as I took the steps two at a time.

9. LIVIN' IT UP WHEN I'M GOING DOWN

Above ground, finally, I walked east down Market Street towards the river. I made my way through traffic against the light and flagged down a cab in front of a hotel. It was the first time I'd set foot in one in years and it was the same as I remembered—a little gross, a little unsafe, but not any more than some dude's busted Kia that somehow passed inspection.

The driver sped to every light and blew not one, but two yellows that just turned red. In between being jolted forward at each stop and pressed against the seat by centrifugal force, I tried for Bollocks. Nothing. Maybelline wasn't answering either, and my calls went straight to voicemail.

We pulled up to Bollocks' building and the driver clicked off the meter. I dug some crumbled bills out of my pocket and handed them over.

***

I took the freight elevator up to Bollocks' loft. The gate opened and I went to his door and pounded on it with the butt of my fist. Again and again.

I tried calling him and I heard his phone go off on the other side of the door. "Fuck," I said and sat down on the floor in the hallway and leaned my head against the wall. The elevator went back down and I listened to it descend, creaking.

"Keith," I said. I waited. "I need you, man." Nothing.

I wondered what would have happened if Keith Richards' human form died. If this was a ghost, or spirit or whatever, he wasn't tethered to the human Keith. I tried to reassure myself with that. I had never thought about that before. I didn't realize how much I came to rely on his presence. He was always there. I didn't think I'd be as grief-stricken as when my parents died or if Bollocks died. But my gut dropped—a cannonball off the plank, pulling me down. Shit—maybe it would affect me more deeply than I thought. I admonished myself for thinking that way. There's no way of knowing if he's gone. Still, I googled Keith Richards again to see if the human version was still alive. He was.

I once asked Keith Richards if his human form knows what he knows. If they were the same or if he was in control of his magical avatar.

"It's more a work of the subconscious," he said.

"Mine or yours?" I asked.

He chuckled and lit a cigarette.

"Like if I met you in real life, would human Keith know who I was?"

"Isn't this real life?" he asked.

"Yeah, but…"

"There's two sides to every story." He took a drag and pointed to my guitar. A beat-up acoustic he made me get at a pawn shop not long after I got the tele. "Run it again. Malagueña. You're almost there kid."

I heard the crank of gears in the elevator shaft. The doors opened. Bollocks stepped out into the hall.

"Is it 5 already?" he asked.

I stood up. "Dude, I've been trying to reach you for hours."

"I just saw you get out of a yellow Uber from down the block."

"I was calling and texting you."

"Sorry man. I left my phone in the apartment." He patted his front leg pocket. "It was real weird at first, but then I felt liberated even though my leg was phantom buzzing all during breakfast."

"You don't eat breakfast."

"Well, I don't. But it's rude not to give the ladies pancakes after they've shared their most sacred of parts with you."

"Since when?"

"Man, just because you don't see it, doesn't mean it doesn't happen."

"Ok, ok. Sir Bollocks, gentleman of Philadelphia, forgive me. I need to see my guitar."

"It's inside."

"I know."

He walked up to the door and turned the knob. The door swung open.

"You don't fucking lock your door?" I asked.

He shrugged.

I walked past him and into the apartment. The place was a mess. Cans and bottles all over the place. I went to his room. Just a bed and some clothes on the floor.

I came back out. "Where'd you put it?"

"In my room," Bollocks said.

"It's not in there."

Bollocks frowned. He went into his room and looked around and then came back out. "Dude, I put it in there last night."

"Did you lock the door to your room?"

He looked at the ground, and his eyes seemed to trace each grain of the wooden planks. "Fuck," he mumbled and then started moving around the room. He checked under the tub and the couch. In the kitchen. "It'll turn up," he said.

I went and sat on the couch. I knew it was gone. And I already had an idea of who took it.

10. THE ONE WITH THE MASTERPLAN GONE TO SHIT

Bollocks checked every unlikely place in his studio. Under the sink. Behind the curtains. It wasn't his fault really, but letting him scramble gave me a small sense of satisfaction. That he was feeling the sting too. Eventually, after triple-checking every inch of the room, he came over and sat on the couch next to me.

Maybelline's phone was still going straight to voicemail, and I had no idea where she lived. I told Bollocks about the dropped call and the urgency in her voice, but he didn't seem too concerned about it.

"She doesn't really know you, so if it was an emergency, she'd probably reach out to someone more important to her. No offense," he said.

"Yeah, I get it. She just sounded in trouble," I said.

"I thought you said you could barely hear her? I wouldn't sweat it, dude. And I definitely wouldn't call her again. Gonna look like a stalker with seventeen missed calls from you."

He had a point. But still, her call and the absence of Keith Richards unsettled me. And with my guitar being stolen on top of it all, I had a bad feeling about this. I never told Bollocks about Keith Richards. I'd wanted to so many times. Was on the verge half of those times. I'd known him since I was a kid. He was my best friend—but after not telling him for so long, it just seemed like I couldn't after 7 years of keeping it a secret. I don't know what came over me last night telling Maybelline. I'd never felt like I could be so open with someone so fast before, but given the trauma of the evening, I chalked it up to near-death jitters, or whatever would've happened had I stuck around the venue.

"So," Bollocks said. "We've got a couple hundred bucks in band and beer funds. And we've got that gig in two days."

"Shit," I said. In all the commotion, I'd forgotten about the gig. It would be our biggest to date. We'd done some other stuff at XPN—they promoted the hell out of our record last month—but this was a gift. The Districts played XPoNential a few years ago, and then they went on to open for The Rolling Stones in Quebec. I got a flutter in my gut that we were following in their footsteps and the thought of opening for The Stones was wild.

"…I mean, it'd be a beater, but it'd work," Bollocks said. I had zoned out thinking about the gig and wasn't paying attention to him.

"What?"

"A guitar from the pawn shop. For the gig."

I sighed and shook my head. "Yeah, sure."

My fucking guitar. Micawber. I had to get it back. There was no way I wasn't going to have my guitar for this gig. From a utilitarian point of view, a guitar is a guitar, as long as it's not a total piece of shit. I could make it through the gig with any guitar if it could stay in tune half-decently. Christ, Kurt Cobain only used pawn shop finds. Still, I had Micawber. I actually bought the fucker and honed my chops on it. This was a huge show for us. Something greater than need drew me to the guitar—I felt like something of tremendous consequence hinged on my having Micawber.

"Who was the weird dude with the one black eye last night?" I asked Bollocks.

"Uh, I don't know. Some dude from Brooklyn, I think. He came in with those dudes from Chicken Nugget Yoga."

"He was at our gig?"

"Not sure. He was here though."

I took out my phone and went to Chicken Nugget Yoga's website.

He wasn't in their band, but I found some links to their social media sites. It took a few minutes of scrolling and some lightweight stalking, but I found him tagged in a picture at a show they did a few weeks back. I followed the links—Tanner Campbell from East Brunswick, NJ. His Facebook cover image was a Mets logo. I'm not a sports guy, per se, but even I knew that was tragic. The eye must've been a contact—I mean, of course it was. Only Bowie had a legit fucked up eye. He was in a band. Everyone from Jersey is in a fucking band. And his was called Divided by Rabies.

They were a bluegrass band, and the singer wore one of those pork pie hats. I checked out their music, and they weren't bad. It's what you'd expect. Classic arena folk—that brand doesn't ever stray too far. Especially when the bass player plays an upright, and the singer, in addition to the hat, has a harmonica slung around his neck. But whatever, they were making strides. That's never easy, even if you're a goddamned thief.

"What'd you find?" Bollocks asked.

I showed him the picture and he agreed it was the same guy.

"Wanna take a ride to Jersey?" I asked.

"And just show people his picture and hope someone knows where he lives?"

"We could get someone to friend him on here and then try to meet up with him. Except we'll be there."

"Would you meet up with someone that just friended you?"

"Do you have any better ideas?"

"We could see if he is on any hook-up apps," Bollocks offered. "We can make a fake account and see if he wants to meet up."

"That's actually not a bad idea," I said. "But, what if he's not gay, or recognizes us?"

"Dude. We're not setting up an account for us. I'll use my sister's pics or something."

"Well, what if he is gay?"

"Then we should make a few accounts."

"This is stupid. Does your sister have an account?"

"Yeah."

"Ask her to swipe on him."

"I don't know man. I don't want to pimp my sister out."

"You were just going to use her pictures."

"That's different. It'd be us. We'd be like Scarlet Johannsen in *Her*."

"What?" I shook my head. "Jesus. Just ask her."

Bollocks called his sister and she instantly shot down our plan. Apparently, you can't search for people on Tinder and she wasn't interested in swiping for hours in the hopes he would pop up. If he was even on it. With our masterplan gone to shit, I checked out Divided by Rabies' webpage again. I clicked on their tour link, which I then realized was the more practical thing to do from the start.

"No fucking way," I said.

Bollocks looked up from his phone.

"That bastard is playing the side stage this weekend," I said.

"At XPoNential?"

"Yep."

"Do you think he knows we're playing?"

"He's going to."

***

An hour passed and still nothing from Maybelline. Nothing from Keith Richards. We drafted a setlist. We had to be careful to pick the perfect songs. They gave us twenty-five minutes, so we couldn't really dick around too much, but we also didn't want to blaze through like a comet either. A staple of our set was "Devil's Haircut" by Beck—it was a good live number, but we cut it for the gig. We had to strike a delicate balance and leave something of substance that wouldn't be completely overshadowed by Beck. And doing a Beck song probably wasn't the way to do that.

As a two-piece band—me on guitar, vocals, and sometimes synth, and Bollocks on drums, synth, and background vocals—we had a lot of room to play. Fortunately, our EP was getting some love still, so we weren't total unknowns taking the stage.

After we finished writing out our setlist, Bollocks let out a long groaning sigh. "Let's hit up the pawn shop, man. We've gotta practice. I mean, that Tele was real nice, and I get it was your main guitar, but you know, you only paid a couple hundred for it. I bet we can find something similar. Onwards and upwards, right?"

I was tempted to come clean but checked myself. Now wasn't the time. Guilt was brewing. I felt like a shitty friend. "Yeah, man. Let's go."

On the way down the elevator, he punched my arm and said, "Don't worry, man. We'll get it back."

11. SOME PRICK IN A BASEMENT THIS WAY COMES

Tanner drew a pentagram on the floor and at each point he lit a candle. He knelt in the center and held Micawber by the body, the neck of the guitar pointing upwards.

"*Lirach tasa vefa wehlic, belial,*" he said and made a circle in the air with the guitar.

He repeated the phrase again, and again. All the while drawing circles in the air.

"*Renich tasa uberaca biasa icar, Lucifer.*" He continued.

"*Ganic tasa fubin, flereous.*" Stabbing the air with the guitar.

"*Jedan tasa hoet naca, leviathan.*" He lowered the guitar. He began the ceremony again.

Keith Richards sat off in the corner smoking a cigarette. He hadn't shown himself to Tanner and he didn't intend to.

"Earth, air, fire, wind," he mumbled to himself. He shook his head. "Bunch of mumbo-jumbo, kid. Ain't gonna reveal me or him to you."

Keith crawled over to the pentagram and took a drag of his cigarette and blew out a candle with the exhale. The ash of his cigarette fell to the floor.

"Who's there?" Tanner said and lowered the guitar. He looked around the room, frantically. He rubbed his finger on the ash and examined it. He began the evocation again.

"Fuuuucck, kid," Keith Richards said and chuckled while slouching back against the wall. "Goddamn wanker."

Keith Richards took another drag of his cigarette. "Come on, Marc. Come on."

12. INTERLUDE: A LEGEND

After the Spaniards and White Man came to America, but before the Trail of Tears saw the mass exodus of Indigenous people, the land in what we would call Mississippi was tended to by tribes of men and women. The Chickasaw tribe was enjoying three generations of peace. However, the men from the north with their rifles and cannons were seen more frequently in their lands, and though they were tolerated and forgiven their trespasses, a change was in the air.

A young chief, Piominko of the Chickasaw tribe, feared the end of his people. Eager to prove himself to his elders, he attempted to band together the surrounding tribes to form an alliance with the new settlers.

One evening, while deep in Quapaw territory, not far off from the Mississippi River, he met with their chieftains. He explained that their culture and way of life hung in the balance and that though they should fight if they were forced to, peace was the only way forward if they wanted their tribes to survive. The Quapaw elders agreed, but before the pact was sealed, a small band of white soldiers stationed in a far outpost came upon the meeting. They drew their weapons. Piominko, who knew their tongue, tried to make peace, but the white men claimed the land was theirs and urged the natives to move.

Fearful for their lives at the sight of such barbarous creatures, the younger Quapaw chiefs let out a battle cry and attacked the white men. There was much bloodshed and, in the end, only

Piominko lived. Broken by the turn of events and the loss of peace, he wailed over the land on which the white man killed his people. Blood sank into the ground while he stamped and spat.

It began to rain, and thunder growled through the air, from under his feet. Lightning struck the ground and the earth opened. A great horned serpent with fire for eyes slithered out of the hole. Piominko fell back and lay amid the bodies. *Sint-Holo*, he gasped.

The serpent reared and towered over Piominko.

It surveyed the landscape and lowered its scaled belly to the ground and slunk around the bodies. With its great horns, it threw the corpses out of the way and wrapped itself around Piominko and held him up. It whispered to him and saw into his soul—Sint-Holo knew Piominko wanted peace. Piominko could have peace, Sint-Holo told him. He could be great and become an advisor and friend to the White Man and their leaders. He could save his people.

***

In the morning, Piominko buried the bodies of the men in the deep hole left from the lightning strike—from where the serpent had appeared. He filled the hole with earth and planted a young sapling in hopes that its roots would prevent the serpent from ever coming forth again. The tree grew strong and it stood for nearly two centuries.

After Piominko left the tree, a pale man with fire for eyes and holding a fiddle appeared out of the dawn mist hanging over the Mississippi river. He danced around the tree while shrieking off violent themes from the fiddle. The tree shook and bent against the storm of melody. Sint-Holo stirred deep beneath the earth. *Your form is returned to you, be at peace* the pale man whispered. *Be at peace*. His bow doubled in ferocity against the instrument.

13. PRESENT: THE BALLAD OF BRAD JOHNSON

"Thank you so much," Maybelline said. "I've wanted this since I started writing."

"Don't mention it," Brad Johnson said. "I knew big things were brewing once that War on Drugs piece went national. Rolling Stone will be lucky to have you."

Maybelline hugged Brad and kissed him on the cheek. Brad blushed and awkwardly hugged her back, patting her gently.

Brad had given his whole adult life to the station—twenty-two years—and had gone as far as he could landing as Program Director. He had given Maybelline her first job as an intern writing for The Key, the station's local music blog, while she studied journalism. After she graduated, she became a staff writer for The Key and WXPN, which didn't come without a little backlash. A public radio station running on a shoe-string budget couldn't just hire people to do jobs that kids in college would do for free. There were rumors that Brad was fucking her. He *was* attracted to her, but under current circumstances he knew he stood about as much of a chance as Bono did at having a successful solo record.

"Sorry, I'm in shock still. This is all so sudden," Maybelline said, letting go of Brad.

"Just make them good again," Brad said. "Just make them good again." He checked his phone. "Shit. I've got a meeting." He smiled and nodded at Maybelline. "You're going to like Beck," he said over his shoulder as he walked away down the hall.

Maybelline took out her phone, and before she realized it, the first person she was calling was Marc.

***

A man in a suit sat in Brad Johnson's office, behind his desk, in his chair. The man was strumming an old acoustic guitar that had been lying around the station since the '80s. The grain in the wood showed and was split, and in places of high friction the finish had worn off leaving thin patches of bare wood. There was a wooden and brass bridge with an electromagnetic pick-up attached where the strings were tied down to the body. There was a secondary sound hole just below the strings that was born out of someone's picking hand beating the hell out of the guitar over the years. Despite the cosmetics, the guitar was solid—still had plenty of mileage left. The legend was that it belonged to Johnny Cash or Willie Nelson, though no one could corroborate either story.

"Well," Brad said, "I just told her. You better not be lying to me, or she'll know real fast."

"Brad, baby," the man said. "You'd be surprised how many people in your industry are willing to make deals with me. So many strings just *begging* to be pulled. I just got off the phone, and it's all good."

The man put the guitar down and stood up. He went over to Brad. "But, what do you want?"

"What do you mean? You know what I want," Brad said.

"Yeah, yeah, yeah. The younger, cute chick to like you. You're her knight in shining armor. Blah, blah, blah. That's boring, Brad. Cliché. Barely worth the price of half a soul. I'd even throw in a sports car if I didn't think you were capable of more."

70

"I don't understand."

"Let's call it tit for tat for Mojo Pin. I need them to get more traction, and you gave them that. Thank you."

"Ok…"

"I want you to fully commit, Brad," the man said and put his hand on Brad's shoulder. "You've been pussyfooting around your whole life. You can have anything you want if you'd stop thinking with your dick. What is it you *really* want? What would you trade your soul for if you were," the man flourished his hand, "hypothetically given the chance."

Brad's forehead wrinkled with concentration. The man lifted Brad's head by his chin and looked into his eyes. He smiled.

"Oh, Bradley, baby. You're a bad boy." He let out a loud, booming laugh. "Now we're talking. Now we are talking."

14. NEWS OF THE WORLD

Practice didn't go too bad considering I was using a cheap student model Telecaster I picked up for a little over a hundred bucks. It stayed in tune enough, which was about as much as I could hope for.

"When I see that dude," Bollocks said, "I'm gonna punch him in the tooth."

"Let me get my guitar back before you get arrested," I said.

"Can't get arrested if no one sees and I don't leave a mark." Bollocks lunged at me and started play punching me in my kidneys. I tackled him on the ground, and he pinched my nipple.

I screamed and pulled his hand off me. "Jesus. What are you, twelve?" I rubbed my nipple. I got up and sat on the couch. "Fuck dude, I think I'm bleeding."

"Just tell people you were running. Runners get bloody nips all the time," he said.

My phone buzzed and I took it out of my pocket. "It's Maybelline."

"Well, fucking answer it, Prefontaine."

"Hello," I said, trying all hell to sound cool and suave and not like a guy who tried calling her seven times.

"Hey, psycho," she said and laughed. "Seven missed calls?"

"Uh," I stammered. "You wouldn't believe the morning I had. I thought you were in trouble. You sounded like you were in trouble. Wait, are you ok?"

"I'm fine. I'm actually better than fine. You wouldn't believe the morning I just had."

I let out a sigh. Two down, one to go. Just waiting on Keith Richards.

"I'm glad to hear that," I said.

"Meet me for a drink," she said.

"Now?"

"Yeah. It's almost happy hour. Let's go be happy and finish the interview. And share our good news."

"I didn't have good news."

"Oh, well I do. Meet me and I'll tell you and then you can bring me down." She let out a laugh—more of a low giggle that killed me.

****

I met Maybelline at a bar under the El. The train roared past overhead and the liquor bottles shook and clinked.

"So," Maybelline said, beaming. "Guess what?"

"You like Taylor Swift in a non-ironic way?" I said.

"There's no such thing as guilty pleasure anymore, Marc. We're in a golden age. There is only pleasure."

"I know, I know. I've been trying to shake it off. Shake it off."

She rolled her eyes. Then smiled at me, her lips hovering just over her beer.

"I just interviewed Beck for Rolling Stone and am working for them now," she said matter-of-factly and took a drink from her beer.

"What?"

She smiled. "You heard me."

"How the fuck did that happen?" I said.

"They liked a piece I wrote and my boss put in a good word for me. They wanted a field reporter for XPoNential this weekend as a sort of welcoming-in, warming-up gig to learn their formatting and procedures."

"That's crazy. Wait. Is Beck cool?"

"So cool."

This all explained why she had her phone off. I felt a little embarrassed, but she didn't seem to be lingering on it, or really think I was a psycho, so I made a note to let it go and not shine a light on that brief episode of madness.

"What was up with your morning?" she asked. "Was it better than mine?"

"Not at all," I said and shook my head. "Someone stole my guitar."

"Oh no. Do you know who?"

"Yeah. I'm pretty sure it was that guy with the weird eye from last night that was right inside the door when got to the party."

"How'd he steal it? There were so many people there."

"That's probably why he was able to." I told her how I left it at Bollocks' apartment, and how we tracked him down on social media, and how his band was playing the side-stage tomorrow.

"How do you know he took it?" she asked.

"He was eyeing me last night, asked me about it, and I bet he saw Bollocks put it in his room. It's a gut feeling. More than that. I just know."

"Do you think he'll bring it tomorrow?"

"I hope so, because I need to get it back if..." I paused.

"What?" she said.

I took a deep breath. "It's about Keith Richards."

"Your imaginary friend?"

"You said you didn't not believe me."

"No, no. I do. I just couldn't resist. What about Keith Richards?"

"I haven't seen him since my guitar went missing. And just before that he told me it was Micawber."

"*The* Micawber?"

"Yeah."

"One of the most famous guitars in rock history?"

"Uh, yeah…," I said. I couldn't tell if she believed me.

"I thought Keith Richards' Telecasters only had five strings? Isn't that his thing?"

"It wasn't built that way. Keith always had the sixth string removed. Someone must've put a tuning peg and string back on."

"So, just so we're on the same page, you're friends with Keith Richards' ghost, and you have his guitar." She put her hand on my shoulder. "Are you sure this isn't some deep-rooted, subconscious hero worship?"

"No. And without that guitar, some bad stuff will happen."

"I still don't not believe you. I'm only onboard with this because of what I saw with my own eyes last night, but you're going to have to prove some of this to me."

"How?"

"Let's get your guitar back and summon Keith Richards."

I let out sigh. "That's the plan," I said.

"Good," she said. "But for now, let's drink."

I raised my glass. "To your promotion."

She clinked her glass against mine. "To magic guitars."

***

We finished our drinks and had a few more. Bullshitting about music and life in general.

"There's no way Elvis would have existed without Chuck Berry," she said, sitting in the amber glow of the half-closed mostly empty bar.

"Elvis was Elvis though. He was a different thing," I said.

"I get that. But The Beatles have more of a debt to Chuck Berry than to Elvis."

"I don't know. I think they owe more to Buddy Holly."

"Buddy Holly," Maybelline said, "played Chuck Berry songs, so…"

I paused mid-drink. Swallowed. "Fuck. You got me there." I raised my glass. "I concede."

"Good. You'll never win an argument about music with me and it's best you learn that now."

"One more?" I asked.

"Citywides?"

We put back the shots of Jim Beam and sipped on the Pabst. Maybelline went to the jukebox. It was the last of a dying breed to still have CDs.

Horns, bass, drums, organ. The unmistakable voice of Al Green.

Maybelline turned around and lowered her eyes to me. She danced slowly, swaying her hips. I went to her, and she put her arms around my neck. Her body was warm. We danced closed. I began to get an erection and backed away, but she pulled me closer and pressed against me. Grinding. Her lips were on my neck. I breathed into her ear. She moaned softly.

"Last call," the bartender said lazily from the other end of the bar.

15. BLACK EYES, BACKSTAGE, AND BUSTING TANNER'S GROOVE

In the morning, Maybelline woke up first. She stretched and her elbow clocked me right in the bone above my eye, waking me up.

"Sorry," she said, interrupting her yawn.

"Goddamnit, that smarts," I said and rubbed my eye.

"Let me see."

I moved my hand away.

"It looks ok," she said. She kissed the spot where she got me.

"I'll probably deserve that sooner than later."

"You better not," she said and kissed me again and then got out of bed. She pulled on her pants. "I've gotta go," she said from inside her shirt, fighting her arms through.

"It's so early."

"It's almost eleven."

"Yeah. Early."

"I'll see you at the event later on."

I yawned. "Ah, gig time. Which t-shirt should I wear?"

She laughed and bent down to put on her shoes. "You better be good. I don't want to have to lie to Rolling Stone during my first week on the job."

"What could possibly go wrong?"

"Exactly," she said and slung her purse over her shoulder and across her body and left my apartment.

I got up and made a shitty cup of instant coffee and texted Bollocks to tell him I'd be over soon to practice. I dumped the last half of my coffee down the sink and showered and left my apartment. I put on my lucky Rolling Stones t-shirt, white with long black sleeves. The word "Altamont" written across the front.

Bollocks was working his chops on a practice pad when I arrived. We ran the set and sung at about fifty percent to preserve our vocals for the main gig. Our scheduled stage time was 7:30 and we had to check-in and load-in by five at the latest. We packed up our gear in the back of Bollocks' twenty-year old Ford Econoline. We took the back seats out long ago, and the bench seat served as a secondary couch in his loft. He bolted it to the floor after it kept tipping over every time someone stood up.

Bollocks started the engine and we headed to the festival.

"I still can't believe we got this gig," I said.

"We've put in the time," Bollocks said. "And someone's looking out for us. Behind every success story there's someone giving someone a break. Or a blowjob."

"Did you blow someone for this?"

"Nah. If it was like Firefly, I'd probably give a handy or something."

"Well, we have to give a big shout-out to the station for the opportunity."

"Work it in during an intro."

I took out my copy of the setlist to see when a good spot would be to work in the nod. There weren't many opportunities between songs. It's a tight balance between being super-robotic and clinical up there or going too far the other way and talking way too damn much. My aunt took me to see Ray LaMontagne a couple of times in the early-2010s when I was a kid. I remember him not saying shit between songs except "Thank you." I was impressed by that—how he let his music do all the talking for him.

We pulled up to the gate and checked in and were given passes attached to lanyards we had to always wear. We drove into the backstage lot. I felt like I was on a movie set, minus the cameras, with all the commotion and wires and speakers and people.

"What the fuck," I said. "I can't believe this."

"I know dude. Let's try to play it cool, though. We belong here." Bollocks slammed on the brakes. "Holy shit, there's Gary Clark Jr." He put his head out of the window, "Gary, I love you," he yelled and honked the horn.

"Knock it off," I said and pulled him back in the window. "What happened to being cool?"

"What? I love him."

"And now he knows it."

"Just don't pee your pants in front of Beck."

"Why would I do that?"

"Just saying it so it doesn't happen. Like how if you think about the worst thing that could happen, it most likely won't."

"Peeing my pants in front of Beck wouldn't be the worst thing. Peeing my pants in front of the audience would be."

Bollocks parked the van near the loading zone. "All right Miles Davis, let's get this stuff backstage."

We got out of the van and a couple of guys wearing event shirts with "STAGE CREW" printed across the front and back came over to us.

"We got it," one of the guys said, pointing to the van.

"We all got it, baby," Bollocks said, winking.

The guy looked confused. "Uh, ok."

Another guy with a clipboard spoke. "You're Mojo Pin?"

"That's us," I said.

"Cool. We'll store your gear backstage. Be back here by 6:45 to set up your kit and dial in your amp, unless you have people to do it for you."

Bollocks looked at me and smiled.

"Ok, we'll see you back here," the guy said. "We'll put your gear onstage and run a line-check before you go out. How many DI's do you need?"

"Just one for my synth," Bollocks said.

"Microphones?"

"One for me, one for him," I said.

"Cool," the guy said. "That'll do it."

We shook his hand, and his crew went to work unloading the van.

We walked away towards the crowd, away from the stage.

"Well, shit," I said. "I can get used to that."

"As could I, young Marcus. As could I," Bollocks said and put his arm around me. We turned the corner around a massive tent and caught a glimpse of the crowd. It was the most people I've ever seen from this side of a stage before in real life. "Fuck," Bollocks said.

"We better not suck," I said.

Bollocks squeezed my shoulder.

"What time is it?" I asked.

"Hammer time," he said. "Let's go."

We set off into the crowd towards the side stage. As we snaked our way through the throng of people, I caught the whiff of cigarette smoke. And bourbon.

16. LIVING IN A GHOST TOWN

Tanner had spent the past two days in his basement trying to summon spirits to no avail. Now he was backstage warming up on Micawber. He was hunched over the guitar, sitting away from the rest of the guys in his band. Divided by Rabies was set to go on in a few minutes.

"Hey, Tanner," the singer said. "You ok, brother?"

"Yeah," Tanner said, absent-mindedly.

The singer looked at the rest of the guys in the band and raised his eyebrows and shrugged.

"Just remember to cut the intro to 'Straw Heart' to two measures," the bass player said. "You know the stuff we went over at practice yesterday. The one you missed."

"I told you I was practicing," Tanner said, looking up.

"What?" The bass player shook his head. "Lose the goddamned contact lens already."

"All right, all right," the singer said. "Let's cool it. We're on soon. We've worked too hard to get here. Let's not let a practice eclipse the past two years of busting our asses."

Tanner stared at the bass player and then back down to his guitar.

The bass player stood up and walked to the edge of the backstage. The stage crew was checking the microphones. Divided by Rabies were taking the stage in a minute. The singer stood next to the bass player.

"We'll deal with him after the set," the singer said to the bass player.

"He's a fucking weirdo. I never liked that guy," the bass player said.

"But he can play."

"Lots of people can play."

The daytime DJ took the stage and announced Divided by Rabies. He pointed his arms towards the wing of the stage and clapped. Tanner stood up with Micawber and the band took the stage.

Tanner plugged in and the drummer clicked off four and they began their first song. Halfway through the first chorus Tanner looked out into the audience. He spotted a guy with a spikey mohawk first, and then a guy he didn't think he'd ever see again. Especially not so soon. Tanner missed a chord change and the bass player yelled across the stage, "F, motherfucker," and stared at him with the side-eye. As the next song's final chord rang out, the two guys moved through the crowd and towards the side of the stage. Tanner started the next song and forgot to cut the intro to two measures. He didn't fare any better through the rest of the set.

When their set was over the singer thanked the audience and left the stage.

"What the fuck?" the bass player said to Tanner once backstage. He pushed him. "Our biggest gig to date and you decide it's time to start fucking up?" He pushed him again.

Tanner shielded the guitar and turned away from the bass player. "Don't push me," Tanner said.

"Fuck you," the bass player said.

The singer jumped in between them.

"Chill out, man," he said to the bass player. "Just chill out. We'll deal with it later."

"Fuck that," the bass player said. "We'll deal with it now. It's either him or me."

"Come on, man. Don't be like that."

The bass player stared at the singer. "Ok. I get it." He looked at Tanner. He looked at the drummer and then the singer. "See you around," he said. He walked away off the stage.

The singer turned to Tanner. "What the fuck, man? What happened up there?"

"I don't know. It's like my fingers forgot how to play."

"Well they better fucking remember." The singer shook his head. "Just lay low. I'm gonna try to sort this out and save this band."

Tanner watched his bandmates walk away. Once they turned a corner, he saw the two guys from the audience sitting on a big amp. The dude with the mohawk was punching his fist into his other hand like a 1950s bully, and the other guy, who was wearing a white t-shirt with long black sleeves, the word "Altamont" written across the chest, was calmly picking at his nails.

"Hi, Tanner," the guy with the mohawk said.

"How's my guitar?" Altamont asked.

Tanner turned towards the stage, but there was nowhere to go. The stage crew was breaking down the gear and setting up for the next band. The other side of the stage dropped straight off to the ground. He thought he could make it, but he wouldn't have much of an advantage trying to move through the crowd with the guitar.

"Hey," a girl's voice called out. "Marc. Bollocks."

A girl in a tank-top, smiling and waving, was half-skipping over to them. She looked at Tanner as she passed him. "Um," she said. "Good set."

"Don't lie to people," Bollocks said. "It's not polite."

Marc made a face like he smelled something. Tanner felt hands on his shoulders pushing him towards the amp. He was lifted and pressed against the back of the tower of speakers, out of view from the audience.

Bollocks hopped off the amp and the girl screamed and put her hands over her mouth.

"What the fuck!" Bollocks said. "What the fuck, what the fuck, what the fuck..."

Keith Richards turned towards the trio. "Let's not react irrationally," he said. Keith Richards looked at the girl. "Pleasure to meet you, darling," he said and then winked at Marc.

Keith Richards pulled out a switchblade from his pocket. "It's been a while since I've had to put the blade to someone, but I still remember how."

Piss trickled down Tanner's leg and puddled on the stage. "You...you're..."

"At your service," Keith Richards said and nodded his head. "Now, I believe you have something that doesn't belong to you."

Marc walked towards Tanner and Keith Richards. He unbuttoned the strap from the guitar and pulled it away. Tanner squirmed, but Keith Richards doubled his grip and lifted him an inch higher off the ground.

"Stop whimpering," Keith Richards said. "Now, normally that'd be the end of this, but I think you have some information that could be valuable to us."

Tanner began to cry.

"Fuuuuccckk, kid," Keith Richards said and lowered him to the ground. "Tell these three what you know. I won't be far." Keith Richards disappeared and Tanner slid to the ground.

"That was fucking Keith Richards," Bollocks said and hit Marc on the arm. "That was fucking Keith Richards." He hit Marc again.

"I know," Marc said.

"Strange things are afoot at the Circle K," the girl said and laughed nervously as she wrapped her arm around Marc's.

17. THE MYTH AND RULES REVEALED

Twenty-five minutes ago, Keith Richards appeared to me in front of the stage where Divided by Rabies was playing. I was relieved to see him, but he told me to be cool and get backstage to cut Tanner off with the guitar. He said he had something planned but he needed to save his energy. Then he disappeared again.

I wasn't expecting him to show himself to Bollocks, Maybelline, and Tanner—but he did, and part of me was relieved that I didn't have to persuade them I wasn't making it up. And to their credit, they were taking it surprisingly well. Maybelline wouldn't let go of me, but if that was a side effect of shock, I could live with that. Bollocks put his arm around Tanner and gripped him tight.

"Let's get a beer," Bollocks said.

"I need to change my pants," Tanner said, almost whimpering still.

"Did you bring an extra pair?" I asked.

"No."

"Than beer and a chat it is."

We grabbed a couple of beers and went back to our van so we could talk privately.

"I get carsick," Tanner said. "We aren't driving are we?" He took a mint out of his pocket and unwrapped it.

"No," Bollocks said. He laid out a towel for Tanner to sit on in the backseat and got in next to him so he couldn't squeak out and get away. "Drink up," Bollocks said and handed him a beer.

I felt sorry for Tanner now that I had my guitar back and he was reduced to a pissed pants kid holding his beer with two hands.

"Why'd you steal my guitar?" I asked. "Not fucking cool, man."

"Not cool at all," Bollocks said.

"Dick move," Maybelline said.

"If you knew what it was, you wouldn't have been so careless with it," Tanner said.

"You blaming *me* for *you* stealing my guitar?" I asked.

"Be cool, Tanner," Bollocks said.

"Yeah, don't be a dick," Maybelline said.

"I'm not. I'm not," he protested. "I could see you didn't know what you had. I spotted it the instant I saw it onstage the other night."

"What's that mean?" I asked.

"Does the name Micawber mean anything to you?" he said.

Maybelline looked at me.

"Yeah," I said.

"How about Number One?"

"Are we still talking guitars here?"

Tanner nodded.

"So, that could be Stevie Ray Vaughn's or Jimmy Page's guitar," I said.

"Both. They both named them that. Stevie's Stratocaster and Page's Les Paul."

"Ok, nerds," Bollocks interrupted. "We get it. Famous guitars. What's this have to do with anything?"

Tanner breathed in deep and exhaled. He shook his head. "Why did Keith Richards just attack me?"

"Probably because you stole his guitar. I mean, my guitar," I said.

"How long have you had it?"

"Eight years."

"Holy shit."

"What?"

"No one's owned any of the Fated Four that long."

"That's a myth," Maybelline said.

We all looked at her.

"What?" she said. "I told you before I know about this stuff." She shook her head. "Fucking boy s club. It's the myth that there are four guitars built from some magic tree that will give their owners musical superpowers."

"That's pretty close," Tanner said and nodded approvingly. "But it's not a myth. I thought so for a long time, but it's not."

"Well, don't keep it to yourself, Nancy Drew," Bollocks said. "Spill the beans."

"How much time do you have?"

I looked at my watch. "Thirty-eight minutes."

Tanner began to tell us how for years he studied the occult. How his aunt owned a bookshop and was really into witchcraft. He spent a lot of time there reading all the books he could in the back of the shop—the *Malleus Maleficarum*, *The Clavicule of Solomon*, *Dragon Rouge*, and countless other grimoires that taught invocation of the Devil and his lieutenants. He studied spells and counter spells. He said his aunt told him that his family had been "good witches" for ages. Something like guardians. Somewhere along the way, he stumbled down the rabbit hole of American folklore and Native American legends which were all white-washed to make it seem like it wasn't the meddling of the Devil in the New World.

"You're a witch?" Bollocks asked.

"He'd be a warlock, right?" I said.

"Either is fine, I guess. It's just how my family's always been," Tanner said. "By the time I came across the legend of the Fated Four, I knew there were other forces out in the world. And seeing Keith Richards today—are you sure it's Keith Richards?" he asked me.

"Yeah?" I said. "Why would you ask that?"

"The Devil and his minions wear many disguises."

"I'm pretty sure it's Keith Richards," I said, but I'd have to admit that a small seed of doubt took some footing.

"All right, Mr. Crowley, what went on in your head?" Bollocks said and tapped his wrist. "We haven't got all day."

"What she said is pretty close," Tanner said.

"Maybelline," Maybelline said.

"Maybelline's pretty close," he said. "There's a Native American legend about a demon, Sint-Holo, coming up from under the earth, and if you met him he would make your deepest desires come true, except at a cost. Supposedly, a chief made the deal, and to prevent Sint-Holo from coming back to claim his soul, he planted a tree over the spot from where the demon escaped and he performed an earth ritual that would protect it from opening up again."

"That doesn't seem like it would work," Bollocks said. "It's the fucking Devil. He can do what he wants."

"Well, it didn't exactly work," Tanner said. "And some variations on the myth suggest it was actually the Devil. Our Devil. That he was grabbing a stronger foothold in the New World. But the prevailing theory is that the tree did act as a conduit of power— it absorbed some of Sint-Holo's power when he tried to come back through that portal. And the tree, which never blossomed, marked a spot where the demon would come to one who called for it."

"Like at the crossroads?" I asked.

"Not 'like'," Tanner said. "Legend says it's *the* spot where the demon made the deal with Robert Johnson."

"Slow down a minute," Maybelline said. "First off, the Johnson and the Devil thing isn't true. The legend grew after he died. He never told anyone that he made a deal with anyone. Second, you keep calling this thing a demon. Isn't it the Devil?"

"The Robert Johnson story is true." Tanner looked at his watch. "You don't have time for me to explain it to you now. But it's true whether you believe it or not. Second, the name 'Devil' is a catchall for the many demons that exist."

"There's more than one? It's not just Satan?" Bollocks asked.

"He's one of the main demons, whatever you want to call him," Tanner said. "But just like there's God and many angels who do different things, there is a 'Satan' and the many demons who do different things for him."

"What do you call him?" I asked.

"Lucifer."

"Ok. So which one put dark magic in the tree?" I added that to the list of sentences I can't believe I have said out loud over the past couple of days.

"No one really knows for sure. I tend to believe it was Lucifer himself given the connection he has to the Fated Four. Some believe it was a lesser demon, but the facts remain that whoever owns one of those guitars, *and* makes a deal with the Devil, will become all powerful rock gods. Not just rock stars."

"What if a guy, I don't know, say, like me," I said, "only owns the guitar and hasn't made the deal?"

"You never really owned it. The only person who can truly own it is the person who made the deal. You never made a deal, right?"

I nodded. "Correct."

"These guitars. They want to slip out of the hands of their owners or whoever has it in their possession. It's why so many rock stars die. They make a deal with one of the Fated Four and then lose the guitar. When the guitar is found, which it always is, and someone makes a deal, which they almost always do, the person who made the previous deal dies and their soul belongs to Lucifer."

"Shit," I said.

"Can you repeat that?" Bollocks said. "Like in real simple terms?"

Tanner took a deep breath. "It's like a reentry stamp. Say you go to a club and then leave and then try to get back. You can with the stamp."

"And you die without it," Maybelline said. "The deal with the Devil is the club. The guitar is the stamp."

"This isn't a good analogy," Bollocks said, "but I think I understand. If you make a deal with the Devil and have the guitar, you need that guitar if you want get out of the deal. If you lose the guitar, you can't get back in the club—you die."

"More or less. There are other ways to enter his realm, but none are as foolproof and put you at an advantage than if you had one of the Four. Problem is most people don't know what they have when they make the deal," Tanner looked at me. "They feel drawn to the power, like Frodo always wanting to slip on the ring, almost subconsciously."

"Did you try and make the deal?" Maybelline asked me.

"The secret chord," I mumbled without thinking.

"What did you say?" Tanner asked.

"Nothing," I said. "I didn't try and make a deal. Wait…"

"Yo, can someone be musically powerful without owning one of these magic guitars? Like is there a magic drumstick?" Bollocks interrupted. "Like, could I have a magic drumstick and not make a deal, but just be like the baddest dude behind a kit?"

"I don't know," Tanner said. "I guess there could be other things made from the tree, but the legend only mentions the guitars. There's lots of variables. But I know for certain that the guitars are special—the bond is stronger and the promise of greatness is more realized than if you just traded your soul without it."

"Like how Harry Potter is still a wizard," Bollocks said, "but, with the elder wand he's a super wizard."

"I mean," Tanner said. "Sort of, I guess."

"Could someone's soul be tethered to one of these guitars?" I asked.

"That's what I've been saying. It's tethered to whoever made a deal with it until the next person does. Wait," Tanner said and looked at me. "When did Keith Richards show up in your life?"

"The same day I got the guitar," I said.

"I fucking knew it."

"Knew what?"

"He's watching over it. Making sure you don't make a deal."

"So you didn't know if I had made a deal or not, right?"

"I assumed you didn't since you were only playing a Thursday at a 300-seat venue."

I ignored the slight. "What were you trying to do with the guitar then? You could have killed me if you made a deal for yourself."

Tanner's eyes widened. "No, no, no. I didn't want to make a deal! I was trying to break the curse on the guitar."

"Did it work?"

Tanner shook his head.

The alarm on Bollocks' phone went off. "It's gig time," he said. "Give me your phone," he said to Tanner.

"Why?" Tanner asked.

"In case we have more questions about the voodoo."

"It's not voodoo," Tanner said.

"Phone," Bollocks said and put his hand out. Tanner reluctantly handed over his phone and Bollocks texted himself Tanner's contact info—address and all. "There we go, Godsmack. Now we're all friends and can get in touch."

We got out of the van and with a touch of what seemed like genuine concern, Tanner turned to me and said, "Be careful."

18. TEMPERATURE'S RISING AT THE ROTTEN OASIS

The band that was on before us, Tripoli, were a quartet from Libya who built their own instruments out of garbage. They weren't half bad and could sing their asses off, but their songs weren't very good. Public radio latched on to their story and within a year they went from political prisoners to a legit touring band with massive radio support. We watched them from backstage as Bollocks tweaked his kit and I dialed in the tone on my amp. I studied them to see which one sold their soul. They finished their last number and took a bow.

And then everything happened fast. The stage crew put our gear in place. The station's daytime DJ came on before we did. He announced us and the audience actually applauded. It seemed half polite and half earnest. I could live with that.

We took the stage and ripped through the first couple of numbers. I thanked XPN, and when I mentioned Beck, the audience applauded the loudest I had heard them all day. We played the next couple of songs, and when we played our single getting airplay, some people were singing along and I could sense the tide turning in our favor.

During the intro to our last song, Bollocks laid down a groove and played a looped bass line on the synth.

"Thanks for coming out," I said. "We're Mojo Pin."

And then my low E string broke. The snap of the string knocked my pick out of my hand. I couldn't find it on the stage. I truly believe there is an alternate universe, a strange portal that is filled with guitar picks. It's a fact that nine out of ten dropped guitar picks disappear into the void. I played it cool and dug into my pocket for an extra. "Marc," a crew member said from the side of the stage, holding up the other guitar, the cheap pawn shop deal I brought.

I turned to Bollocks. "Loop it again," I said while still digging in my pocket. "My fucking string broke. I'm gonna switch guitars real quick."

"I got you," he said.

My fingers were loose magnets drawn to a particular pick. Keith Richards appeared next to me, sitting on the drum riser. "Play it with five strings," he said and winked. "I'm here, kid," he said.

Suddenly, a bolt of lightning coursed through my body—a mysterious force in my veins surged inside of me up through the soles of my feet. I felt like I could do anything and before I knew what I was doing I waved off the stage crew guy.

I'd never played our songs with five strings before. We needed that low end with just the two of us. But I had played all the Rolling Stones songs that Keith had tuned that way, so I wasn't a stranger to the feeling. I touched the pick to the strings and that feeling hit me again—I looked down at Micawber and then turned towards the audience as the intro came back around. I raised my pick hand high, straight up to the sky, the little wooden pick vibrating at the end of my fingers, and with a windmill that would make Pete Townshend jealous, I swung out the first three chords to the song and we were fucking off.

The song played itself, and I was its steward, its frame. The song was a kite that pulled—I its master. We pushed the song and performance to greatness—we had made a contract with glory.

When it was over, the audience flipped the fuck out. They cheered for an encore. I thanked them and as if they couldn't get any louder, they did. I looked to my left and Beck was dancing out on to the stage. He put his arm around me and grabbed the mic.

"Let's do one more," he said. "What do you say?"

The stage shook from the sheer volume of the audience. I looked at Bollocks. His face was cracked wide open with a smile. His fingers danced on the synth, dialing in the new patches, and then he clicked off four.

"This is a good choice," Beck said and laughed as I played the riff on my guitar.

"*Somethin's wrong cause my mind is fading, and everywhere I look there's a dead end waiting,*" Beck sang.

Halfway through the song I saw Keith Richards rocking his head, a smoking cigarette in his hand. He was grinning. I saw Maybelline in the wings of the stage. She waved at me and blew me a kiss. I kept my composure this time.

19. SILVER LININGS SLAY BOOK

Beck congratulated us backstage, and Maybelline staged a photo with the three of us and then went off with Beck to grab a few quotes to dovetail the interview from earlier with the show.

"What the fuck happened up there?" Bollocks said.

"I don't even know. This jolt ran through me, and it was like everything I'd ever learned and practiced with the guitar and singing was heightened. I felt like I could do anything."

"Dude, you went limitless!"

"What?"

"You were like Bradley Cooper in that movie where he took a drug and he had no limits."

"Oh. Yeah, sort of. Except I didn't take any drugs."

Maybelline finished with Beck and came back over to us. "What the hell was that?" she said.

"He went limitless," Bollocks said. "Like Bradley Cooper in that movie where…"

"I know what that is," Maybelline, cutting him off and laughing. "There was something unreal about that performance. You looked like you were floating up there."

"I sure felt like it," I said. I put my hand in my pocket and pulled the pick out. "I think it was this."

Maybelline and Bollocks huddled around, looking at the wooden pick.

"It's a little small, isn't it?" Maybelline asked.

"Dude. Has Louis C.K. taught us nothing? You can't be whipping out your pick all nonchalant-like. Especially if it's that tiny."

"All right," I said, dragging the words out.

"Where'd you get it?" Maybelline asked.

I told them the story of the subway, and honoring my word to Johnny Newman, I said that I found the pick on the ground. And for added scent-throwing off, I said that it looked like the pick Scotty Moore used.

"Elvis' guitar player?" Maybelline asked.

"Yeah," I said, and lest this white lie get out of hand, I added, "but he mostly used a thumb pick, so it's definitely *not* his."

"So, let me get this straight," Bollocks said, ignoring my last statement. "You've got Keith Richards' magic guitar and maybe Scotty Moore's magic guitar pick?"

"It seems so."

"Dude, you've got two thirds of the musical Deathly Hallows."

"This Harry Potter thing again?"

"There's the elder wand, the most powerful wand in the world. That's Micawber. The resurrection stone which can bring anyone back to life. That's the pick." Bollocks' mouth dropped open. "Oh shit, dude! You have the Pick of Destiny!" He jumped up and down and clapped his hands together. "Ok, ok. The third thing was the invisibility cloak so death can't find you. That's probably something like a mask from one of those dudes from KISS."

"That's ridiculous. And KISS wore makeup, not masks."

"Well, it's probably *something*. I just think it's cool that you're almost like a wizard," Bollocks said and then mumbled to himself, "I wonder what the third thing is."

"I don't know. He might be on to something," Maybelline said. "The two are definitely linked together. Do you think it's a coincidence that you have Micawber, found that pick, and the first time you use the two together your performance is transcendent?"

All of this seemed to be a bit of an overload. I put the pick away and took a deep breath.

"I guess not," I said. "But what the hell am I supposed to do with these things?"

Bollocks and Maybelline went a little pale and were staring over my shoulder.

"You could start by asking him," Bollocks said and pointed to Keith Richards who was standing right behind me.

"You can still see him?"

"It's ok, kid," Keith Richards said. "We're gonna need all the help we can get. Ron and Hermione over here seem like they'll fit the bill."

Bollocks smiled. "Told you," he said.

"Keith," I said. "We need to have an honest talk later on."

"I think so, too," he said. He pointed to Micawber. "Keep a tight eye on her?"

***

Keith Richards disappeared and Bollocks and I went out into the crowd to watch Beck. I put Micawber back in its case and kept the guitar with me as we slipped through the crowd and managed a spot upfront. During one point of his performance, Beck thanked the radio station and the other bands on the bill with a general acknowledgment.

"And," Beck said. "How about Mojo Pin? Thanks guys. That was a real treat." He pointed down to us. "Let's give it up for Mojo Pin."

The audience applauded and Beck counted off, "two, three, four," and began his last song. My heart raced and I nudged Bollocks in the side. He put his arms around me and kissed me on the cheek.

"Knock it off," I said, wiping my face.

***

After Beck finished, Bollocks and I went backstage to load up our gear in the van while Maybelline went off to interview Gary Clark Jr. She heard Neko Case was kicking about, and despite the uncoolness of a journalist fawning over an artist, she was going to make up an excuse to talk to her and have a picture taken with her.

"Dude," Bollocks said. "We just fucking destroyed out there."

"I know," I laughed. Bollocks wouldn't stop mentioning it. "We'll have to send a gift basket to Brad."

"With that guitar and pick, we're going to be unstoppable."

I sensed a small tinge of desire—a longing in his voice. The tone was off for him.

"I think we should be careful," I said. I did feel on the edge of something great. Like all the pieces were starting to fall into place after a couple of years of slogging it out.

But I was torn. On one hand, I had the tools to catapult to rock glory. On the other, it was a dangerous line to walk, flirting with the Devil and temptation.

"Dude, as long as you don't try to make a deal with the Devil, we're golden," Bollocks said. "We could be headliners for Bonnaroo or Made in America by this time next year."

"I don't know man. If what Tanner says is true, this guitar and the other ones have taken out a lot of musicians."

"That's because they probably tried to handle it alone." Bollocks sat down on the bumper of the van. "You've got motherfucking Keith Richards on your side. And Maybelline. Dude, it's all good. You're not alone." His settled into a familiar tone, the one I knew was the true Bollocks. Then with a slight British accent, "Don't worry, Mr. Marco. I'll be your Samwise. I'll be your fat hobbit."

20. BACK IN NEW JERSEY: NO TIME FOR THE CORNER BOYS

Tanner apologized to his bandmates on the ride back to New Jersey. The singer seemed to get the bass player to cool off and he rejoined the band with the caveat that if Tanner fucked up again, one of them would have to go.

Tanner stayed up all night searching his books and the internet for information on the secret chord. He knew he heard Marc say it. Marc hadn't meant to say it, but he did. Tanner had been searching for it for years, but he thought that with Micawber in his possession the simple invocation would have worked. That he could have vanquished the demon from ever doing harm through the guitar again.

He turned back to Leonard Cohen's "Hallelujah." It was the only outright mention of the secret chord in a song. Cohen must've known it and never used it, or found a way to slither his poet-talking ass out of the deal. He probably set up Jeff Buckley to take over for his soul. Buckley died way too young at thirty years old. Drowned in the Wolf Creek while swimming. An accident.

Tanner looked up live versions of Jeff Buckley playing "Hallelujah." Again. *The secret chord couldn't just be an A minor?* he thought. *That'd be ludicrous—every guitar player knows that chord. There was one difference between Cohen's version and Buckley's. After the secret chord lyric, the instructions are to play the fourth, the fifth, then a minor, then a major—and then the difference: Cohen plays an*

E minor, whereas Buckley plays an inverted E major, borrowing from the harmonic minor for one chord.

Tanner grabbed his guitar and played the song over and over. The fourth, fifth, minor, major, inverted dominant. Nothing. He tried it Leonard's way. Still nothing.

Fuck it, he thought. *I'd probably need Micawber. That's if Leonard and Jeff even knew the goddamn thing. The lyrics say they've only "heard" of it.*

Tanner shook his head. *This isn't it. It doesn't make sense. Every asshole at an open mic singing "Hallelujah" would be summoning a demon.*

Tanner wasn't sure what he was doing anymore. He was being careless without having Micawber as his Excalibur. He was a kid pushing a button just to see what would happen. He knew that if Marc pushed the button he'd be pegged. Hounded. There'd be no escape until he relented or vanquished the demon, but he knew Marc wouldn't have the first clue how to go about it—Keith Richards or not. He had Micawber and didn't even know it.

Fuck, Tanner thought. Invoking a demon for himself was one thing, but maybe it's because he was in the Boy Scouts, or had Canadian ancestry, he couldn't let Marc lose his soul without knowing it. He knew in his heart he had to help him.

21. SELFISH IS AS SELFISH DOES

Brad was back at the radio station after filing payroll for the overtime shifts from the festival. He picked up the acoustic guitar in his office and sat down on the couch. People always asked him about the instrument after the rumor that it belonged to Johnny Cash began to circulate, and he didn't do much to dissuade them. The truth was the guitar had always been there. Johnny Cash had never been in the studio. When the station opened and Brad took his office, he found the guitar in the back of a closet, old and dusty. The deed to the building at large, before it was chopped up into offices and the station, once housed a large music store and a luthier's studio back in the '40s and '50s. Brad thought it was a leftover from a time forgotten. Though, having people think the guitar belonged to Johnny Cash was way cooler.

Brad strummed the guitar. He never learned to play the instrument very well, but shit, neither did the Sex Pistols or the Ramones. Half of rock music was just attitude shoved into leather. Brad was too old for leather and skin—that shipped had sailed, and if you don't get onboard when you're young and thin, it's best to avoid that port no matter how strong it calls.

He fingerpicked a solemn number on the guitar and began to sing. His voice sounded full and throaty, the kind of voice people would pay to hear—not the usual thin, whiny twang it had yesterday. He laughed out loud and then put the guitar down. He pulled out his phone and called his connection at Rolling Stone. The one the Devil set him up with to get Maybelline the job.

"There's a new band I think you should check out. I think Maybelline would be perfect for the assignment if you could spare her next weekend. They're calling him the next Jeff Buckley or Bruce Springsteen."

When he hung up the phone with Rolling Stone, he dialed Maybelline's number.

22. A PLAN IS FORMED

Maybelline, Bollocks, and I went out after the gig to celebrate. We ended up at a burger joint, Lucky's Last Chance, in Queen Village that had a killer draft lineup. Spending $8 a beer wasn't our usual mode, but I had a sweet tooth for imperial stouts and Bollocks knew it. He was friends with the bartender and our tab was often minimal. Bollocks put back pounder after pounder of High Life while I sipped my stout and had an Irish whiskey. Maybelline ordered an Old Fashioned.

"Redemption, lemon rind, no cherry, not too sweet," she said. "On the rocks."

"And don't you dare bruise the fucking bitters," Bollocks said and pointed his finger at the bartender.

We split a basket of tots. And then another.

I kept Micawber under my arm the whole evening. There was no way I was letting it out of my sight again. Not until we straightened everything out.

"So, what's the next move?" Bollocks asked. "Tour?"

"I'd have to see if I can get my shifts covered," I said. "I'd probably get fired if I took off again." We'd just come back from a little jaunt in the spring down the coast and it was hell to get all my shifts covered for two weeks without being able to make them up. I had been contemplating quitting anyway—stocking shelves overnight wasn't going to be my career.

"Dude, we've got to capitalize on this momentum," Bollocks said.

"I agree," Maybelline said. "You've got to really want it if you want to make it. People don't realize that. I've seen so many bands put so much work in and really hustle the local scene, and then when it comes time to make the big jump, they chicken out. They can't get off the pot. It's like 'Do you really want it? Or do you just like to play once in a while and say you really want it and then get all bitter when a kingmaker doesn't show up?'"

"I know, I know," I said. "I do want it. It's just this is all of a sudden. And with Keith Richards and the Devil on my trail, it seems weird to think of my career right now."

"Settle down, Robert Johnson," Bollocks said. "The Devil isn't on your trail."

Maybelline gave me a look. I never told Bollocks about the other night.

"About that," I said. I told Bollocks everything and holy hell did it feel good to finally come clean to him.

"Well, shit," Bollocks said. "Why'd you play something called 'the fucking secret chord?'"

"It was an accident," I said. "After what Tanner just said, I think the guitar wanted me to play it."

"Is he going to come after you forever, or was it a one-time thing? Like a knock and run?"

"I sure hope it's a one and done, though a lot of weird shit has happened since."

"Maybe it's all coincidence," Maybelline offered. "Maybe it isn't all related. I mean, you didn't make a deal with the Devil, so that's good. Right?"

"I sure as shit didn't make a deal, and I don't plan on it either."

"So," Bollocks said, "essentially, you've got this magic guitar and pick that makes you awesome, but the downside is the Devil is coming after you. Maybe."

"That sounds about right."

"Well, it seems pretty straightforward if you ask me."

"I'm glad you're feeling so enlightened."

"Dude, relax. All we gotta do is vanquish the Devil and then he won't be after you anymore."

"Vanquish the Devil? How the fuck do you propose we do that?"

"I don't know. Call a priest?" Bollocks shrugged.

"You believe in God now?"

"I didn't believe in ghosts or the Devil until today."

"I don't know man. This isn't a movie."

"Well, priests aside, that guitar seems to be the thing drawing him to you."

"I'm not getting rid of it," I said. "I can't knowingly let someone else have it and lose their souls."

"Not get rid of it," Bollocks said. "Destroy it."

"It ain't that easy," a voice said next to Maybelline.

"Jesus," Maybelline said, spitting out her drink on the bar.

Beside her, Keith Richards wiped his finger on the bar and licked it.

"Ohh," he said. "You're a fun one."

"I'm not sure whether to freak out or shit my pants," Bollocks said, staring.

"You'll get used to it," Keith Richards said.

"Where have you been?" I asked.

"Around. My energy's been waning lately."

"That ever happen before?"

"Not like this."

"When did it start?" Maybelline asked, regaining her composure.

"After Marc played the secret chord. That night, after the Devil, I noticed it."

"That's when the guitar was stolen," I said.

"Hmm…" Keith Richards said.

"What?"

"I'm tethered to the guitar because of the deal I made."

"No one else has made a deal though. You should still be strong."

"It seems that you playing the chord and that kid with candles have broke its hold on me. Like the guitar is pulling away from me."

"Tanner only said you're in trouble if I make a deal with the guitar. What do you think will happen if it pulls away from you completely?"

"I'm not sure, and I don't want to find out before we battle the Devil."

"I told you we had to battle the Devil," Bollocks said and hit me in the arm.

"We've got to go to the crossroads," Keith said. "As far as I know that's the only place we can enter the underworld to cut heads."

"So, we just casually go down to the crossroads and battle the Devil to save your soul?"

"With that guitar I can win," Keith said.

"What about me?"

"You're golden, kid," Keith said and nodded at me. "I've got your back. I'll arrange for you and your lot."

"You said it wasn't that easy," Maybelline said. "Destroying the guitar is the objective, but now it seems like you just want to play it."

"Gotta free my soul before we destroy it, don't I?" Keith said.

"Seems fair."

"How will we destroy it after?" I asked.

"Drop it back down to Hell," Keith said matter-of-factly.

"From whence it came, it shall remain, until you are complete again," Bollocks said.

"What?" I said.

"Tenacious D, dude. Their battle with the Beezleboss. I bet that was autobiographical."

"Come on, man. Everything isn't related to pop-culture."

"How else do you explain two overweight dudes with acoustic guitars becoming rock stars? I bet they actually had the Pick of Destiny."

"They never had it," Keith said and lit a cigarette. "But Grohl did."

"I told you," Bollocks said. "Again." He jumped up and down again. "Grohl had that pick!"

"One of 'em, anyway," Keith said.

"There's more than one?" Bollocks rubbed his hands together. "Fuck yeah. There's definitely magic drumsticks."

"Chill out," I said. "None of this matters. We're going to the crossroads to save our souls and make sure this guitar doesn't take anyone else's."

"So, tour?" Bollocks asked.

"I guess fucking so."

Maybelline's phone rang. "It's Brad," she said.

"Answer that shit," Bollocks said. "Thank him for us."

Maybelline stepped away. Bollocks and I talked about what venues we could hit up on the way down to the crossroads and what bands we were cool with on that circuit.

Maybelline slid back onto her barstool. "Well," she said. "It looks like I'm heading to Austin. Mind if I tag along?"

23. GUITARS AND PICKS AND LEATHER JACKETS, OH MY!

Tanner threw a duffel bag into the trunk of his Honda Civic and closed the hatch. He got into the driver's seat and started the ignition. He texted Bollocks. Again. Told him he'd be in Philly in a few hours—please call back. He popped a mint into his mouth and put the wrapper in his pocket.

He pulled away and made his way to the interstate.

He ran through all the incantations he could remember for banishing a spirit, but he knew they wouldn't be enough. Marc had to battle the Devil himself and Micawber was the key. He was pretty sure Marc had a talisman pick. No one just finds those. Helper spirits or guides only give those to the people who are marked. Everyone gets a choice and the tools to enact change, even if they aren't aware of it at the time.

The jacket—if Marc hoped to vanquish the Devil, he'd need the jacket too. Tanner wasn't initially sure if he believed the legend of the guitar and pick and jacket, but the events of the past few days squashed any doubts he had.

The legend said Piominko, the young chief, was wearing a large shawl made of buffalo hide when *Sint-Holo* burst forth from the ground. The blood of his people soaked the garment. Magic was transferred when the earth was electrified. The shawl was passed down. It was tanned. Cut. Pieces of it used to make leather pants.

Jackets. Hats. Gloves. The largest swatch belonged to Elvis, then Pete Best, then Joey Ramone, in the form of a leather jacket.

And if Tanner was right, and he was pretty sure he was, that leather jacket hung in the Hard Rock Café in New York City. Thought to be the jacket George Harrison wore during the Beatles' Hamburg days. Truth was it belonged to Best who chucked it aside after the Decca sessions proved fruitless—and with it any chance of rock glory. Ramone somehow ended up with it and lost it during their tour in support of *Ramones*. After that it slipped through history until a collector misappropriated it and sold it to the restaurant chain.

Tanner pieced it together—followed the jacket through photographs and known locations. This had to be it. Most people who studied the occult and wrote about the legends thought the jacket was John Lennon's from the Rubber Soul album cover, given Lennon's tragic end. But, there was no mysticism behind the work of a crazed fan. Tanner knew that. He also knew that he was embarking upon something special that joined the two worlds he cared most about: rock and roll and black magic.

"Alexa," Tanner said. "Play Zeppelin IV."

He stepped on the gas.

24. CROSSROADS, BUT MAKE IT FASHION

Maybelline went home to pack, and Bollocks and I went back to his apartment to reach out to venues along the way towards Austin.

"Remember, though," Keith Richards said. "Austin isn't the aim."

"Well, if we can a get gig while we're hot, I'd say it is the aim," Bollocks said. "After we vanquish the Devil, that is."

"What's the name of the promoter in Memphis?" I asked. "That'll put us right near Clarksdale."

Bollocks took out his phone and began swiping his finger on the screen.

Keith Richards let out a quiet grunt.

"What?"

"Rosedale," he said.

"The crossroads are in Clarksdale," I said. "Aren't they?"

"Yeah, they put a real pretty little lamppost up too," Keith chuckled again. "Trust me, kid. It's in Rosedale." Keith Richards lit a cigarette. "Everyone thought it was at US 61 and 49. I did too for the longest. But the true bluesman—them motherfuckers with soul—they know Clarksdale is nothing but a diversion. The place where men go to decide if they *really* want to go on to the *real* crossroads. In that sense, it is a crossroads, but it's not *the* crossroads."

Bollocks was looking at his phone. "Ok. Rosedale, Clarksdale, wherever it is, we shall go." He looked at me. "So, remember how I liked not having my phone yesterday?"

"Yeah," I said.

"I put it on 'Do Not Disturb' earlier."

"I'm proud of you."

"I mean, everyone I knew, I was with, so I didn't really need it. It was great and…"

"The point, kid," Keith Richards said.

"Tanner sent me a hundred messages," Bollocks said. "I think we should wait for him."

"For what?"

Bollocks tossed me his phone.

"Yer a wizard, Marky," he said.

***

I scanned the messages. Tanner said he wanted to help us with the Devil and save my soul. He said that having just the guitar, or just the pick might be enough, but to truly be prepared I'd need some legendary leather jacket. A jacket that would protect me from the Devil's magic in the underworld.

I gave Bollocks his phone back. "How do we know he isn't just angling to get the guitar back for himself? With my pick?"

"We don't," Bollocks said. "But he seems to know his shit."

"Let's just keep an eye on him," Keith Richards said. "I know what I have to do. If that wanker thinks he can help you free your soul, sure, let's bring him along."

"And if he can't help us, or starts acting funny," Bollocks said while punching his fist into his hand, "it's curtains for Smeagol."

"I thought you were all 'Harry Potter' for this?" I said. "Now it's back to 'Lord of the Rings?'"

"Why can't it be both?"

I shook my head and dialed the number to the promoter in Memphis.

Bollocks looked at Keith Richards and shrugged. "It can be both," he mumbled.

Keith Richards leaned back, smoked his cigarette and exhaled. "I don't get you, kid. But sure. It can be both." He chuckled to himself. "It can be both."

25. NEW YORK CITY—HARD ROCK CAFÉ: INDIANA WAS THE DOG'S NAME!

"Ok, ok," Tanner said. "I was just looking! Take it easy!"

The manager and a bartender from the Hard Rock Café had their hands on Tanner's arms, and one hand each around the back of his neck.

"Don't come back," they said as they lifted him up off the ground and threw him out onto the sidewalk on 7th Ave in Times Square.

"Fucking fake ass, corny, watered-down tourist bullshit," he said to himself, straightening his shirt from being bunched up around his collar and under his arms. He looked at the entrance to the Rock Shop and all the tourists going in. He rubbed his neck.

He walked around the block. "Think, Tanner," he said to himself. There had to be a way in. He felt a little nauseous and pulled out a mint, unwrapped it, and put it in his mouth. He put the wrapper in his pocket and felt a small stockpile of wrappers. He crinkled them and looked around. There weren't any trashcans in sight. He walked around the block again, hoping to find a service entrance to the building. *Probably near the dumpsters*, he thought. He didn't recall seeing any dumpsters on his first walk around and his second trip confirmed his recollection.

Where do people put their trash? It *was* New York, but he looked around and it was surprisingly litter-free for the most part. He looked towards Times Square. There was a heavy police presence at all the corners and intersections. An officer across the street had a K-9 on a leash. There were cameras, orbicular domes watching, recording everything.

Of course there are no trashcans. People could hide bombs in them. The realization and reminder that the world in which he lived had its own problems not caused by the Devil—and were mostly done in the name of the good guy—was short lived and shattered when a voice above him boomed, "Hop on the Meat Train to Tastyville! Open your mouths, baby birds, the sky is dripping with deliciosity!"

Irritated, Tanner looked up. Gustave Bovarie's digital circle beard and white spiked hair loomed over him. "First stop, Disco Potatoes! Glamtastic!"

What the fuck is he even saying? Tanner thought. He felt the wrappers in his pocket again. He looked at Gustave—*this better be worth it*—and opened the door to Gustave Bovarie's Bistro Américain.

26. 3 AM— NEW YORK CITY—HARD ROCK CAFÉ: FUCKING NEW GUY

Tanner stretched his legs and pushed a pile of cardboard off his body. He had spent the past 10 hours sliding in and out of the kitchen to the Hard Rock Café—mostly out—not meeting anyone's eyes and pretending he didn't understand English whenever someone spoke to him.

"New guy," he'd say with an accent crossing the line somewhere between Russian and Michael Caine and then point to himself. He couldn't believe it, but his plan worked. All of it. So far.

He had went into Gustave Bovarie's for an order of Slamabama Sliders, slipped out the backdoor, and into Hard Rock's stockroom where he found a box of uniforms. He spent most of his time in the utility closet or hallway. There was a lot of staff, and the fast-paced kitchen allowed him to operate unbothered as long as he was cleaning something when he was in the kitchen.

When he took the last load of trash to the dumpster he came back and broke down a large empty box. When no one was looking, he climbed in the big gray trash wheelbarrow, just inside the backdoor, pulled the cardboard on top of himself, and nestled snugly in the bottom. The cool sensation of trash juice soaking through his pants and sliming its way against his body almost made him vomit. The cloyingly sweet smell of the trash juice *did* make him throw up in his mouth. He chewed it back and took long, slow deep breaths from his mouth and waited. And waited. And thought about how only two days ago he was living a very normal life. Safe from harm. Working a nine-to-five. Gigs on the weekend.

Then he found one of the most significant guitars in rock history. And now he was trying to steal a leather jacket to help someone defeat the Devil. It was the right thing to do, he told himself. *It's the right thing to do. I'm doing the right thing,* he repeated to himself as he climbed out of the dumpster, as silent as the mice circling the bain-marie in search of leftover scraps.

The kitchen was dark except for the red EXIT sign above the door, and the ghostly glow of the pilot lights twinkling from the burners under the grill. Tanner crept slowly to the edge of the kitchen door. His best bet would be to leave through the back. Grab the jacket and bolt like hell before the cops came. The chairs were up in the restaurant, and he expected an alarm to go off as soon as he set foot in the dining room. He could see the jacket hanging on the wall in an enclosed glass frame, just above the booth and table he climbed up on earlier to see how he could get the jacket. The frame was bolted to the wall and wouldn't budge when he pulled on it. He'd have to smash the glass, grab the jacket, and run. He looked around for something to break the case. Plates. Pots. Pans.

He spotted a fire extinguisher hanging on the wall. *That could work.* He took it off the wall and tiptoed back to the edge of the doorway. His eye on the prize. A woman's giggle echoed through the place.

He darted across the small expanse between the kitchen and a pillar. As quietly as a madman at midnight, he moved his head around the pillar.

Two people at the end of the bar. A man and woman. Through the honeyed haze of the dimmed lights and neon signs over the bar he vaguely recognized them as the bartender, and he thought, one of the waitresses. They had glasses of something and were smoking cigarettes. Her hand was on his leg. She giggled again. He put his hand on her back and leaned in and kissed her. A moan, and then a giggle.

Tanner hid behind the pillar. *Fuck*, he thought again. *Think, think.*

The distant sound of mumbling, moaning, and giggling came in small waves across the empty room. He stood there deciding how to make his move. The mumbling stopped. The giggling stopped. Low moans.

He peeked his head back around and the girl had her shirt off.

Holy titties! Tanner thought. The bartender had his hand down her pants.

Tanner stared at the half nude woman moaning and felt a small sense of arousal and shame, and a little like a pervert. A trash juiced soggy pervert. He re-hid behind the pillar.

Eye on the prize, he said again. He saw a fire alarm on the wall, just in arms reach. *Eye on the fucking prize.*

He poked his head back around towards the bar. The waitress unbuckled the bartender's pants. They clumsily laid on top of a table, crashing the chairs onto the floor. *C'mon, c'mon.*

The waitress reached down and pulled her feet out of her pants. Tanner couldn't see over the rail and chair legs obstructing his view of the table, but once the moaning assured him the lovers were sufficiently docked and entangled, he took two quick and deliberate steps towards the jacket, lining it up, and hurled the heavy metal extinguisher, butt end first. The glass shattered and fell. He jumped up on the booth and grabbed the jacket off the wall and darted towards the kitchen.

"Hey!" a voice yelled. He glanced back and for a split second saw a man tripping over his pants legs and falling. Tanner hit the fire alarm and a sharp, blunt signal ripped through the building, lights flashing.

No water?! Goddamnit. Hoping for maximum confusion to cover his escape, he pulled the trip to the Ansul system in the kitchen by the door. Behind him, the sound of foam burst forth from the nozzles over the grills, oven, and fryers and floor, covering everything in a 2-inch fire retardant layer.

He hauled ass down the hallway towards the dumpsters. His heart was no longer part of his body—it was a weight thumping inside him, propelling him forward, a black hole sucking him in. He ripped off the Hard Rock Café shirt and tossed it into the dumpster and put on the leather jacket in full stride. He punched the "open" button to lift the metal gates that lead to the street. They creaked and opened slowly. *C'mon, c'mon, c'mon.* He bounced on the balls of his feet.

The gate raised just enough to roll under. He stood up and dusted himself off and walked casually away down the block.

Adrenaline coursed through his body, and to his surprise he didn't piss himself. His body was lead, but he felt a light confidence washing over him with each step he took. His gait loosened. A siren was in the background. His heart slowed. A policeman on the beat walked towards him from 8th Avenue. Tanner nodded at the cop, said, "Evening, officer." The cop ignored him as if he didn't even register Tanner was there.

Tanner laughed and crossed the street. He walked a block and crossed up towards 46th where he parked his car. All the nervousness and doubt had left his body. He caught his reflection in a window and laughed again to himself. He felt a strange calm and *not-give-a-fuck-edness* feeling he had never felt before. He felt cool.

Across the street from where he parked his car a couple of guys were outside of a bar, smoking cigarettes.

"Hey, new guy," one of them yelled.

Tanner looked over.

"It's the fucking new guy," the other said.

Tanner walked over to them. He put his fist out and they gave him a pound.

"Cigarette?" Tanner said and pointed.

One of the guys gave him a cigarette and they talked to him about work and asked him where he was from. Tanner didn't say shit. He smiled and smoked the cigarette and pointed to himself and said, "New guy."

They invited him in for a drink by way of pantomime.

They asked him what he wanted, and he replied in the same odd and broken English, "Wheeskee."

He put back the shot of whiskey and left the bar without saying a word. He could hear the two guys behind him, laughing. "Fucking new guy."

He got in his car and drove off through the neon lit streets of New York that gave way to the waterfront and the Lincoln Tunnel. He merged on to I-95 and began the drive towards Philadelphia.

27. RECYCLE-ATORS, MOUNT UP!

Bollocks showed me the text Tanner sent in the middle of the night. He included a jacket and thumbs up emoji. We didn't have a gig until tomorrow, but figured we'd get on the road and figure shit out. At least with moving we'd feel like we were making progress, even if we didn't exactly have a plan yet.

It was almost 9am and Keith Richards hadn't shown up. We weren't sure when Tanner would get here. Bollocks texted him and he only responded with "omw$."

Bollocks ran out to the corner store and loaded up on jerky, bread, peanut butter, bananas, and raisins for the road. On our last tour in the spring, Bollocks only ate peanut butter, banana, and raisin sandwiches, which meant that's all I ate.

"Again?" I said.

"One small bite will fill the stomach of a grown man," he said.

"Sigh," I said. "Maybelline will be here in a few minutes."

"Cool, we should get going soon," he said. "Are you going to sit in the back with her while I drive?"

"Uh…" The thought hadn't crossed my mind.

"I'm just fucking with you. But, we should arrange for a pee-tent."

"For a what?"

He went to the pile of supplies by the door and held up an empty plastic gallon carton, the kind for milk or water.

"Yeah, we're not gonna bring that this time," I said.

"Dude, you know I gotta go like every hour."

"We'll stop."

"We're never gonna get there," he said and shook his head. "I thought you liked it."

"I said it was a good idea."

"And now it's not?"

"What's a good idea?" Maybelline asked from the doorway, walking in the room.

"Maybelline," Bollocks said. "How do you feel about reducing, reusing, and recycling?"

"Pretty good," she said. "I'm for it."

"Maybelline," I said. "How do you feel about Bollocks peeing into a jug in the back seat of the van while we drive across the country?"

She looked at Bollocks holding the jug. He held it up a little bit and made a puppy-dog face. "I have a small bladder."

"Gross. We'll stop," she said.

"We're never gonna get there," Bollocks said again and tossed the jug across the room.

"Sorry," Maybelline said. "What time are we thinking about heading out?"

"As soon as Tanner gets here."

"He's coming?"

"He said he has a special jacket for me," I said.

"Marc's pretty much Harry Potter now," Bollocks said.

"That's if it even does anything."

"After all that's happened, you still doubt that the jacket could be magic?"

"Well, I mean it could. But it could also just be a jacket."

"Oh, it does some things," Tanner said, leaning against the doorframe. He dropped a duffel bag at his feet. "Boy does it do some things."

***

Tanner explained how once he got on I-95 and approached the Garden State Parkway he was compelled to go to Atlantic City.

"Where'd you go?" I asked.

"I was real thirsty, so I went to Margaritaville 'cause I was kinda feeling like an asshole too. I ordered a '5 O'Clock Somewhere' drink in a sippy cup."

"You really were feeling like an asshole," Bollocks said.

Tanner shrugged. "So I walked right out of the bar and across the street to the Hard Rock Café."

"Wait a minute. You just robbed the Hard Rock Café in New York, and you walk right into the one in Atlantic City?" I asked.

"I walked right in and no one carded me or anything. I mean look at me. I'm not even wearing a fucking shirt!"

"Yeah, we're gonna fix that," Bollocks said.

"I walked right up to the roulette table and put everything I had on black. Like $53. Black hit and I doubled back down on black. I did that shit seven times, cause seven is a lucky number."

"Nice," Bollocks said. "How much did you win?"

"I'm not done. Then I took all my chips and put them on 00."

"What happened?" Bollocks asked, biting his fingernails.

Tanner opened his duffel bag and pulled out a plastic bag bursting at the seams and smiled. "237,440 dollars happened."

"Holy shit! Why didn't you just stay and bet more and retire?"

"I don't know. I felt like it was time to go after that and come here."

"You think it's the jacket?" I asked.

"Have you met me?"

"That's a lot of fucking dough. What are you going to do with it?"

"I don't know. It doesn't seem like it's mine. I feel like it's—the jacket and the money—are destined for something."

"What do you think, Maybelline?"

"That's a lot of gas money," she said.

"Maybelline!" Tanner said, as if just realizing she was there. He dug into the bag and pulled out a small rectangular box and tossed it to her.

"Salt water taffy?"

"I only felt like an asshole in the casino."

"Uh, thanks."

"You got it. I have to pee. Can I use your shower?" Tanner asked.

"Are you going to pee in my shower?" Bollocks asked.

"You guys are pee obsessed today," Maybelline said.

"Just go," Bollocks said. "We're leaving in 15."

Tanner went to the bathroom.

Maybelline held up the box. "I don't even like salt water taffy."

"Nobody actually does," I said.

Tanner leaned his naked torso out of the doorway. "Hey, can you hang this up so the steam doesn't ruin it. The leather is precious."

I walked over to Tanner and took the leather jacket from him. "Be careful," he said. He ducked back in the bathroom and pulled the door shut.

"Did he just fucking call that jacket his 'precious'?" Bollocks asked.

"Not exactly, Samwise," I said and laughed.

28. SOMEWHERE IN THE BETWEEN

Keith Richards sat cross-legged, guitar on lap, on the trunk of a tree that had fallen beside the Mississippi. He looked out into the great waters and blew a long thin stream of smoke from his cigarette. It had been a lifetime since he was here as a young man. But it had been a good life. He couldn't complain. He had a family. He loved. He was a guitar player for the ages.

Loss?

Yeah, he had that too.

He thought of Tara. His boy who died while the Stones were on tour. Was it Anita's fault? Would it have been different had he been home? That was a road he couldn't go down. It ended the same no matter which way he landed.

Thinking back on his life and all that he carried was like looking at a long shadow he could not escape. Not if he kept going the way he was.

A breeze. The trees swayed and the low branches of the willows dipped into the river.

"Devil-Man," Keith said.

"I didn't think you'd actually show up," a figure said. Its skin was waxy. It glowed and shifted then settled into a form resembling a man in a suit.

"You needn't on my behalf."

"I like this shape. It's done me well."

"Suit yourself," Keith said and then chuckled.

"Stop protecting the boy. Give him to me," the Devil said.

"Ain't mine to give."

"You picked him. Told him the chord. Groomed him to take over for you."

"No one's taking over for me."

"Of course not. You're mad, bad, and dangerous to know. No one can replace you."

"That's your bag, baby. Not mine."

"Keith. You had a long run. A good run. You can have your soul back and go to wherever it is after, free. Not many are given the choice or live long enough."

Keith Richards took another drag off his cigarette and looked past the Devil and into the water.

"You're on your last life, cat-man," the Devil said. "I counted three at Nellcôte alone. It's amazing you've made it this far." The Devil studied Keith Richards, sizing him up.

"I've got a remarkable immune system," Keith said. He flicked his cigarette into the Mississippi and then lit another one, dipping his head, and cupping his hand around the flame.

"Be it as it may, you're only human. Why the change of heart?"

"Leave the kid alone."

"Deal. It's your soul and we're done here." The Devil adjusted his tie and put on a hat manifested from his fingertips.

"There's gotta be another way," Keith said. "You've used plenty of my soul. Let's call it even."

The Devil laughed—a boom that shattered the open sky and echoed. The atmosphere darkened. The trees shivered and the landscape seemed to diminish, blood in the river.

"Keith. Keef. Mr. Richards. Ain't nothing even. Not in this game." The Devil snapped his fingers and everything was normal again. "I'll see you soon."

"Leave the kid alone," Keith Richards said again and adjusted his guitar. "Or else."

The Devil's eyes flashed plague and disaster. Then he disappeared. His form sucked up and gone. In the same instant he was in all places, a snake curling around every molecule, wrapping itself inside Keith, knocking him and his guitar to the ground. A whisper, a hiss—*threats? Cute. I expected more out of you.*

Keith tried to stand up, to reach for his guitar just out of reach. The grip tightened.

Excuse me. Someone knocked and it'd be rude to leave my guests waiting.

29. PHILADELPHIA: THE CITY OF BROTHERLY LOVE, LOVE, LOVE—LOVE IS ALL YOU NEED

I put on the leather jacket I took from Tanner.

"Leather in the summer?" Bollocks said and then shrugged. "Fashion over function, I've always said."

"I think he looks hot," Maybelline said and pinched my ass.

"Settle down," Bollocks said.

Maybelline blushed.

"Hot?" I asked.

"Just saying what I'm saying."

"Ok, Rico Suave," Bollocks said. "You do look cool, but don't let it go to your head. We've got a lot of work to do."

Tanner came out of the bathroom and looked at me. "Oh. You're gonna wear it now?"

"You got it for me, didn't you?" I said.

"Well, yeah. But I thought I could wear it for you a little bit. Just until you needed it."

"I'm good with it now. Thanks."

"If I get cold can I wear it?"

Bollocks stepped up to Tanner. "Relax, my dude."

Tanner put his hands up. "I'm relaxing, I'm relaxing."

"Ok boys," Maybelline said. "Let's go. Your first gig is in Memphis, right?"

"Yeah. We should be there by tomorrow if we don't feel like driving all day," I said.

"Sooo, my cousin is in Baltimore right now if we wanted to stop for lunch. If you guys are cool with that."

"Sure. I like crabs. Does he live there?" Bollocks said.

"No. He's on tour drumming with The Stewford Brothers."

"Eww."

"Are they the band with that song that goes 'bang, bang' and has claps and then stops in the chorus?" I asked.

"Yeah. That song's annoying," Maybelline said. "He did some session work for their label and is touring with them now."

"Can't hate on a dude for making some dough," Bollocks said.

"Thanks guys. I'll text him and let him know. I was supposed to see him in Philly tomorrow, but since we're leaving today…"

"It's all good," I said. "Let's go get lunch with your cousin."

Bollocks picked up his duffel bag and handed it to Tanner who was already holding his own. "Here you go, Sméags. Lead the way."

***

We drove and it wasn't long before Bollocks asked to pull over so he could go to the bathroom. And then it wasn't long after that he asked if we could stop at a liquor store to get some tax-free booze in Delaware.

"I love bargains," Bollocks said. "And booze."

"Well, you're in luck," I said as I pulled into the parking lot of the first liquor store that popped up on our GPS—a non-descript white building that had *Fine Liquors* written on the wall.

"No top shelf shenanigans this time," Bollocks said to me. "We can't blow our road load on the first day."

"It was one time," I said.

"I'm just saying." Bollocks turned to Maybelline. "Last tour he was too embarrassed to put the bottle back, so he blew like ninety bucks on a scotch he didn't even like."

"Are you still upset?" I asked.

"Oh, it's cool. I just had a flashback and remembered I had to drink it all."

"You didn't have to."

"It wasn't going to drink itself, Marc."

"Guys," Tanner said. "There's nothing you can buy that can't be bought," he sung to the tune of "All You Need is Love" and held up a stack of dough he pulled from his bag.

"My man, Ringo. Love a little help from my friends," Bollocks said and took a few bills. And then a few more.

"I don't think we should be spending all that on booze," Maybelline said. "Or maybe at all."

"It's just a little bit."

"Doesn't magic come back three-fold or something?"

"It did. I got the jacket and my $53 turned into this," Tanner said.

Maybelline frowned and took off her seat belt.

Tanner handed me a small stack. I took it sheepishly and put it in my pocket.

We grabbed a shopping cart and went into the store.

"A shopping cart?" Maybelline asked.

Bollocks shrugged. "It's partly for riding," he said and leaned over the handle-rail and pushed off the ground, gliding through the doors. He went right to the register and asked where the bathroom was. Top 40 music played through the store.

"I don't care what anyone says," I said. "Bryan Adams is so much better than Ryan Adams. Man, those sweet Canadian pipes."

"Easy," Maybelline said.

We walked around and Maybelline grabbed a bottle of Jameson.

"No offence to John Jameson and his pirate-fighting family," I said, "but why?" and waved my arm towards the wall of whisky.

"It's for my cousin. It's what he likes," she said.

"That's fair."

We filled the shopping cart with bottles of whisky and rum. And a few boxes of wine. There wasn't anyone else in the store.

"I thought this place would be busier," I said.

"It's before noon," Tanner said.

"You've clearly never been to a liquor store in the city."

He looked around. "Well, it is a little odd, I guess."

We went to the register and the clerk eyed us as he rang the bottles. Slowly. The guy was wearing a straw hat and leaning on a cane. He was so old I swear I could hear his joints disintegrating to dust with each movement.

"Expensive taste," he said. "Where're you fellas going with all this fine liquor?"

"To fight the Devil at the crossroads," Bollocks said.

The clerk crossed himself. "Speak of the Devil and he shall appear."

"I'm just kidding. We're lovers, not fighters," Bollocks said and kissed me on the cheek.

The clerk shook his head. "How're you kids paying for this? Cash or credit?"

Tanner reached in between us and laid down a large pack of loose tobacco and a stack of bills. "Cash."

"You smoke?" I asked.

Tanner looked at me. "No."

The clerk counted the bills and put them in the register. One at a time. He held our change and looked at Tanner. The music playing throughout the store stopped. I looked up to the speaker as if I'd find an answer.

Bollocks cleared his throat.

The clerk eyed us again.

Bollocks cleared his throat louder and held out his hand.

Nothing.

Bollocks coughed *can we have our change* and held out his hand farther.

"You kids want to see something?" the clerk said. "Special?"

"Uh, we're good, Sandusky," Bollocks said. "Just the change."

"You talk a lot, son," the clerk said. "I'm talking whisky. *Good* whisky."

"Is this shit?" Tanner asked and pointed to the cart. I didn't know Tanner well at all, but he had an authoritative, questioning tone to his voice that I hadn't heard before. Cautious too. I couldn't place it.

"That'll do you all right. But it ain't special. Anyone can buy that. I'm talking something special. Rare."

"We good on time?" I asked Maybelline.

"Yeah, but I don't think we need any more liquor," she said and leaned into me and grabbed my arm. "We should get back on the road…"

"Will only take but a minute. Who knows when you'll have such fortunes again," the clerk said and looked at Tanner.

Tanner studied him. "Show us."

The clerk smiled. "This way," he said and moved from behind the register with a bit more grace and ease then he had when ringing us up. "I'm going to lock the door, if you don't mind."

Bollocks put his hands over his butt and leveled his gaze at the clerk. "Alright, just don't try anything funny."

The old man led us into the storeroom. Cardboard boxes full of bottles were stacked on shelves and skids. He leaned his cane against the wall and maneuvered a hand-operated pallet mover. "Watch your toes," he said as he swung it around and slid the forks under a stack of dusty and cobwebbed wooden pallets against the back side of the wall. The pallets creaked and behind them was an alcove covered over with an iron gate. Just inside, out of arm's reach were bottles on shelves. Short wide bottles, long skinny bottles. Some wrapped in twine. Blue, green. One red bottle. Two identical bottles in a small cage. All covered in varying amounts of dust.

"Now, this," the clerk said and stood upright with his hands on his hips, "is *whisky*." The old man produced a pipe from his pocket and lit it. He took his cane from against the wall and sat down on some crates. One hand on his cane, the other holding his pipe.

Tanner approached the alcove.

"Don't get too close, Fortunato," Bollocks said. "Is any of that Amontillado?"

"Amonti-what?" the old man said.

"Nothing," Tanner said. "Talk to me about these."

"Pre-prohibition bottles mostly. Two bottles salvaged from a shipwreck."

Tanner scanned the bottles. He ran his finger across the rows, in the air, and stopped mid-shelf, transfixed by a brown bottle. "What's that one with the handwritten label?" he said.

The man grinned.

"That's a good bottle," Bollocks said, leaning in. "Simple. The bottle of a carpenter." He put his arm around Tanner. "You've chosen wisely."

Tanner smirked at Bollocks.

A draft seemed to come from everywhere. I shivered.

"This guy is fucking with us. Let's get out of here," I said.

"Fine by me," Maybelline said.

"That one there belonged to Thomas Jefferson," the man said.

"Do you know what's in it?" Tanner asked, turning his head towards the man.

"I do."

"Then you know that it doesn't exist."

"I know that the slaves at Shadwell made off with more than just his fiddle when the building burned," the man said with a tone bordering on impatience.

"No one's ever seen one of the bottles. Not in almost 200 years."

"Consider it an honor then."

"I do." He eyed up the man. I was starting to get an uneasy feeling and inched my way back towards the storefront with Maybelline.

"Well, you guys are getting weird and this is getting boring. How much for the shipwreck bottle? I want to drink some booty," Bollocks said.

"I want the Jefferson bottle," Tanner said.

The old man's mouth opened, a wide smile revealing two rows of the whitest teeth I've ever seen. I swore I saw the glint of a fang before he closed his mouth. And for the first time I noticed a small tattoo on his neck, under his ear, an upside down cross. "You know it's not for sale then."

Tanner went into his bag and pulled out two bottles of rum and the large packet of tobacco. He handed the items to the man. All the air sucked out of the room as if a vacuum was turned on.

30. BRAD JOHNSON'S APARTMENT: ONE HAND IN MY POCKET AND THE OTHER'S...

Brad was furiously masturbating in his bathroom with one hand while swiping through pictures of celebrity nip-slips on his iPad with his other. His phone rang and the alert redirected to his tablet just as he was about to climax. He sat there, on his toilet, looking at a picture of the program director of the sister station, WBBR, in Austin. He tried to swipe it away but ended up connecting the call via Facetime.

"Hey, Brad," Michelle said.

Brad let out a low, uncomfortable moan. "Hey."

"Are you shitting?"

"No."

"You're in your bathroom."

"Let me call you back."

"It's ok, I'll look away. I just wanted to tell you that we've got that backing band you asked for. Pretty much the Wrecking Crew of Austin."

"Thanks. I'll see you tomorrow."

"We'll touch base then. Make sure to wash your hands," Michelle said in a sing-song voice and disconnected.

Brad cleaned up and went to his living room. He sat down on his couch and picked up his guitar. He strummed a C chord, then an A minor. He played each chord for six beats. He sang. *Well I heard there was a secret chord…*

"Don't be an asshole," the Devil said, sitting across from Brad. "This isn't an open mic."

"I like it," Brad said.

"That song's debt has been paid."

"But you came."

"Pure chance. I had something to run by you. A favor."

"Uh, sure. But what can I do for you that you can't yourself?"

"Not much, really. I can pull strings, massage, and persuade. But, there is still free will."

Brad raised his eyebrows.

"To a limited extent," the Devil said. "I can whisper in ears, but there are certain things I can't do for myself in the," the Devil waved his hand, "physical world."

"What's in it for me?"

"There's the selfish prick I knew you could be." The Devil smirked. "If we pull it off, we'll call it even."

"I can keep my soul?"

"If we pull it off."

31. A LIQUOR STORE OFF I-95 SOMEWHERE NORTH OF BALTIMORE

"Holy shit!" Bollocks said and kept saying as we ran through the store. Maybelline was way ahead of us and she unlocked the door that led to the parking lot.

"Keys," she yelled.

I threw the keys to her across the entrance of the store.

"Let's go," I yelled behind me.

"Holy shit," Bollocks said again, the shopping cart crashing against a metal post in front of the store. "Don't leave the booze!"

He grabbed two bags, the bottles clinking against each other. I doubled back and grabbed two boxes of wine. Tanner closed up the rear of our pack, clutching a dusty bottle to his chest.

We bolted across the lot and jumped in the van and tore off.

"What the fuck," Maybelline said looking at the building in the rearview mirror. It collapsed in on itself, spiraling, just like the stage. Smoke. The parking lot began to crumble, reaching out for our tires.

"Faster, Maybelline!"

"Holy shit, holy shit, holy shit," Bollocks said looking over the back seat. The ground fell away behind our tires. It caught up with the back passenger tire and the van dipped just as Maybelline cranked the wheel hard, took to the highway, and skidded into traffic, righting our course.

The liquor store was back. There were cars in the parking lot. I blinked. There *was* a fucking parking lot again.

"Tanner," I said, out of breath, "you've got some fucking explaining to do."

Chains and smoke.

"That was stupid, kid," Keith Richards said. "But, you did good." He took a bottle of whiskey out of a bag and looked at it. He opened it and took a drink. "You did good."

Bollocks looked at Keith Richards, drinking right next to him. "Guys. Can we pull over soon? I'm gonna piss my pants."

Maybelline tossed an empty water bottle to the back seat. "No." She pressed the gas pedal harder.

32. INTERLUDE: A JEFFERSONIAN LEGEND

In 1991, archeological research revealed a deep hole in the foundation of what is believed to be the original house built by Peter Jefferson in Shadwell—the house where Thomas Jefferson was born. The blueprints did not survive, but it was uncustomary for a house of that time, in America, to have a privy on the premises. To further complicate the mystery, the hole was not against a wall or chimney where a tunnel for the waste would have been easier to build and clean out—where an indoor privy would likely have been located. It was in the very center of the basement in what was believed to be the wine cellar. Furthermore, less than 100 paces from the property *was* the privy, rich with the non-biodegradable waste from the Jefferson household. In the hole in the middle of the basement, archeologists found large pieces of black tourmaline wrapped in a soiled hemp sack.

***

A young Thomas Jefferson had all the advantages a man could ask for. His father owned land, which meant that he, the younger Jefferson, the first son, would eventually own land. He had an education. Tutors. The best schooling and all the books he could want for. An inheritance at 21 secured his position among the wealthy and powerful of Virginia. These are the facts—the rest is known: Governor, The Revolution, The Declaration, The Swivel Chair, The Presidency.

However, a much-underreported advantage has faded from history. Jefferson's grandmother, Jane Rogers, came from England—and a long lineage of witches. The women were run out of Newcastle after an incident with Lord Abraham Cutter Burnip involving some farm animals, a stottie cake, and a snorker, but the fine intricacies of that matter have sadly been lost. The Rogers women sought refuge in the London parish of Shadwell. Jane Rogers bewitched and married Isham Randolph and secured her passage out of England to the New World shortly after her daughter, Jefferson's mother, was born.

Witchcraft in the colonies was under much scrutiny. Salem was only the spectacle. Every colony and community had their own coven of the accused. Most accusations were born of property disagreements and poor luck and were forgiven in court—but not without penalty. An ocean did not give Jane impunity. She practiced in private and passed on her knowledge and customs to her daughters.

Her grandson, Thomas, was the first boy born to her daughter, also Jane, and Colonel Peter Jefferson. Peter wanted a boy. An heir. Jane had given birth to three girls before Thomas came along.

Jane practiced a placenta ceremony in the basement of the newly built house bearing the name of the plantation: Shadwell— after the parish where she was christened. She called upon the earth god. The air god. The god of water and longevity. The god of soil and deceit. The god of fire and instinct. She wrapped the placenta in a sack and buried it deep in the ground, an offering. One she unwittingly made that would put Thomas directly in the Devil's sight.

This would have been forgotten if not for Jefferson himself. Ever the devout learner—one who believed and studied all languages and religions—Jefferson, in his more curious and vulnerable years, gave himself wholly to the practice of what we would now call the occult. No one is certain of the deal Jefferson later made with the Devil, or if he lifted his curse or passed it on, but scholars believe he died with a free soul. His journals and diaries, locked up in Monticello, tell all.

February 3rd, 1770

Dr. Ensloy,

It is with the greatest displeasure I write to you with news that Shadwell burned to the ground, two days ago, on the first of this month. I arrived while the ruins were still smoldering, my dear mother having escaped before the blaze took over. The slaves, not living in the house, did their best to save what they could, but they report that the fire was quick and voracious and consumed the whole of the building in such a quick period of time methinks if it weren't for their otherwise congenial nature and the verity with which they have conducted themselves in every other matter up to this point, one would suspect foul play. The head negro approached me as I stood at the blackened ruin and upon the inquiry of my books, he proclaimed they had all burned but my fiddle had been saved—that it lay in its case unscathed and cool—as if the lick of the flames did not dare ignite that precious instrument. I was informed the other slaves were heard whispering of Devils and figures in the flames, laughing and crying—wretched forms. But, during great trauma, one's faculties can leave and deceive and the mind creates fancies. Of this I am not concerned. Time will pass, Monticello is under way, and we will build a new home for my mother at Shadwell and their minds will come back to a peaceful balance. But, my books! I have lost every paper I had in the world, and almost every book. On a reasonable estimate I calculate the cost of the books burned to have been £200 sterling. Would to god it had been the money; then had it never cost me a sigh!

I have one task left before I can depart for Richmond to meet you whereat I hope, if I am afforded this last comfort, you will see able to remedy my situation. I will write again before I depart.

Your friend and humble servant,

Th. Jefferson

February 12th, 1770

Dr. Ensloy,

Forgive the brevity and curtness with which I conduct myself in this letter. The post must be sent today with news I am, and with great relief, able to share. I have in the past week searched myself the remains of Shadwell. Having sent my servants away I toiled among the ruins for what hope against hope I have prayed for—the bottles! Found this afternoon! I think that among what was lost I can now discount the heavy weight this loss would have had upon my soul. I calculate the New Moon on the 25th of this month. I will delay my departure with the intention, with your willingness, to enter a new phase, reinvigorated after ceremony on this purest of Sundays. I write in haste—I will see you soon.

your very hble servt.,

Th. Jefferson

February 20th, 1770

Dr. Ensloy,

I will depart the day after tomorrow. I will be en route by the time you receive this letter. Why did you in your last letter, dated the 16ᵗʰ, say the bottles will no longer be needed? Is there another way with which we can proceed? Say nothing in letter. We will speak soon in person. My friend, father, companion—thank you for your reassurance in hastening my return to form as it were. You said there would be a way for me to repay you and I need not concern myself at present. Thank you for this small comfort, as you who know me and my condition so well can attest to my constancy in our shared faith and my desire to repay you when fortunes turn favorable upon me once again.

I am Dear Sir, Your affectionate friend,
Th. Jefferson

[Date unintelligible], 1821
Dr. Ensloy,

[illegible text]…great comfort these last weeks in the promise of obtaining a release from that contract with which I, as an eager young man (perhaps too eager?) had entered with the promise of greatness. I am not sure that ideal was achieved. I see much imperfection in this Union and I feel it all around me—there is too much to do, so much work to be done, but where one life ends, another begins, and I feel that framework has been laid, a framework that exists in no small part because of our endeavors. I will see you in a few short days where I am eager to meet that man from Richmond, Mr. John Allan. [illegible text]…this contract at his behest inspires in me a solemn joy. To be free of this duty and charge and to be taken up by one so willingly is worth the sum he asks. I have kept the bottles, which now number six—I dare not part with those. But more on that in person.

your very hble servt.,

Th. Jefferson

33. BALTIMORE: SUDDENLY THERE CAME A TAPPING

"Wait," Bollocks said. "Are you telling me that those two bottles are filled with Thomas Jefferson's soul?"

"No. Not his soul," Tanner said.

Bollocks hit me in the arm. "Fucking horcruxes."

"They kept his soul intact. The rumor based off the legend—" Tanner looked at each of us in the diner booth. "Keep in mind this is really far-fetched. The legend is that Jefferson had to drink one bottle per year. He was going to make more wine and infuse it with whatever magic he and Dr. Ensloy were conjuring, but someone stole the last two bottles, and he died before he could make more."

"So what are we going to do with the bottles?" I asked.

"If worse comes to worst, you can drink them to preserve your soul. If that's…"

"I didn't sell it yet!"

"*If*, Marc, *if.* Alternatively, it's been said that whoever drinks the draught will be granted special protections or powers."

"Which is it?"

"No one knows. No one has ever seen them before."

"Then how'd you know?"

"They spoke to me."

"Get out of here," Bollocks said.

"It wasn't words, but they were like calling to me. Somehow. I just knew."

"So you got a gut feeling and we're going with that?"

Tanner shrugged. "That whole fucking thing was weird. I'm so out of my comfort zone to be honest. All I know is a lot of strange shit has been happening since I saw you with Micawber."

Maybelline cleared her throat. She had been noticeably quiet during the car ride after the liquor shop while Tanner told us about Thomas Jefferson. "What about the dude taking over his contract?" she asked.

"No one is really sure if that ever happened," Tanner said. "The life of John Allan is marked by much sorrow and…"

"Yo, yo, yo, motherfuckers!" a voice said, booming over Tanner and approaching our table.

Maybelline smiled the brightest smile I've ever seen on her. The whole diner glowed. She stood up and barreled into a dude with a small afro who was wearing a leather jacket and sunglasses. She threw her arms around him. "Matthew!"

"Primito," he said and hugged her back, lifting her off the ground and spinning her around. He set her down. "It's been too long, cuz."

Matthew turned to us. "Yo," he nodded. "I'm Drix." He put out his fist for each of us to bump and then sat down after we introduced ourselves.

"I got you something," Maybelline said and pulled out the bottle of Jameson from her bag.

"Niiice," Drix said, admiring the bottle. "My medicine." He ordered a coffee and after the waitress left, he dumped a healthy pour of liquor into the cup, then offered us all some.

"It's all good," I said. "We've got a small distillery in the van."

"Slow your roll there, Speed Racer," Bollocks said and extended his cup towards Drix. "I would love some medicine. I've been feeling rather sickly."

"Dig," Drix said and poured some booze into Bollocks' cup. "Gotta get your humors in balance."

Drix took a big drink of coffee and then poured more booze into his cup. "Sorry I'm late."

Maybelline waved his comment off.

"Nah, that ain't my style. I apologize. But I was meeting up with a dude over on the other side of town getting a reload on some pot for the guys in the band. Those motherfuckers smoked out the whole tour bus last night as a celebration of the last gig. Then they remembered that tonight's the last gig, and they still got a couple days ride back to the West Coast so I was all 'I gotchu' and called a dude who knew a dude. Anyway, long story getting longer I was walking up this street and I passed a graveyard and you know what I saw right inside the gate? Fucking Edgar Allan Poe's tombstone. That dude was my boy. Only shit I remember from high school English, really. I mean, I've since bridged that gap with all the downtime on the road, but I was all 'Once upon a midnight dreary' and shit. It all came back to me. I had to pay my respects to my man. So I'm in the graveyard and this dude comes up to me, says his name is Reynolds or some shit. He was there paying his respects as well, but he was like 'I saw you last night' and went on about congratulating me and saying I'm good. Then I was like 'thank you, man,' and he was all, 'no, thank you.' Dude tells me he's in the biz for some label I've never heard of. He puts his business card in my pocket and is all 'call me if you want to go to the next level' but I've been hearing dudes say that shit ever since I moved out to L.A. But this dude had a seriousness about him. He didn't seem like a sleazeball. So I'm all 'all right man, thanks' and then he gets somber as shit and starts talking about Edgar Allan Poe. Dude had a cane and pointed it at the grave and was going on about how Eddie had his own demons and couldn't get out of the way of them to realize his full potential. Then he tucked his hair behind his ear to put on this straw hat he was carrying—motherfucker was wearing a straw hat! When he did that, I noticed he had an upside down cross tattooed behind his ear like he was in Black Sabbath or some shit. Didn't really bother me, I see all sorts of weird stuff in L.A. But then I swear the dude vanished. Like I know he didn't vanish. I heard a caw or some shit behind me so I turned around, but then when I turned back, dude was gone. I thought maybe I was still tripping but I knew I wasn't and I still had his business card. Anyway, I searched around for a minute for the dude and couldn't find him and that's why I'm late. So, I do apologize."

I looked to Tanner. After what we'd just been through and seen, this encounter at the cemetery seemed really weird and didn't sit right with me. It sounded like it was the same guy. But it couldn't have been. Tanner didn't meet my eyes. He was laser focused on Drix.

"What did he say to you exactly?" Tanner said.

"Just what I told you. He might have said some specific shit I'm forgetting, but that was the gist."

"Let me see that business card."

Drix shrugged and tossed the card across the table. "You know him?"

Tanner looked at the card. "It just say 'Reynolds' and has a number."

"Weird, right?" Drix said.

"What're you thinking?" I asked Tanner.

"Nothing." Tanner gave the card back to Drix. He held Drix's gaze. "Be careful."

"Thanks for the concern, man. I mean that shit," Drix said.

"Sooo, tell me about this gig," Maybelline said, breaking the tension. "It sounds pretty awesome."

"Ah. Just some dudes I got hooked up with through this studio I do session work out of. They needed a drummer and my man at the studio knew of my versatility. Doing that wagon wheel shit ain't my everyday jam, but for the dough these cats were paying me, I tucked that particular peccadillo away. You ever hear of The Stewford Brothers?" Drix asked, and before any of us could answer he continued, "Yo, dig this, those motherfuckers aren't even brothers. Can you believe that?"

"It's unbelievable," Bollocks said.

"Right?" Drix said. "Like homies all look alike. Anyway, it doesn't really matter. They got an image and I can dig that. We're finishing up this East Coast jaunt and then I'm headed back to L.A. Something else came down the pipe. Man, I'll tell you. When it rains it pours. But I'm thankful as shit. Thankful as shit. So. What are you doing?" Drix looked towards Maybelline and me.

"We're headed to Austin," I said. "Trying to line up a couple of gigs along the way to keep sharp."

"Right on. Lots of cool clubs. Gonna be a little early for City Limits, but still worth playing, man. You know where you're gonna be?"

"Uh," I said. "Bollocks, did we even get confirmation on a venue?"

"I think it's the Hole in the White Horse or something," Bollocks said.

"That's two clubs. Hole in the Wall and The White Horse. You playing both?" Drix said.

"I think so," Bollocks said.

"You just tagging along with these dudes?" Drix asked Maybelline.

"Yes," she said. Then smiled. "But, I'm actually field reporting for Rolling Stone."

"The magazine?"

Maybelline nodded.

Drix gave her a fist bump. "Right the fuck on, little cuz! When'd that happen?"

"Yesterday."

"We must celebrate! Come to the show tonight?"

Maybelline looked around at us. "Do we have time?"

"I think so," I said.

"We'll just have to burn through a day driving," Bollocks said. "I'm cool if you're cool."

"Nice. I'll leave tickets at the box office for you," Drix said and finished the rest of his coffee. "Listen, I gotta roll out and get to sound check. Raincheck on lunch?"

"Not a problem," Maybelline said.

Drix gave us all a fist bump again and hugged Maybelline. And then he was gone.

"That might be the coolest dude I've ever met," Bollocks said.

"You'll get to see him again later on," Maybelline said and laughed.

"I gotta find something to wear."

"I think something bad is going to happen," Tanner said.

"You felt that too?" I asked Tanner.

"What did you feel?" he asked.

"I can't explain it. Tension? A weird anxiety."

"What do you guys mean?" Maybelline asked. "Is my cousin in trouble or something?"

"I don't know," Tanner said.

"Let's figure this out," I said.

"Can I still get crab cakes?" Bollocks asked.

"It's gonna be tough fighting the Devil on an empty stomach."

34. AN UNEXPECTED PARTY

We went back to the van to talk and try to catch a nap before the show. Tanner told us all about John Allan. How his wife died. How he had financial troubles and sought to remedy that by consorting with Jefferson and black magic. How he may have marked his un-adopted son, Edgar, as his successor with the deal he made with the Devil.

"Like Edgar Allan Poe?" Bollocks asked.

"Yeah," Tanner said. "You know what his last words were?"

We all looked at each other. I shrugged.

"Lord help my poor soul," Tanner said.

"So?" Maybelline said.

"Poe was not a religious man. There's no evidence of his faith. Why would he appeal to God before his death?"

"Lots of people do," I said.

"Yeah, but before he died he called out for one 'Reynolds' over and over. No one knows who that is."

"That's the name of the dude at Poe's grave," Bollocks said.

"Correct," Tanner said. "And also an anagram for 'Dr. Ensloy'—the mysterious man that Jefferson was writing to."

"They can't be the same person," Maybelline said. "That's years apart."

"Jefferson died in 1825. Poe died in 1849. Jefferson's Dr. Ensloy *could* be the same Reynolds. It's unlikely—he'd be really, really old. 105 if he was the same age as Jefferson. But it's not impossible."

"Unless he doesn't age," Keith Richards said.

Bollocks jumped. "You gotta stop doing that!"

"I'm limited in my approach," Keith said.

"What do you know about this, Keith?" I asked.

"That that bastard's been around a long time and is capable of a lot more than what we've seen so far."

"Like?"

"It ain't so easy to walk away from ol' Beelzebub once he pegs you. And this Reynolds is just one name for that man you're all getting tangled up with."

My stomach dropped.

"If this is true," Maybelline said, "then my cousin was just talking to him."

Keith grunted.

"We don't know that for sure," Tanner said.

"We've got to warn him."

"How?" I asked. "Do you think he would believe us?"

"We have to make him believe," she said. "Keith, can you show yourself to him?"

"I'll try my best, love."

"You can't just show yourself to whoever you wanted? Like you did at the festival? Like you are now?"

"I'm tethered to the guitar and Marc's quest somehow. I just know there are things I can and can't do. That took considerable energy."

"Well, muster it. I'm not going to let my cousin get wrapped up in this too."

"Ok," Keith said softly and lit a cigarette. "I'll try."

Keith smoked quietly while we figured out what route to take after the gig that night. We'd have to hit the road right away to make it to Memphis in time.

"The bottle," Keith said.

"Yeah?" Tanner looked at him.

"Why would Reynolds want you to have it?"

"I've been working that out myself."

"He didn't exactly give it to us," I said.

"But he gave you the opportunity. Why?"

Tanner shrugged.

"If it can help protect you from the Devil, why would the Devil give you the opportunity to get it?"

We all looked at the bottle.

"I don't know," Tanner said.

"If it were me," Keith said. "I wouldn't touch that thing. Not if my life depended on it."

***

Drix's band finished their set. Despite Bollocks' constant lamenting that he was going to give up drumming after seeing Drix play, it was a good distraction from the more serious business we were dealing with the past couple of days. There's nothing like a good show to remind you of the power of music.

"He's too good," Bollocks said. "It's like there's good, and then there's something after that." He shook his head. "You know how I feel about drum solos—but that was…" Bollocks shook his head and then held his hands up and looked at his palms. "They look

159

like big, good, strong hands, don't they? I always thought that's what they were."

I took one hand off my guitar case and put it on his shoulder. "He's got chops. I'll give him that," I said. "But you're good too."

"Those weren't chops, friend. That was coming from somewhere else. Something deeper than rudiments."

"When's the last time you saw him play?" Tanner asked Maybelline.

"I don't know. A year or two ago when he passed through," she said.

"Was he always that good?"

Maybelline shrugged. "Yeah. Drumming has always been his thing."

Tanner narrowed his eyes at the stage. "Ok," he said, slowly rocking his head.

"Last call," Bollocks said. "If we're going to make up some time driving, we'll have to get started in about an hour. Who's got first shift?"

"I'll do it," I said. "You can drink with your hero, and Maybelline can celebrate with her cousin."

"I'll ride shotgun," Tanner said. "I have some research I want to do. I'll take second shift."

We went to the bar and ordered a couple of beers and stale coffees and waited for Drix to come out after the floor cleared. The bartender gave us a hard time saying they had to close real soon, but Tanner slipped him a $100 and told him we were with the band.

"I know they say money is the root of all evil, but I like this," Bollocks said.

"I still think you shouldn't be spending it haphazardly," Maybelline said.

"It was won fair and square," Tanner said.

"Still…" Maybelline said and look off towards the stage.

"Do you think you should get Keith Richards here?" Bollocks asked.

"He's around. I saw him earlier," I said.

"When?"

"Before the set. He was on stage checking out the guitar amp, but then he was gone, and The Stewford Brothers came on."

"You should call him," Maybelline said. "Drix is coming out." She waved at Drix, walking from around the side of the stage and out to us.

"Keith," I said.

Nothing.

"Keith," I said again, louder.

"Yo, yo, yo, motherfuckers," Drix said. He hugged Maybelline again. I noticed he had a pair of drumsticks in his back pocket. They seemed weathered, tarred.

"That was amazing," Bollocks said. "I've never seen drumming like that before."

"Thanks, brother," Drix said. "I appreciate that."

"Can I touch your drumsticks to get some of your powers?" Bollocks asked and reached his hand out towards the sticks.

"Ah, ah, ah," Drix said and playfully smacked Bollocks' hand. "Buy me dinner first."

"I'm sorry."

"I'm just fucking with you. These aren't mine anyway. I think they're from the opening acts or some shit. Gonna put them in the lost and found." Drix pulled down over a stool and ordered a beer. He turned to Maybelline. "So, tell me about this Rolling Stone gig."

"There's not much more to say than what I did earlier. I was doing good work at XPN and the right people noticed."

"You good, cuz?" Drix said.

"Yeah." Maybelline looked at me and then Tanner.

"What's on your mind? Our time is short, don't keep that shit in," Drix said.

Maybelline took a deep breath. "Can we go somewhere private?"

Drix grabbed his beer and stood up. "Yeah, little weirdo. I got a dressing room I can clear out. I think the dudes are on the bus anyway."

We all stood up.

"These cats coming to our family meeting?"

"Yeah," Maybelline said. "I've got something to tell you that you might not believe. I need them there." She looked at me. "All of them."

"Come on, Keith," I whispered on the way backstage. "Come on."

***

Keith Richards didn't show up.

Maybelline told Drix about that first night. The stolen guitar. The liquor store. Everything. We corroborated and assured him she wasn't lying.

"Get the fuck out of here, cuz," Drix said laughing his ass off. "You dudes are fucking with me. You had me going for a second with all that shit about dude at the liquor store, but I just told you what homey looked like at the cemetery."

"She's not lying," Tanner said and pulled the Jefferson bottle out of his bag. "Those two guys were the same guy."

"Cause they both had hats and tattoos?"

"It's more than that."

"And where's Keith Richards?"

"Well, it's his spirit or ghost."

Drix lit a cigarette. "Right, right, right. His ghost," he said. He made his eyes big on the word ghost and laughed again. "Let me see that bottle," Drix said and reached over and took it from Tanner. He looked at all of us. "I admire your commitment to the cause here. I can't wait to tell the guys in the van. They're all stoned out of their fucking minds. They'll believe this shit and it's going to be hilarious." He held the bottle up to the light. "So what, this has Jefferson's soul or some shit in it?"

"I thought it was protection," Tanner said. "But we're not sure anymore."

"It doesn't seem like magic," Drix said and put the bottle on the ground next to his chair.

"Call Keith Richards again," Maybelline said to me. Pleading in her eyes.

I frowned. "I'll try." I called out. I took out Micawber and strummed some chords. Some Keith Richards licks. The lights went out in the room. They flickered and then came back on.

We looked around. No Keith.

Drix laughed. "Yo, that was freaky, dude."

"I'm sorry," I said to Maybelline. "Something is wrong. I can feel it."

A loud knock on the door. We all jumped.

The Stewford Brothers' manager came into the room.

"Damn, motherfucker," Drix said. "You ever hear of knocking?"

"I did," the manager said. "We're rolling out in 5. Long drive ahead of us."

"All right," Drix said. "I'll be right out."

Maybelline stood up. She put her hands on Drix's shoulders. "I know it sounds crazy, but I'm telling you the truth. I love you. I don't want you to get wrapped up in this shit and…" her voice cracked. She looked away.

Drix took her hands and stood up and hugged her. "There, there, little primito. It's all good. I can tell this shit is important to you." He held her back and wiped her face with his thumbs. He kissed her on the forehead. "Listen. I'm gonna hook up with these dudes out in L.A. or San Francisco or some shit to do some session work for a little bit. If things goes well I might be able to tag along on their tour and I'll probably swing back out this way. Keep in touch and we'll hook up real soon so you can write about your awesome cousin for Rolling fucking Stone. I promise if some weird shit starts happening, I'll call you and we'll sort it out. I promise."

Maybelline nodded. They hugged again.

"Take care of her," Drix said to us. "Lots of slimy motherfuckers in this world. Don't be one of them."

He gave us all fist bumps. Bollocks hugged him. "We doin' this?" Drix said, caught off guard. "Bring that shit in motherfucker."

Tanner picked up the bottle on the floor and looked at it. He furrowed his brow.

"What's up?" I asked him on our way through the venue.

"I don't know. Probably nothing." He tucked the bottle back in his bag.

We left the venue and went to our van, leaving Drix behind with his band and whatever uncertain future lay ahead.

"Make sure to pee before you leave," I told Bollocks. "We've got a long night."

***

"You did good," a man in a suit said to Drix. The man held up a bottle.

"Yo, I don't like lying my to cousin. Especially don't like stealing either. This shit better be worth it."

"Did you like how you played and felt tonight?"

Drix didn't say anything. The man smiled. "And it only gets better from that."

"What's so special about that anyway?" Drix asked, pointing to the bottle. "And where's dude I talked to earlier?"

"So many questions. Understandable." The man sat down. "This?" He snapped his fingers and the bottle disappeared. "It's nothing now. Too precious to waste."

"And dude?"

"*Dude* is a friend of mine…of sorts. He offers guidance. The choice. Nothing more than an intermediary."

Drix nodded.

"Are you satisfied?" the man asked.

"What next?"

"Go. Be great. Enjoy it all. Your part in this story is over."

"My cousin ain't gonna be wrapped up in this shit?"

"Everyone has a choice."

"That wasn't part of the deal, motherfucker."

The man shifted. Glowed red and formless. The room darkened. Back to normal.

"I like you," he said and smiled. "Such spunk. I have no desires for your cousin. It's the boy who's been marked."

"We're rolling out now, Drix," the manager yelled from the hall.

The man was gone.

Drix was alone. He took a deep breath and exhaled slowly. He took the drumsticks out of his back pocket and gave them a twirl between his fingers and left the room—heading towards the hall, the van, and his life of promised greatness.

35. INTERLUDE: A JEFFERSONIAN LEGEND CONT'D

Thomas Jefferson's last words are lost to history. In the early morning hours before he died, he called in his servants for what most believe were farewells. He had been in and out of consciousness for two days before his death on July 4, 1826—50 years after the signing of the Declaration of Independence. It's documented that, despite the sweltering heat at Monticello, a fire had been lit in his room.

Recent scholarship suggests that Jefferson ordered one of his servants to burn a small chest full of letters and manuscripts in the fireplace. What these contained no one knows for certain.

Many years later, Isaac Granger—who was enslaved by Jefferson, given to Jefferson's daughter as a wedding gift, and later gained his freedom—spoke about that last day of the Founding Father's life. Granger recounted how a different enslaved servant was directed to a hidden alcove in the wine cellar and told to bring the bottles kept in a locked iron cage. A cage that Granger himself had wrought as chief blacksmith at Monticello. The cage was empty, and the servant thinking the request was made by the muddied mind of a dying old man, reported back to Jefferson with two bottles of port from the cellar. Jefferson, satisfied, died a few hours later.

36. FLIGHT FROM PHILADELPHIA TO AUSTIN: MOTHER'S LITTLE HELPER

Brad Johnson, reclining comfortably in first-class, closed his laptop. He had just sent an email to the program director of every public, independent, and college radio station in his contacts. There was a solo album, recorded secretly by the lead singer of a major rock band, and he was using all his pull within the industry to get people onboard. A risky move considering he was using those same contacts to covertly gain some buzz for himself. But, he made a deal. If he could have stardom *and* keep his soul, blasting a few emails out was worth it. He hadn't heard this new album yet, but the man in the suit, the Devil, promised it would be great. Brad sure hoped it would be. He really wanted to keep his soul. Ever since he made the deal he felt a small twinge deep in his core, scratching at something he didn't have a name for.

He put in his earbuds and listened back to the live session he recorded at the studio last evening before he left work. The songs poured out of him. All the yearning he had felt as a young man came flooding through him. The pull to encapsulate what it meant to be alive and want more out of life and put it to song. He never had the musical talent or wordplay to truly realize that vision. But now, what a gift he had been given. It would take some genius marketing to promote an over forty newcomer to the scene, but he was up for it. And if the Devil would pull through on his deepest wish—to not only become a voice for the ages, but to dominate the musical world by writing songs for young popstars, to create a harem of musical ingénues all under his thumb—it would mean immortality. History would remember Bach, Beethoven, The Beatles, Beyoncé, and next in line—Brad Johnson. Forever.

His eyes drifted towards the overhead compartment above him. Where he stowed his guitar. The old acoustic from the studio. His number one he said to himself.

37. PETE FOREVER, RINGO NEVER!

Somewhere between Roanoke and the Tennessee border, just before dawn, the van pulled off route 81 for gas. The service station was nestled in a valley formed by the foothills of the Appalachian Mountains. An Arby's sign burned red against the black night in one direction, in the other, just at the edge of the horizon over the mountains, a translucent sliver of burnt orange crested.

Marc pumped the gas while Bollocks and Maybelline were asleep in the backseat. Spread out, head to toe. Tanner got out of the car and stretched.

"I'm going to grab a coffee," he said to Marc. "You want anything?"

"I'm good, thanks."

"I'll take the next shift."

Marc nodded.

The store was brightly lit and smelled like burnt coffee, beef jerky, and the confusing freshness of air-conditioning mixed with mop water.

He poured a large coffee, dumped in a few ounces of French vanilla creamer to make it appealing, and bought a roll of mints. The clerk, half asleep, rung him up. Tanner was head down into his phone on his way out of the store, thumbing through the last article on the crossroads he liberated from behind JSTOR's paywall. He was hoping to find any new or overlooked information on Robert Johnson and any mention of the Devil. The myths and folklore often told more than they let on. Lots of things were random, but when dealing with the Devil, he had a feeling that lots of things weren't either. Johnson never escaped an early death, but there had to be clues in the sum of his life.

Two men in camouflage and orange vests walked into the gas station. They were talking to each other and didn't notice Tanner not noticing them. It was a hot and creamy collision.

Coffee everywhere—on them and the floor.

"What the fuck," the first man said, jumping back—the damage done.

"I'm so sorry," Tanner said. "I'm so sorry."

"You gotta watch where the fuck you're going," the man who'd taken the brunt of the coffee said. He shook his arms and hands down, dripping. "Why is this so sticky?" He looked to his friend. "We gotta go back so I can change. The scent will give us away for miles."

"These fucking kids," the other man said. He reached across and slapped the phone out of Tanner's hands. It clanged against the floor.

"Hey, I said I was sorry," Tanner said as he bent down to pick up his phone. Then added, "Dickhead."

"What?" The man pushed Tanner to the ground. "You spill shit on us and we're the dickheads?"

Tanner crawled back crab-style a few feet. "I only called *you* a dickhead."

"This fucking kid," the man said to his pal. "Get up. We're going for a walk."

The man lifted Tanner off the ground and took him outside.

Marc looked over from the van and saw Tanner being dragged out of the store. He got out of the passenger side seat. He thought about waking up Bollocks, but that feeling vanished before it fully formed. He was moving towards the melee. Free—light. Confidant. Instinctual.

"Hey, camouflage pumpkins. I'd suggest you let him go," Marc said to the man holding Tanner. The other man, soaked through with coffee, getting ready to punch Tanner, stopped, turned around, and said, "Nice jacket, dork. Beat it."

Marc put his hand on the man's shoulder. The man swung at Marc. He sidestepped it gracefully, barely moving. Another swing. Another miss. "Look at me," Marc said. He leveled his gaze at the swinging man. The man froze. Marc smiled. "I think you should leave."

"I think we should leave," the man said to his pal.

Marc looked at the other man. "Let him go. Leave."

"Yeah, let's get out of here," the man holding Tanner said. He released his grip on Tanner and straightened his shirt for him. "Sorry about that. We don't want any trouble."

The men went to their truck.

"What the fuck was that?" Tanner said. He looked at the jacket. "I knew it."

Marc shook his head. He lifted his arms and appraised the jacket. "I'm never taking this off."

***

Tanner made another coffee and took over driving for the next shift. Marc sat in the passenger seat.

"Did you feel like this when you were wearing it?" Marc asked.

"Yeah—pretty much invincible," Tanner said.

"Why would anyone give this thing up?"

"It was stolen a few times I'm sure. Lost a couple of other times."

"But what about Pete Best? You told me he got rid of it."

"I've been thinking about that. The best I can come up with is that he didn't know what he had. He didn't know that it should enhance whatever he was trying to manifest. Like me—I was trying to get away undetected and then win at gambling. I had intention. You, back there, were trying to intimidate and sway Roscoe and Ace."

"But he was in the fucking Beatles."

"And John and Paul kicked him out. Had nothing to do with him, really."

"They should've kept his jacket and given it to Ringo."

"What's wrong with Ringo?" Bollocks mumbled from the backseat.

"Nothing, sweety," Marc said. "Go back to sleep."

Bollocks rolled over as much as he could and pulled a blanket up over his face.

"You have service out here?" Tanner asked Marc.

Marc pulled out his phone. "Yeah."

"It's funny you mentioned Pete Best. I was just researching Robert Johnson. He died on August 16th. When did Pete Best get kicked out of The Beatles? I'm rusty on my Beatles history, but I know it was in August. There might be a connection."

"Of all things, why do you know that?"

"I did a report on him in high school."

Marc tapped away at his phone. "Why?" he laughed.

"For music class. My teacher was a huge Beatles fan. I thought it'd be funny. He didn't."

"Holy shit," Marc said. "August 16th."

"Fuck."

"Apparently it's the same day Elvis died, too," Maybelline said from the backseat, holding up her phone. "Look at all this stuff that happened on the 16th."

"You're awake?"

"Obviously," she said and then stretched.

"Do you think it's just a coincidence?" Marc asked.

"That Pete and Elvis were the owners of the jacket?" Tanner said.

"Yeah? Do you think Johnson had it?"

"Probably not," Maybelline said. "He wore suits. Leather wasn't the fashion."

"But he had a deal, so maybe he didn't need the jacket to be linked to the Devil," Marc said. "Or a guitar, or pick…"

"Maybe August 16th is a day of reckoning," Tanner said

"Best didn't die then, though."

"A reckoning doesn't mean death. He got rid of the jacket and missed out on an opportunity by getting fired. It's possible it's all just a big, creepy coincidence. It's also possible that one of the other Beatles had a deal."

"Ringo has lived a blessed life," Maybelline said.

"Well, I sure hope it doesn't mean death," Marc said. "Because today is the 14th."

Maybelline reached up between the door and passenger side seat and gave Marc's arm a light squeeze. "We'll be okay," she said.

"Or we'll get kicked out of the Beatles," Tanner said.

"It feels like the further down this road we're going, the harder it's going to be to come back."

"Just don't make a deal," Tanner said to Marc. "No matter what. That's your mantra."

38. SOMEWHERE IN THE BETWEEN

"Papa Legba," the Devil said.

An old man leaning on a black Lincoln Continental and wearing a straw hat nodded to the Devil. "Evening." He inhaled his pipe, smoke billowing up into the ether.

"You've been busy."

"Bored."

"That young man, the drummer. He was a good addition."

"He was hungry."

The Devil held up a bottle. "You want to explain this?"

Papa Legba smirked. "I told you I was bored."

"Do you know what they could have done with this?"

"That depends."

"I need you tell me, just so I understand that you *do* understand."

The old man yawned. He pulled his pipe out of his mouth. "If one who is marked drank it, he would become unmarked, never to be called on again."

"And…" The Devil crossed his arms.

"If one who already sold their soul drank it," the old man put his pipe back in his mouth, "they would become an archangel."

The Devil glowed, bursting, "So you do see the problem!"

Legba pulled on his pipe again. "It was my intention to persuade them to another more," he paused, "sinister bottle.

Something that would weaken their resolve. Four souls for the price of one."

"But that didn't happen."

"I didn't know they were traveling with one versed in our ways and magic. I'm a sucker for gifts, and he paid the toll."

"You're the trickster. Why didn't you stop them?"

"I sensed some form of protection surrounding them."

"That damn Keith Richards is entangled in all this."

Legba raised an eyebrow. "That so?" He shifted his weight, looking at the Devil. "It seemed more than him."

"What do you mean?"

"You're distracted. This should have been done with. I wouldn't take the duel lightly."

"I'm not worried about the kid. And let's remember you were the one who was taken by the man from Virginia. You helped the bastard make this damn thing." The Devil held up the bottle.

"A trick on his part. And a lapse that's been paid for many souls over."

The Devil sighed. He handed the bottle over. "Lock this back up."

Legba took the bottle. He twisted around and put the bottle in the glove box of his car.

39. INTERLUDE: ANOTHER LEGEND

When she was a very young girl, Alice Crow Lee's family died in a barn fire. She loved her family very much and sadness etched itself unto her bones and heart. She went to live with her great uncle, her only living relative, deep in the Mississippi River Delta. He was a superstitious man and a devout practitioner of natural magic. He taught her the arts which he studied—the arts of nature and of the spirit world. She was a good student and absorbed each lesson. She would disappear for days and live off fish she pulled from the bayou while she practiced and became very powerful.

One day some years later, her uncle, while on his deathbed, told her of a burial ground to which a secret portal beneath a tree to the underworld existed. The portal existed only while the tree stood. To which one could go, like Orpheus, and reclaim their dead. Angry that her uncle had kept this from her—that he only told her now in hopes that she would extend his life, that he had not gone to bring back her family—she uttered a spell and all life was extinguished from his body.

The next day she set off up the river, as she was instructed. The tree, shaped like a horned serpent, stood alone on a plain. When the wind blew through its branches it would sing and howl.

She met a young man on her journey. A poor, but very eager, traveling musician named Charles Dodd who played very well and had a voice that seemed to vibrate every fiber of her being. Alice felt a stir in her heart that she had never felt before. He was headed north, as she was, and, unaccustomed to the ways of men, she allowed him to travel with her. One night, she took the drink he offered her while the cold winds blew around them. A drink called whiskey that would keep you warm. She drank and drank and after a time she found herself telling Charles about the tree—how she intended to bring back her family.

Charles laughed at her for believing in such superstitions. Alice, in a moment of clarity, realized she had said too much and laughed with him. He kissed her head. Not long after she fell asleep, and in the morning he was gone.

Alice continued on her journey, and after a few days she found the tree. She began the incantation and the tree lifted high out of the ground. In the distance, an engine roared. Alice's concentration broke and the tree slammed down on its side against the earth. She looked towards the truck, almost upon her now, and levelled her fury at the vehicle. The vehicle stopped violently as if it struck an invisible pylon, and Charles fell out of the open door. Her anger disappeared and was replaced with confusion when she recognized the man. Charles, laying on the ground, took out a pistol and shot her in the stomach.

While she lay there bleeding to death, he told her the night before he met her a man had come to him and said that a woman would come and speak of a tree. If he built a guitar out of the tree, he would have no rivals. But there must be a soul sacrifice. And it wasn't going to be his.

He pushed her body into the hole in the ground and filled it with the surrounding soil.

40. REHEARSAL STUDIO IN AUSTIN: TRIGGER HAPPY

Brad Johnson's band just finished running their set for the second time. They worked out the kinks—the musicians were pros and Brad somehow held his own.

"That was pretty great," Brad said. "Why don't you boys take fifteen and we'll hit it one more time."

The drummer, bassist, and keyboardist left the studio to catch a smoke. The pedal steel player pulled out his phone and stepped into the hallway. The electric guitarist put his guitar down and went over to Brad. "Hey, man," he said. "What's holding that guitar together?" He pointed to Brad's guitar cradled in a stand next to him.

"Lot's of glue, Hank," Brad said and laughed.

"She sounds fantastic. May I?"

Brad tensed. "I'd prefer not," and then hastily added, "if that's cool. She's just real fragile. Need to take her to the shop after the gig. Bridge is loose."

"It's all good man. No worries," Hank said and put his hands up. "I can dig it."

Brad put his hand on the guitar.

Hank looked at it again. "I've got a '67 D-28 if you want to use it for the gig. She sounds amazing. Solid body."

"I appreciate the offer," Brad said. "I'm kind of attached to…"

"Trigger!"

"What?"

"That's what it is. You've got Willie Nelson's guitar!"

"Nah, man," Brad said. "This has been kicking around the studio since the '80s. I found it in my office when I took over the station in '08." A joyous panic flooded his body. *Were the stories actually true? Was this Willie Nelson's guitar?* There was a certain electricity he felt when he played it—a strange surge that he never felt with other instruments. Earlier in the sessions he played a telecaster for an upbeat rocker he wrote. His playing was good, but he felt like he lost a step when he swapped instruments.

"Well, it sure looks like it," Hank said. "They made some repros in the 90s." He crouched down. Looked at the guitar more closely. "Maybe someone relic'd this one. Looks just like it."

"Martin makes really good guitars, so…"

"They do. She sounds good, repro or not."

"True tone comes from the player," Brad offered.

"Yes it does, friend. Yes it does." He stretched. "I'm gonna piss. Let's try to double that lead on 'Mockingbird,' yeah?"

"Sure thing," Brad said.

Hank left the studio.

Brad's phone buzzed. A promoter who owed him a favor put lines out to get Brad in festivals starting next week until November. There was a possible support spot with Eddie Vedder in Europe for a winter tour. *Book it all* Brad responded.

The band all came back in the studio.

"All right boys," Brad said, straightening himself, smiling and tucking his phone away.. "Hank wants to try and double that lead on 'Mockingbird' and then we'll run the set again. Cool?"

They played through each song—even better than the last time. Brad was going to kill in two days.

41. MEMPHIS: MARCH OF THE PIGS

Mojo Pin loaded up their gear in the green room before their gig. They had a couple of hours to burn before they were set to play. Marc kept Micawber with him and they went to explore Beale St. The sound of music and the smell of roasting meats, barbecue, and fried onions spilled into the street.

"I want BBQ," Bollocks said.

"Me too," Maybelline said.

"Thirdsies," Tanner said.

Marc pointed across the street. "That place has a neon pig. It's gotta be good."

Bollocks put his hand on Marc's chest. "Woah, woah, woah. Slow your roll there, Porky. Two things: We aren't eating before we play. And, we're not eating on Beale Street. It's tourist central."

"Yeah, let's check Yelp! or something for the best place," Tanner said.

"Tanner, Tanny, T-Bone," Bollocks said. "Yelp! is for assholes."

"I'd give this place no stars if I could," Maybelline said in an airy voice. "I was there on Saturday afternoon and decided to be a real dick."

"See, Maybelline gets it," Bollocks said. "We need to find someone who really knows this place. Someone who looks like they know barbecue. Someone with molasses in their bones and mesquite coursing through their hemoglobins."

Marc laughed. "What does that person look like?" he asked.

"Like pornography and douchebags, we'll know them when we see them."

"Ok, well let's keep an eye out."

The group walked down the street and stopped for a picture in front of the Elvis Presley Statue.

"Long live the king," Marc said. He looked down the street towards the Mississippi river. "I want to go check out the water."

"Gotta waz?" Bollocks asked.

"I think that's the spot Jeff Buckley…"

"Oh, yeah!" Bollocks interrupted. "Didn't he live here?"

"Our band is named after one of his songs," Marc said. "I'm going to give you a minute to remember the answer."

"I feel like you mentioned it once or a hundred times," Bollocks offered. He furrowed his brow. "I'm going with, 'Yes. He lived here.'" Bollocks smiled.

"Yeah," Tanner said. "He drowned in the river there…"

"Ah, snap," Bollocks said and stopped smiling.

"And his body washed up on the shore at the bottom of Beale St.," Marc added.

"Let us make the pilgrimage," Bollocks said. He put his arm around Marc and they set off down the street.

The four of them stood on the banks of the Mississippi, along the small channel of water called the Wolf River. Mud Island, a large land mass, a peninsula jutting into the river, stood maybe 100 yards away.

"The water seems so calm," Maybelline said.

"You could probably swim across if you wanted to," Bollocks said.

"That's what Jeff thought," Tanner said.

"Fucking undertow," Marc said. "And mud."

"He was there and then he wasn't." Tanner shook his head.

"Singing some Zeppelin."

"Whole Lotta Love."

"Are you two Buckley Buds?" Bollocks asked.

Marc looked at Tanner. "I think we might be."

"He probably had a deal with the Devil," Tanner said. "Or I've suspected it since he sings about the secret chord."

"You know about the chord?" Marc said.

"Well, yeah. I thought you mentioned it. And, it explains why the Devil is after you."

Marc sighed. He nodded. "Jeff didn't have a deal." He looked out to the water.

"How do you know?"

"I asked Keith Richards."

"Fuck," Tanner said. "That makes it even more tragic."

"Um," Maybelline said. "Speaking of Keith Richards…"

Marc looked at her and shook his head.

A wind blew in off the water. Marc pulled one of his old plastic picks out of his pocket. He kneeled and buried it. He placed his hand on the sand over the spot for a few moments and then stood up. "Let's do 'Everybody Here Wants You,'" he said to Bollocks.

"Oohh, yeah," Bollocks said. "People are gonna be fuckin' tonight."

***

Mojo Pin finished their set at Calliope's. A half venue, half restaurant that looked like it was once a factory. The audience was wild for them. The local radio station was plugging the gig hard the past two days. Fresh off the success of opening for Beck, they were able to garner a small draw—not a ton, but the band they opened for, The Merkin Men, pulled their weight and brought a crowd.

Marc played with the leather jacket on and that same surge from the XPoNential gig electrified him. That mysterious force was doubled and seemed to hum out of his pores when he played. He was unstoppable on stage. There wasn't a note he couldn't hit, or a lick he couldn't play. He was a man possessed, wrangling the songs out of his guitar with the grace of a snake charmer and the precarious control of a flame twirler.

"Potter's glasses!" Bollocks said backstage. "That was incredible. The air was static up there."

"You felt that?" Marc said, wiping down Micawber and sticking her back in the case.

"It felt like the sound Velcro makes. But like, really good. I was feeding off that shit."

"I was radiating."

"I fucking know it. Gotta get some iodine at the nearest drugstore."

The guys from The Merkin Men hustled past Marc and Bollocks on their way to the stage. "Good shit!" the singer said. "Usually I just say that, but I mean it tonight. That was incredible." The drummer fist bumped them and the bass player and guitar player nodded to them and gave them a pat on the shoulder.

Marc and Bollocks made their way into the crowd to meet up with Maybelline and Tanner. Tanner offered to go onstage and break down Marc's rig and Bollocks' cymbals, snare, and bass pedal.

"Uh, I'm not gonna say no to a roadie," Bollocks said.

"Gotta earn my keep," Tanner said.

"You got us thousands and thousands of dollars," Marc said.

"Lower your anchor, sailor. No need to talk him out of it," Bollocks said.

Marc shrugged. "Ok. Thanks, man."

Tanner walked past them to the stage.

"That was somehow better than two days ago," Maybelline said. "Light years from last week's gig."

"That seems like a lifetime ago," Marc said.

"I feel like I haven't eaten in a lifetime," Bollocks said. "Did you guys see the bouncer?"

"The guy that stamped us earlier?"

The group looked back towards the door at the entrance to the venue. There was a big guy sitting on a stool. Shaved head. Tattoo of a skull on his skull. Black beard. Tank top. Chewing on a toothpick.

"I smelled him," Bollocks said.

"That's not weird," Maybelline asked.

"I had to know."

"And?"

"Vinegar and smoke. Charcoal. A hint of brown sugar."

"Right," Marc said. "Since when do you have super smell?"

"I'm telling you, he's our man." Bollocks looked to the guy. "And, he was wearing a shirt for a BBQ place. The Rendezvous."

"Ok," Marc said. "Lead the way."

The three of them went to the bouncer. Some of the people in the crowd gave Marc and Bollocks high-fives and pats on the back. Most people just ignored them.

"Hey," Bollocks said. "How's it going?"

The bouncer looked up from his phone. "Bathrooms are to your right. Smoking is outside."

"Oh, I don't smoke. I was wondering if you knew where the best place to get BBQ is? I don't trust the internet for food reviews."

"Ok." The bouncer eyed Bollocks.

"If you were only able to have one last meal, where would it be?"

"BBQ?"

"Yeah."

"I don't mess with that stuff. I'm a vegetarian."

"Shit," Bollocks said to himself.

Marc and Maybelline laughed. "Sorry," Maybelline said to the bouncer. "We're not laughing at you. We're laughing at him." She pointed to Bollocks.

"It's good," the bouncer said. He looked back at his phone and swiped at the screen and then put the phone in his pocket. He eyed the group and slowly took the toothpick out of his mouth. "Hamiel."

"What?"

"You want to speak to Hamiel."

"Hamiel?" Marc asked. "Who's that?"

"Runs our kitchen. If it's good, he'll know where to get it…if he can't make it." The bouncer looked towards the back of the venue, to where the kitchen was. "You boys just played, right?"

"Yep," Bollocks said and showed the band stamp on his inner wrist.

The bouncer picked up his walkie and pressed a button. A static chirp. "Yo, is Hamiel around?"

A garbled response came back—paper covered in tinfoil being crumpled.

"Cool," the bouncer said. "He'll be out in a second."

"The cook's name is 'Hamiel?'" Bollocks asked.

"That's his name," the bouncer said. He put his toothpick back in his mouth. "Don't be weird about it."

"My name is 'Bollocks.' Nothing but respect."

"Well, 'Bollocks Nothing But Respect' there's your man."

A skinny guy in kitchen whites with a thin mustache and crooked chef's hat approached the group. "What can I do for you?"

"These boys and girl want BBQ," the bouncer said and pointed to the group.

Bollocks put out his hand. "Pleased to meet you, Hamiel."

Hamiel looked at the bouncer. "John, you motherfucker."

John spit his toothpick out and threw his head back with a roar of a laugh. He slapped his leg.

"My name is 'Daniel,'" Hamiel said. "This joker thinks he's funny."

John wiped his eyes.

"Bad nicknames really tickle him," Hamiel Daniel said.

John put his hand on Hamiel's shoulder. "Last weekend he got so drunk and said when you eat ham you get the power of the hog." John wheezed out the last part of the sentence before letting out a thunderous outburst again.

"I have respect for the animals that die so that we may eat them and live," Hamiel Daniel said.

John caught his breath. "And then he went all Bubba Gump. Ham sandwich, ham steak, ham salad…this motherfucker was pontificating on the merits of ham and hog meat for an hour."

Hamiel Daniel shook John's hand off his shoulder. "I care more about the animals we eat than this Sunday vegetarian."

"What's that supposed to mean?" John said.

"I saw you in my stew."

"Naw, man. That wasn't me…" John said and pulled out another toothpick from his pocket and put it in his mouth.

"I am sorry for this rude, rude man," Hamiel Daniel said to Bollocks, Maybelline, and Marc. "How can I help you?"

"Uh," Bollocks said. "I'm sorry he made fun of your reverence. We are but pilgrims looking for the best BBQ in Memphis."

"It's late," Hamiel Daniel said. He surveyed the group. "I could send you to the Rendezvous. Central or Corky's."

"Are they close?"

Hamiel ignored the question. "But, you said you wanted the best."

"We do."

Hamiel Daniel nodded. "Sit."

***

Hamiel brought out a feast—every portion of what was left from that day's service. Racks of dry and muddy. Brisket. Pulled pork. And the crème de la crème: a small silver dish with brown lumps of meat resting in a brown sauce surrounded by fanned out miniature carrots. "Pig's cheek," Hamiel said with a flourish of his hand.

The four of them ate heartily. Bollocks cleaned the plates with cornbread.

They left the venue and stood outside of their van which Tanner had parked out front after loading up their gear.

"You know," Marc said. "For as much as I ate, I don't feel gross. I actually feel great."

"Do you feel like you have the power of the hog?" Bollocks asked.

"Kind of."

"The pig is a symbol of strength and fertility in some cultures," Tanner said.

"I do feel strong and sexy," Bollocks said and flexed his bicep.

"It's also forbidden and associated with the Devil in others, so…" Tanner added.

"Well, I don't think there was anything weird about that," Marc said. "Did you?"

"Not really," Tanner said. "Chefs are weird, so there's really no telling. But, no."

"Let's find a motel. We have to go to Rosedale tomorrow."

"What are we going to do without Keith Richards?" Maybelline asked. "The whole reason we're going there is because of him."

"I don't know," Marc said.

"Do you think you're going to try on your own? Without Keith Richards you don't really have anything to do with Rosedale. You could just, I don't know. Dodge the Devil."

"For the rest of my life? I'm marked, Maybelline."

She sighed. "I know, I know. I just…" She shook her head. "We were going to help Keith Richards. But without him, do we even know what we are supposed to do? Are we even able to do what we have to?"

"I've never felt like this before. I feel…powerful," Marc said and squared his shoulders, "like I can beat him. Keith has been training me almost my whole life and now with the jacket, pick, and guitar, I really don't think there's a thing I can't do musically."

A car horn honked. On the street was a black Lincoln Continental convertible. The top was down. "You folks need a ride?" an old man said—a man wearing a straw hat and holding a pipe in his hand.

"What the fuck," Bollocks said and jumped back. The rest of the group braced their stances.

"Ah," the old man said. "Don't be afraid, now." He took a drag off his pipe.

"You almost swallowed us in the ground the last time we met," Marc said. He laid the guitar case on the ground and un-latched the clasps. He threw Micawber around his neck.

"Easy there," the man said.

Marc took a step forward.

"Marc," Maybelline said. "What are you doing?"

Marc played a lick on the guitar, an old blues riff. His guitar wasn't plugged in, but the sound resonated through the air, electrified by some unknown current. The man winced and the car slid sideways. He threw the transmission in park and put his hands up.

"Easy there, goddamnit," he said. "I'm only here to deliver a message."

Tanner stepped up next to Marc. He put his hand on his shoulder. "Let him speak."

"You sure?" Marc asked.

"I think I know who he is now."

"What do you want?" Marc said to the man.

"We can end all of this tonight," the man said. "If you like." He smiled—rows of teeth glistening in the light of the streetlamps.

"You're the trickster. Intermediary. Legba," Tanner said.

Legba tilted his hat towards the group. "At your service."

"We outsmarted you before and we're stronger now. What do you want?"

"I can see," Legba said. "I was foolish last time. I underestimated you."

"What do you want? The bottle?"

Legba laughed. "Useless to me. You earned it fair and square."

Tanner took the bottle out of his bag. He held it up. "Tell me what it is."

"You know what it is."

"I knew what it was. This isn't it anymore."

Legba smiled. "Now why would you go and say that?"

"This bottle is dead."

Legba appraised Tanner. "And perhaps I still underestimate you." He smiled. "It's a shame you aren't calling. There's still time." He looked at Bollocks and Maybelline. "For all of you."

"We're good," Bollocks said. "No one's playing grab ass with you, Legolas."

"Let's make a deal. You agree to come with me and I'll tell you what's in the bottle."

"Why would we go with you?" Marc said.

"Because I know where Keith Richards is."

Marc gripped the neck of Micawber and shredded off a riff, doubled it and bent the strings. "Let him go," he yelled. Legba retreated into the corner of the seat and door. He dropped his pipe. When Marc stopped, Legba slumped, and his hat fell off and lay in his lap. Marc took a few steps towards the car. "Let him go."

"Easy, easy, easy," Legba said. His tired voice crackled. "I get it. You're strong." He sat up in the car. "I don't have him. I'm only bringing a message."

"Speak." Marc's eyes flashed.

"If you agree to cut heads, tonight, you can save Keith," Legba said. He put his hat on. "And yourself."

"Name the place."

Legba's teeth shimmered again. He was back to himself. He put his pipe in his mouth and puffed. "Sun Studio. Midnight."

42. SOMEWHERE IN THE BETWEEN: BEAST OF BURDEN BROKEN

Keith Richards sat at the bar of an empty juke joint smoking a cigarette. The wooden floorboards were in a permanent exhalation of dust, a weary fog hovering. There wasn't a right angle in the place, the building's beams long ago bent and resigned under their own weight. There was a stage—a jetty sticking out from the darkness, made from the same wood as the floor, supported by barrels acting as the pilings.

Keith had no idea how long he'd been there. Time was irrelevant where he was. All he knew was that he wasn't on earth. One moment he was beside Marc, and the next he felt like he was evaporating like mist, burning off and being pulled beyond the veil.

Behind the bar were countless rows of hourglasses at various states of fill. Hundreds. Thousands. He couldn't count them all stacked up and shoved in the shelves as they were. Some emptied very quickly, and some dropped grains at an imperceptible rate. He had a hunch about what they were, and he sincerely hoped he was one of the slow ones. Every so often one would crack, the glass orbs releasing a soft pop, and then the hourglass would disappear sending a small trail of dust to the floor. Others echoed their banishment and demise in the far crevices of the deep and endless shelving.

He had his guitar. An old nylon stringed beater his grandfather gave him when he was a boy. There was magic in that old guitar still. He looked at his hands. Gnarled and knotted and burred as the branches of a river tree. He picked up the guitar and plucked out a blues tune. An old one that came from someplace beyond memory—that came from the stuff that watered memory's roots.

There was no door in the building. No escape to the mortal world. The walls were covered in windows of different sizes and angles. Small diamond shaped ones and large ones like a glass movie screen. Some were so pin perfect he had to get his eye right up to the wall to look through. The windows flashed, shooting beams like a car's headlights passing by at night. How long had he spent looking through them? A lifetime? Lifetimes? They replayed every moment he had experienced. Buying candy and chocolates for the first time when the sweets rationing ended years after the war. Weekends at his grandparents' house. Singing with his aunts. His mother—his mate. He relived all these moments. There was no chronology. They were presented by the mysterious force of memory. One thing leading to the other.

Meeting Mick Jagger in primary school. Reconnecting again waiting for the train at Dartford Station. Little Boy Blue and the Blue Boys. Drugs. Getting busted in Arkansas. Anita. The touring. Oh god, all the touring. Jamaica. Falling. He pitied himself, strung out, a needle in his arm. Cold turkey. More drugs. Every drug. Shepherd's pie. Cutting the junk in the bathroom and dosing it out. His children. Brian Jones. He lingered over a meeting on the banks of the Mississippi on that first US tour. He shook his head. Nothing to be done about events already lived. Flames shooting out of a microphone stand, almost dying from electrocution. Patti. First birthdays. Missed birthdays. Grandkids. All these events swirled and replayed. Things remembered and things forgotten—things he wished had never happened.

Only the Devil knows how he wept and for how long at the window of his boy, Tara, newborn, in his arms. He long ago gave up on the idea that angels could hear him where he was.

He tapped his fingers on the bar. He lit another cigarette. How he wished for a drink. He thought of Marc. He had seen that show already, many times. He shook his head and began that old song one more time.

43. SUN STUDIO: JUST BEFORE MIDNIGHT

The studio's neons were glowing when they pulled up. "Sun Studio" burned red in one window, "Memphis Recording Service" in blue and red repeated in another set of windows farther down the building—above, the word "Sun" was illuminated, a red arch on the side of the building, welcoming and guiding them through the dark.

They parked around back and walked up the alley at the side of the building. There were pictures of the greats who had recorded there enlarged and stuck to the wall, covered and framed in plexiglass. Jerry Lee Lewis, Johnny Cash, Carl Perkins, Roy Orbison. And of course, The King—Elvis Presley.

"Are we here to cut a track?" Bollocks said. "Why this place?"

"I don't know," Marc said. "But we'll be all right. I promise."

Marc looked over to Maybelline. She had been quiet lately. Ever since they left Drix. "You writing all this down?" Marc asked. "It'll make a good cover story when we're done."

She smiled weakly. "I just want it to be done."

"Soon."

"Yo, Tanner," Bollocks said. "You ready to glamour the Devil or something if we need you to?"

"Charms aren't going to do much," Tanner said.

"That's a shame."

"It's all good," Marc said. "I can handle this."

"Did you see dude's car?"

They all looked around. The car wasn't anywhere to be seen.

"You think this is a trick?" Bollocks asked.

"It'd be a lame trick if it was," Marc said.

Bollocks pulled on the door at the end of the building. It was locked. Inside the building was dark as far as we could tell.

"What time is it?" Maybelline asked.

Tanner pulled out his phone. "11:58."

"He said midnight."

Marc bounced on the balls of his feet. "I'm fucking ready to do this."

"Don't be too cocky," Maybelline said.

"I agree," Tanner said. "You might feel powerful, but the Devil is tricky. Legba is tricky. And there's a lot on the line."

"You think I don't fucking know that?" Marc said "It's my goddamn soul he's after. I can feel him clawing at me."

"We just want you to be ok, Master Frodo," Bollocks said putting his hand on Marc's shoulder. "We're entering Minas Morgul."

"What?" Marc said.

"It's how Frodo and Sam entered Mordor," Tanner said.

Marc sighed. "As long as a giant spider doesn't get us, we'll be ok."

"They encountered Shelob before they entered Minas Vale…"

Bollocks shook his head. "Now's not the time for specifics. We've got to get his head in the game." Bollocks squared up with Marc. "Ok, what's the sickest riff you know?"

The sound of an engine roared behind them on the street. Maybelline and Bollocks, who were closest to the curb, jumped. A black Lincoln Continental was there, seemingly from nowhere. The lights in the building burst on, the whole place came alive with electricity. A translucent aura shrouded the walls.

"You made it," Legba said, killing the ignition and getting out of the car. "Right this way."

He motioned toward the locked door and pulled on the handle, opening it up. They stepped into what looked like a cross between a gift shop and a diner from the '50s. Red stools along a counter. Black and white checkered tile floors. Pictures and merchandise everywhere.

Legba looked up at an old sign that said "Crown Elec. Co." He motioned with his cane towards it. "You know what that is?"

"It's where Elvis worked," Maybelline said.

Legba smiled. "Good."

"Wait," Tanner said. "Is that a test?" He looked at all of us. "Don't answer any questions unless we know."

Legba laughed. "No. That one wasn't a test. People seem to like to know that when they come here. That's all. I'll give you a tour later on." He laughed to himself again. "We're in a neutral zone right now. No harm will befall you in this room."

Legba went around the counter behind the bar. "We're going to get started soon. Can I get you folks anything from the café while Marc is next door?" He reached for a stack of menus behind the counter.

"He's going alone?" Maybelline said.

"We're going with him," Bollocks said.

"Only those marked or have a deal can enter," Legba said. He smiled again. "That can be arranged."

"Guys," Tanner said. He shook his head. "He's right. Marc has to go alone."

"What would happen if we went next door?" Bollocks said, standing in front of Marc.

Legba shrugged. "You'd be in an empty studio in the middle of the night. The alarm would go off. The police would come."

"I'll be ok," Marc said to Bollocks. He turned towards Maybelline and Tanner and nodded.

"Well, we best go over the rules before we go. He's waiting." Legba handed out the menus. "First side is the rules, drinks and snacks on the back."

They each took a menu. Bollocks flipped his over twice. Legba lit his pipe.

The Rules

Marc, herein referred to as "The Marked," will cut heads three times.

+ *Each confrontation will take place beginning at midnight, starting tonight.*

+ *Each confrontation The Marked will cut heads with a different adversary.*

+ *If The Marked loses, The Marked loses. The Marked cannot face-off against the others—those prizes are forfeit.*

+ *If The Marked loses, he forfeits Micawber, the pick, and the leather jacket.*

+ *It costs $3 a side if The Marked would like a copy of each performance.*

"Three?" Marc said. "Why three battles?"

"One for your soul. One for Keith Richards." Legba said. He took a drag off his pipe and raised his eyebrow. "And finally, for us to leave your friends alone."

"What the fuck?" Bollocks said. "Why the hell are you after me?"

"You're implicated. You know. Knowledge is power."

Tanner sighed. "I was afraid of this. I knew it when we started but didn't want to believe it."

"What the fuck does that mean?"

"It means since we've seen it, we can't walk away from it. We'll be tempted and tested for the rest of our lives."

"But we didn't make any deals or call the Devil," Maybelline said.

"You entered this of your own volition when you came, freely and not against your will, I might add, into my lair at the liquor store," Legba said. "You gave yourselves the knowledge. I asked you. No one forced you."

"But we didn't know," Bollocks said.

"One of you did," Legba said.

"What happens if Marc loses?" Tanner asked quickly. "We can't fight for our own souls? To be left alone?"

"You sure can. Just come calling or make a deal," Legba said. "You think any of you are ready to do that?"

A deep bell sounded, a pitch so low it was felt more than heard. No one said anything. Every molecule in the room was constricted and expanding—strained filaments, magnetic, reaching out and being pulled from both ends.

"What's the order?" Marc finally asked, his voice a lead ball in the bottom of a steel drum.

"You'll discuss that inside. That's out of my realm," Legba said. He pulled a watch out of his pocket. He pointed to a doorway at the end of the café that led to the studio. "You have to go."

"Who do I pay?" Marc asked and put his menu down on the counter.

"You'll pay the man," Legba said. "You always pay the man."

Marc turned around to Bollocks and gave him a pat on the side of his arm. He nodded to Tanner. Maybelline hugged him and kissed him hard. "Be careful," she said.

Marc walked toward the door at the end of the café. He threw his guitar case on the counter and opened the latches. He lifted out his guitar and ran his hand along the back of the neck. Over the body. He slung Micawber over his shoulder and turned to the group. "I can win," he said. "For all of us." Marc stepped away from the counter and the café and his friends, alone, and into the darkness.

"What's in the bottle?" Tanner said to Legba. "You promised."

"Oh," Legba said. "Dr. Pib. The real one is safe and sound."

"Motherfucker," Bollocks said. "Get me a chocolate milkshake."

44. A COASTAL MANSION IN KILLINEY, IRELAND

"Aye…aye…good fer 'er."

The man wandered around his spartan office overlooking the Irish Sea, a cell phone pressed to his ear.

"I'll be there, no problem…fer sure."

The man rested against the edge of his desk.

"You sorted out the details?…grand…yep, Austin…ok…grand…"

He lowered his phone. The waves splashed gently against the rocks below. He had lived a good life. He had everything he could have dreamed of by anyone else's standards. But, there was a lot of work to do still that would affect his personal and professional life. He lifted his phone and tapped away at the screen.

Just heard about the Rolling Stone gig. Nice job. I'll be in Austin this weekend. Pint?

45. SOMEWHERE IN THE BETWEEN, BUT ALSO SUN STUDIO: COME HERE BOY, THERE AIN'T NOTHIN' FOR FREE

I walked through a doorway separating the café from the studio. A thin veil passed through me, as if I were wading in gossamer. It was quiet—an oppressive silence, deep and weighty. I gripped Micawber tighter and a weird gravity grounded my feet little by little with each step. The floor of the studio became firm under me. The tiles were yellowed and worn smooth, as if they had been waxed, reflecting the lights of the room. Three were three black Xs taped to the ground in a triangular formation. I ran the tip of my shoe across a divot in the tile next to one of the Xs. White soundproofing tiles covered the walls, floor to ceiling, set in a wave-like pattern. There were pictures all over the place—mostly of Elvis. A slew of instruments lined the wall. An upright bass in the corner. The far end of the room had a glass window which looked into a control room. There was a door next to the window, and I went to it and turned the handle and pushed it open. I stuck my head in.

"You're late," a voice said from behind me.

I pulled my head out of the door quickly and turned around, my hands on Micawber, ready to blast off a lick.

"Easy," the man said and put his hand up. He was wearing a suit. His shoes were shiny, piano black, a sharp counterpoint to the floor.

"Where's Keith Richards?" I demanded.

"You haven't earned him yet," the man said impatiently. "Everyone's in such a big damn hurry these days." The man approached me with his hand out. "I think we should introduce ourselves properly."

I looked at his hand. There was no way in hell I was going to shake it. That clawing I had felt earlier seemed to intensify. An anxiety buried deep in my chest, siphoning some essential part of me.

"You know who I am," I said.

"Of course. And you know who I am?"

"I do."

He dropped his arm. "Well, I would have loved to meet you under different circumstances. You have such potential. But, you came calling and I had to show up. I don't like to keep people waiting."

"It was an accident."

The man smiled. "Was it, Marc?" He raised his eyebrow. "Was it?" He walked around the room. He pointed to the black X near my foot. "That's where Elvis stood when he sold his soul." He pointed to another X. "Scotty Moore." Then the other. "Bill Black."

"I thought you had to go to the crossroads?" I asked.

"You weren't at the crossroads, were you?"

I didn't say anything.

"All one has to do is have desire in their heart," he said. "But you knew that."

"Lots of people have desire. You telling me that you're disrupting everyone's lives?"

"You're a man of the people, now? No, Marc. The desire must be pure. Not some half-assed wish to be famous. If I gave this great opportunity to just anybody I'd have the most pathetic army of talentless YouTube personalities and SoundCloud rappers." He sneered. "Though, I can't say I haven't snatched a few in one of my more careless moods. It's too easy. Those souls are as useless to me in my realm as they are in yours. You're special, Marc. You have great abilities, and the possibilities for you could be endless if you let me help you. You could be great."

I released my grip on Micawber slightly. I felt a small ease wash over me as he talked, like a knot slowly unraveling. He moved closer to me. "You could be one of the greats." He put his hand on my shoulder. I looked into his eyes.

I saw myself on stages—Wimbledon. O2. Maracaná. Knebworth. The Parkway. A floating stage in the ocean with half a million people. I saw money. Maybelline beside me. Bollocks happy. I breathed in and felt the essence of having made a difference. That I had helped people with my music and made the world a better place—that my music gave comfort to those who needed it. I had a goat farm. A mansion in Rittenhouse.

He removed his hand from my shoulder. "All yours," he whispered, the words dripping into my ear, wrapping themselves around my mind and dreams, cradling me. I dropped my hands from Micawber. "Why fight?" he said.

I looked down at my feet. Inches away from where Elvis stood. I could be Elvis. I thought of black hair and jumpsuits. Cars. Screaming fans. Fried chicken. Peanut butter, banana, and bacon sandwiches.

The Devil moved away from me and reached out for a mic on a stand. One of those old-timey grilled chrome deals that looked like the front of a car. "Elvis' microphone. He used this to record in this room, right where you're standing. We could start a session right now instead of fighting."

I touched the microphone. A slow current ran through me— soft and warm as cotton candy. Then a brief flash, a sharp tack on my finger that sent a pain up my arm and into my head. It drained down my body, fast, from my crown to my face and cheeks, neck and into my body, my gut dropping out.

A vision: Elvis alone. His left arm folded under his body, right arm out, his underwear around his calves. Cold tile against his cheek. A pool of vomit forming a cruel halo about his head, shit and piss spreading out on the floor beneath his body.

I jerked back from the microphone. "What happens at the end? What happens to my soul when I die?"

"Your soul? Tell me about your soul. What is it to you?" The man said.

I didn't actually have an answer. At least a specific one I could articulate. I knew that it was mine. If it was valuable to the Devil then it must be worth keeping, especially after seeing the torment it put Keith Richards through.

"That's what I thought," the man said. "You don't even understand what you're trying to protect."

"I understand enough. What happens?"

"You're asking too much," the man said.

"Try."

"Imagine a womb. It's that feeling."

"Then why do you have to collect souls?"

He walked around the room and ran his finger along a piano against the wall. He tinkled out a discordant melody, then pointed to a brown mark at the end of the keyboard. "Jerry Lee Lewis. He put out his cigar after we partnered up." He looked back at me. "Let's say I'm lonely."

"You're lonely? You need friends?"

"Do you need me to tell the old story?"

"I want you to leave me and my friends alone."

"It's not as bad as they're saying, you know."

"You having my soul?" I said and gripped Micawber.

"It's not torment. It's more like…wandering through a palace of pleasure."

"That sounds like heaven."

His eyes flared. His form grew and turned pale, translucent and silhouetted by fire. Horns, wings. He shrank. "It is not heaven," he spit out. "It is something honest for those who deserve it. Not those blind thoughtless hypocrites who follow Him."

"Then why's everyone dead or trying to get out the deal? Why is Keith Richards trying to free himself?"

He was silent and simmering. His chest heaved and he shook his head. "You have no idea what I've done for Keith. How do you think Mötley Crüe survived? Jimmy Page? You think Steve Jobs lived for 8 years by accident after he was given cancer? I helped him. The cancer wasn't me. The overdoses weren't me."

"You telling me it was god?"

"I'm telling you it wasn't me. I liked those guys. I liked Steve. He was good."

Everything I've ever heard about Steve Jobs was that he was an asshole in his personal life. "*Was* good? *Liked?* I thought they're wandering around the womb of pleasure."

"I told you you wouldn't understand."

"I'll take my chances. I'm keeping my soul." I narrowed my eyes and flexed my fingers.

He stared at me. "We'll see."

The room spun. The gear ignited. Micawber hummed. Its frequency was pouring out of the walls. A man with leather pants and a 7-string electric guitar appeared in the center of the room.

"A PRS?" I said and shook my head.

"What's wrong with a PRS?" the Devil asked genuinely.

"Nothing if you're an asshole. He could at least play a Strat like a gentleman."

The Devil shook his head. "This is Martone Hawkins," he said. "You will duel for your friends first. Then your soul. And then Keith's."

I pulled the old wooden pick out of my pocket. "Bring it."

The Devil took a hat down from off a shelf. He held it out to me.

"I'm guessing you don't accept Venmo?" I said.

He smirked. "My account's frozen."

I dug into my pocket and dropped in a $20. "That's for the whole session."

Martone blasted into a fast pentatonic riff that ascended the fretboard and squealed out up top. I copied the lick and ended it with a pick scrape against the low A string while I hammered on a repeating loop with my left hand.

Martone picked up my lick and two-hand tapped out some bullshit '80s shredder nonsense. It was a dirty trick devoid of musicality. I felt a tug in my chest. My hands didn't move that way. I could hear Keith Richards in my ear. *Come on, kid. It's never how many or fast the notes are. It's gotta be the right notes, at the right time.*

I took a deep breath and slinked my fingers around the fretboard, pulling out a slithering melody, long and slow like a hungry snake from a sack.

Martone copied me again and divebombed at the end to try and one up me. I rephrased the melody, this time using two notes at a time, creating a harmony and contrary bass line. The type of shit I had to do since Bollocks and I were a two-piece band.

Martone tapped out a bad copy. It squawked and I felt him diminish—I could tell he wasn't up for it. I felt like I was growing. Enlarged by energy.

I bent my strings hard and plucked them, releasing the bent note, creating a backwards scream out of the notes and finessing a variation of the melody downwards into the low end of my guitar. I dragged the final line out slow and grinding and ended with a grip chord in the middle of the neck, right at the sweet spot.

Martone Hawkins couldn't hack it. He tried for the melody but could only come up with the mechanical clinkings of a slave to the metronome and musical gymnastics. He began to dissolve, a hurried look of worry and panic on his face. His form stretched and disappeared.

"Hmm," the Devil said. "Well, that one was easy." He waved away what luminescence remained of his guitar player. "Your friends weren't committed. The next one will be harder. You fight for your soul."

With that the room went dark and I was standing in the doorway to the café. Bollocks, Maybelline, and Tanner looked over from a table in the corner. I smiled at them. "And to answer that ancient question put forth by the great Alaskan chanteuse, Jewel: It's me. I will save your souls."

46. SOMEWHERE IN THE BETWEEN

Keith Richards sat at the bar, his guitar resting on his lap. The windows howled at him—driving him mad. He was losing himself, slipping. He had run out of cigarettes a while back—or maybe he just did. Time was funny in this place. Something deep in him plummeted long ago and rolled over. Stirred and yanked at him like a hook caught on the bottom of the ocean.

The door to the bar opened. A man in a suit.

Keith looked at him. "You haven't any smokes do ya, Devil-Man?" he said.

The Devil flicked his finger.

Keith pat his pocket. A full pack. "Much obliged." Keith lit a cigarette and sucked in the smoke, deep and long and exhaled full and slow.

"Those things'll kill you," the Devil said.

Keith grunted. "I ain't close to it being here?"

"Oh, no. Not yet. This is a holding cell of sorts. It's all in the user agreement you signed."

"A bar without booze seems torturous to me. And those windows…" Keith looked down and shook his head. "No man should have to relive his life that way."

"I didn't think you'd be one for regrets."

Keith looked at the Devil. "What do you want with me here?"

"I just wanted to keep you out of the way for a couple of days."

"A couple of days?" Keith said. "I've been here ages."

"Oh, Keith. It's barely been two days on Earth," the Devil said.

Keith sighed. He ran his hand over his face. "Why am I here?" he said through his teeth.

"It's a holiday weekend," the Devil said and shrugged. "In the olden days folks would celebrate me. They'd have great parties and orgies and sacrifices culminating with a great giving of spirits on the 15th of the month. It was always such glorious fun." The Devil looked up as if he were lost in that other time, reminiscing at all the bloodletting and worship. He sighed. "Then on the 16th I'd go back to work and claim all the souls that had been sold or enact whatever penance was befitting. Those days are long gone, however. Now, I'm just overseeing some good old-fashioned head cutting."

"Neat story, Beelze. What's any of that got to do with me? Why'd you need me out of the way?"

"Because your boy is fighting for his friends…and his soul."

Keith tensed and gripped his guitar.

"Easy, now."

"He's going to beat you," Keith said.

"Maybe. Maybe not," the Devil said and ran his finger along the edge of the bar. "He's also fighting for your soul. Hence, the reason you're here. Can't have you interfering."

Keith's face sank. "Oh, Marc. No," Keith said to himself.

"He's pretty good. I'll give him that," the Devil said. "He could be truly great if he'd let me help him."

"He don't need the kind of help you can give."

"Well, we'll know when we win," the Devil said.

"We?" Keith said, his eyes dark. "I'm not helping you, Devil-Man." He spat on the ground at the feet of the Devil.

The Devil waved his hand and an orb appeared. Globulous and translucent, folding in and over on itself like waves pulled in every direction. The ectoplasmic shape approached Keith Richards.

Keith Richards stood up from his chair and the Devil motioned again with his hand. Keith was thrown hard and tight against the bar, pinned by two barstools. He dropped his cigarette. His guitar fell to the ground and cried out a hopeless clang, the strings unable to harmonize. The form wrapped itself around Keith Richards and muffled his screams and cries. It worked on him for a few moments more and then slowly fell away like slime down a window.

It puddled on the ground and began to take shape and rise. It grew to Keith Richards' height. Features began to appear. A young man turning old. Wrinkles and eyeliner. Bracelets and rings. The smell of smoke and bourbon.

All strength left Keith Richards' legs and he fell against the bar and slid to the ground.

The form looked down at him. "You got a cigarette, bub?" it said in a deep grumbling and guttural voice.

47. SOMEWHERE IN THE BETWEEN, BUT ALSO SUN STUDIO: AND IF I SAY TO YOU TOMORROW?

"You saved our souls?" Bollocks said and ran over and hugged Marc. Marc hugged him back. "Yeah. Piece of cake."

Maybelline kissed him. "Now that's some old-fashioned chivalry."

"What can I say? I'm a sucker for a smart gal."

"Gal?"

"Ok, ok," Tanner said breaking up their lovefest.

"What?" Marc said, a little annoyed.

"The next round will be harder," Tanner said from the booth.

"You said, 'Thank you' wrong," Bollocks said to Tanner.

"Thank you, Marc. The next round will be harder," Tanner said. "There wasn't as much on the line. The Devil is more invested in your soul. And he is fully invested in keeping Keith Richards' soul."

Papa Legba cleared his throat from behind the counter. The group looked over to him.

"What?" he said.

"Something you want to tell us?" Bollocks said.

Legba shrugged and shifted his weight to his cane and moved from behind the counter. He sat down on a stool and lit his pipe with a match and waved it out.

"Take your time," Marc said. "By all means."

Legba blew out a cloud of smoke. "Tanner is right."

"That's it?"

Legba nodded. "You'd better go shed kid if you want to save your soul." He pulled a pocket watch out of his vest. "It's almost time."

"Almost time? I just fucking came out," Marc said.

"And yet the bell is nearly tolling," Legba said.

"It doesn't matter," Marc said and shrugged. "I got this."

"Why do you care?" Maybelline asked Legba.

Legba shrugged. "Bored I guess. Maybe I'm feeling a little rebellious amidst all this. He always gets his way, and it's really got little to do with you, but sometimes I like to see the world burn."

"His world or ours, Heath?" Bollocks asked.

"His'll do for now."

Marc rolled his shoulders. "Ok. I'll practice. For us. Not for you."

"Better get to it," Legba said.

"Is there time for a cup of tea?"

"Of course."

"Marc," Maybelline said. "Are you ok?"

"Yeah. I feel great. Why?" Marc said.

"You seem different."

"I just beat the Devil. I'm feeling pretty good."

"There's something else." She shook her head.

"I'm ok," he said.

"Be careful."

"Your tea," Legba said.

Marc backed away from Maybelline. He ran a quick and dirty lick off the fretboard. "It's them that need to be careful." He slung Micawber behind himself and moved to the counter and picked up his tea. He blew on it and took a sip. That deep bell sounded again. "Keep this warm," he said to Legba. "I'll be back in a minute."

Marc stepped away from the counter and walked past his friends and back through the doorway leading to the studio.

Bollocks put his hand on Maybelline's shoulder. "He'll be ok."

"I hope so," she said.

48. SOMEWHERE IN THE BETWEEN, BUT ALSO SUN STUDIO: I WOKE UP THIS MORNING AND THE BLUES WAS WALKING LIKE A MAN

The room was empty. Again.

"Hello," I yelled to the back of the studio. Nothing. I pushed the white door open farther and stepped up into the control room. There was an old reel-to-reel 4-track in the back tucked up against two tape machines. Under the window, next to the massive console, was a Mac running Pro Tools. There were three rack units outfitted with compressors, audio interfaces, effect processors, a power conditioner, and a bunch of other units I'd never seen.

I looked out into the room. This was the view Sam Phillips had when he was recording Elvis, B.B. King, and Johnny Cash. I sat down in the chair with my guitar in my lap. I ran my hands along the console. This was a newer unit, but I bet U2 recorded on it.

"We're gonna run that one back, boys," I said into the talkback mic. "Whenever you're ready." I laughed to myself. The room grew cold.

"Having fun?" a voice said behind me.

I turned around. "Yes," I said, looking down the Devil.

"Here's your wax. I cut it to 33 1/3. All three sessions will be on the A-side," he said and handed me a 10-inch record in a plain white paper sleeve.

"Thanks." I took it. "What's on the B-side?"

"A hidden message."

"Funny."

"Marc," he said and sighed. "You care about your friends. I respect that. I really do."

He moved to the console, past me, and leaned over to the computer. "Can I show you something?"

"Do I have a choice?"

He shrugged. "Not really." He minimized Pro Tools and typed my name in the Google search bar and hit enter. The search results came back with a few articles and links to Mojo Pin. Most of the hits were unrelated to me.

"Ok?" I said.

"'Unremarkable' is more apt," he said.

"Your point?"

"It doesn't have to be." He snapped his fingers and refreshed the search. Links to Rolling Stone, Billboard, The Grammys, Paste, Spin. There were thumbnails to videos of performances at Coachella, a Tiny Desk Concert, and an interview with Jimmy Fallon. There I was sitting across from Marc Maron.

"Cool trick," I said. "But if selling my soul means I have to do Carpool fucking Karaoke, I'd rather wither away in obscurity."

The Devil laughed. "That's exactly why I like you, Marc! You've got integrity. You don't know how many people would do whatever I asked just for the glamour. You really are special."

I picked up Micawber from my lap and pushed the chair back, past The Devil. "I am special." I stood up. "And that's why I'm going to beat you, and still get all of that."

He closed the small distance between us and put his hand on my shoulder. "I'd really like it if you'd reconsider. Things aren't the way you think they are." He spoke low. Slow.

"Then how are they?"

"They could be great for you. Serving me isn't that bad."

I felt that unseen pull again, something under the surface spreading through me, wrapping itself around what I guess was my soul, my being, desire. Flashes of greatness again. Then the image crumbled and burned and I saw myself driving an old Honda Civic that had rusted around the wheel well. Spilling coffee out of a leaky tumbler onto my tucked in short sleeved shirt I was wearing with a tie. Stacks of unpaid bills. A guitar that wasn't Micawber with rusty strings and a dusty headstock leaning against the wall in the corner of a living room. Gray hairs in my beard. Getting yelled at by a guy in a bad suit. Fluorescent lights.

I shook it off. Stepped away, feeling his hand fall, that invisible grasp loosen. "Hondas are very reliable," I said. "And I'm glad I'll finally be able to grow facial hair."

I took the pick out of my pocket and rolled my shoulders, readjusting my guitar. The leather of the jacket creaked pleasantly. "Your tricks won't work on me."

The Devil's eyes flared briefly. "We'll see." He snapped his fingers and we were in the live room. There was an old man in the corner, sitting on a Fender '65 Princeton amplifier and holding a Gibson ES-335. As soon as I took a step he let out the sweetest guitar lick I think I'd ever heard, dripping with the delta, full of such sorrow and resignation. This was the stuff Keith always talked about. The stuff he was training me for. I knew where this bluesman was playing from—a place born from loss. I thought of my parents. The years of feeling utterly alone. The deep sense of abandonment always tucked away in my heart crept out and flooded my body. I took a seat across from the old bluesman gave it right back to him.

"Hey guys," I said and waved to Maybelline, Bollocks, and Tanner.

"Holy shit," Bollocks said. "That was fast. You like just left."

Maybelline stood up. "Are you ok?"

I took a deep breath. "Not really," I said and looked down. "Just had to go somewhere I hadn't been in a long time."

Bollocks excused himself past Maybelline. "Come here, brother," he said and hugged me. "What happened?"

"He's fucking with my head."

It all came flooding back to those early days and weeks and months when Bollocks had been a rock when I lost my parents. He always somehow knew when I was low about them. I let him hug me—I needed it. I hugged him back.

Maybelline rubbed my back. I sighed and wiped my eyes. I patted Bollocks on his arms and stepped back. "I'm good. I'm good," I said.

"You're free," Legba said with amusement in his voice.

"I am."

"No one wins them all," he said.

"Watch me."

"He tried to pull on your emotions this time. It'll only get worse. The next test will be the hardest of them all."

I furrowed my brow. "I don't see how," I said. "Besides, I can't play any wrong notes. It's impossible."

Legba took a puff on his pipe. He shrugged one shoulder and motioned with his head as if he almost believed me.

I went to the table and set my record down and picked up my tea. Tanner zeroed in on the vinyl. "May I?" he asked.

I nodded and sipped from my cup. Tanner slipped it out of the sleeve and ran his fingers over the grooves. He turned it over and brought the record close to his face. "That's weird," he mumbled to himself.

"Third session is gonna start soon," Legba said.

"This is some weird ass *Christmas Carol* shit," Bollocks said.

"Where do you think he got the idea from?"

"You're kidding," Maybelline said. "Did everybody fucking sell their souls?"

"I never met the man. Not my jurisdiction. But writing, publishing, and getting a book to market all within six weeks is nothing short of a dark miracle."

A deep bell sounded once again. I stared at my tea.

"It's time, young fella," Legba said.

I took one last drink and walked towards the studio. I felt lighter than before. Powerful still but shook. I tried not to think of what I saw last time when the old bluesman played his licks. I didn't know if I could handle that again. The twisted metal and flames. The screams. The awful loneliness. It somehow fueled and depleted me. But now, as I was on the verge of securing Keith Richards' soul, a whispering uncertainty I hadn't felt the last two battles was tugging at me. *Just one more time,* I said to myself. *Just one more time.* And then I'd be free. We'd all be free to follow our paths unhounded. I stepped through the veil once again.

***

"You kids want a tour of the studio?" Legba asked after Marc stepped through the doorway.

"What?" Bollocks said.

"A tour. We've got some time to kill. I haven't been here in a while and I thought you'd like to check it out."

"You're a weird motherfucker," Bollocks said.

"I'd like a tour," Tanner said from the booth, his face blue from the glow of his phone, the record in his hand.

"Atta boy," Legba said and smiled. He looked at Maybelline and Bollocks. "I know you don't trust me, but really, you are safe here. Nothing will happen to you, and whatever claim he might have had on your souls has been released. What do you say?"

"How long will it take?" Bollocks asked.

"However long you want. Time is what you want it to be if you haven't noticed. You'll be back before Marc is finished no matter how long or short you wish the tour to be."

"There's nothing we can do for him here," Tanner said. "Might as well get a private tour."

Maybelline scanned Tanner for a few seconds. He nodded. Barely.

"Ok," she said. "Sure."

"Can we take pictures?" Bollocks asked.

"No videos. No flash photography."

"Fair enough."

Legba smiled. "I used to do this so much more in the '80s. Not many guitarists want to cut heads these days. Not like they used to. Thank you for the opportunity." He stood up slowly from the stool with the help of his cane and motioned with his arm to the wall in the café. "The sign you've already seen. If you'll follow me we'll start upstairs before going into the studio."

"Isn't Marc in there?" Bollocks asked.

"Yes and no. But for our part, no."

"Lead the way."

The three of them followed Legba to a set of stairs in the back of the café.

Maybelline fell back a step and walked with Tanner.

"What are you thinking?" she whispered.

"I'm not sure. I'll know it when I see it…I hope."

***

"And Sam Phillips, after recording Elvis' first hit 'That's All Right Mama,' brought the record to Dewey Phillips, no relation, at WHBQ," Papa Legba said. He pointed to a record console with a microphone behind glass. "And on July 7, 1954, Dewey Phillips played the record 14 times during his program on that record player right there. He received over forty phone calls. Elvis didn't become a sensation overnight, but that lit the spark."

They all leaned in close to the glass to get a better look.

"Come this way," Legba said.

Tanner touched Maybelline's arm. Bollocks and Legba moved on.

"What's up?" she whispered, hanging back.

"The console," Tanner said. "I found an old photo of Dewey Phillips playing Elvis' record."

Maybelline tilted her head towards the console and squinted. "Okay?"

"The record was upside down."

"How could you tell?"

"There weren't any grooves on it."

"It's probably just a prop photo. What kind of record wouldn't have grooves?"

"I don't know," Tanner said and shook his head. He looked at the console again. "One that could catapult an unknown singer's career and start a movement."

Papa Legba's voice yelled back to them from the next room.

"I'm tying my shoe," Tanner yelled back. "Coming."

"What should we do?" Maybelline asked.

"I'm not sure. I think that record player has something to do with the smooth records."

Tanner showed Maybelline the B side to Marc's record.

"The same feeling I had in the liquor store with the bottle, I'm getting from this." He rubbed his finger across the smooth vinyl. "I think there's something to this side of the record."

"Like what?" Maybelline touched the record and angled her head. "Smooth as glass."

"A hidden track? A spell? I don't know. I just know there's no way the Devil is going to let Marc win three times without any catches. Elvis totally sold his soul and I think that record or the console has something to do with it. With all of this." Tanner took a deep breath. "There are so many stories about people becoming hypnotized by Elvis when they heard him—especially when they saw him. How many kids decided to pick up a guitar because of Elvis?"

"Are you suggesting that the song had a magic spell or incantation on it?"

"It's what's it's telling me." Tanner held up the record.

They moved on to the next room where Legba was telling Bollocks about the Million Dollar Quartet. "Now, I don't do this for just anyone, but I like you," Legba said. "Wanna hear the original tapes from that session?"

"What's the Million Dollar Quartet?" Tanner asked.

Maybelline saw the slightest twitch of Tanner's eye.

"How do you not know that?" Maybelline asked. "Of all the things you know, you don't know about that?"

"To be fair," Bollocks said, "I just learned about it. Elvis, Johnny Cash, Jerry Lee Lewis, and Carl something or other got high and jammed out while the tape rolled."

"Perkins," Legba said. "Carl Perkins."

"My man, CP," Bollocks said. "He makes good flapjacks."

"Not that Perkins," Legba said and shook his head. "Everything's a joke with you, isn't it?"

"I never joke about flapjacks," Bollocks said and crossed his arms.

"I want to hear the tapes," Tanner said.

Legba smiled. He went to a cabinet and pulled out a small, flat, circular tin canister. "We'll have to go to the control room where the reel-to-reel machine is."

Legba was already shuffling away down the hall. "Mind your step," he said and turned down a flight of stairs.

"It's cold in here," Maybelline said and rubbed her arms.

"An occupational hazard of being in the Between. Sorry," Legba said. He set the tape on the console and removed the lid. He lifted out the tape reel and placed it on the empty spindle of the machine and fed the end of the tape into the reel beside it. The two reels spun like vertical plates when Legba powered on the machine. The crackle of sound being picked up fell out of the speakers attached to the device.

"This is the closest to time travel you'll ever get," Legba said and leaned against the console. "No other reproduction will get you as close to that room as this."

"I didn't know you were a studio hound," Tanner said, mildly impressed.

"A man needs hobbies if they're facing down eternity. You think I only like doing his bidding?"

The sound of a jangly piano. Drums and twang fed guitar.

Tanner nudged Maybelline and then made a show of patting his pockets and looking on the ground.

"What's up?" she said.

"My inhaler," he said. "I lost my inhaler. I think I dropped it when I was tying my shoes."

"You know, I thought I saw you put it down now that you mention it," Maybelline said.

"We'll go back up in a minute," Legba said. "Let's listen some more."

Maybelline looked at him. "He can't breathe without his inhaler."

"I need to go check. I'll be right back."

Legba sighed. "Your loss, young man."

"I'll be back in a minute."

***

The Devil was already waiting for me when I went to the live room. "I guess it won't do to offer you one last chance to join me now that you're free?" he said.

"No. I'm here for Keith."

The Devil smiled and laughed. "Well, we mustn't keep you waiting." He waved his fingers and a dark iridescent cloud shifted and rolled into the room and in on itself like a sandstorm.

"Hey, kid," the cloud form said as it turned into Keith Richards.

"Keith?" I said.

"The one and only."

"We'll be out of here soon. I just need to beat one more chump and we'll both be free of this asshole forever."

Keith lit a cigarette and then conjured a telecaster.

"Ready?" The Devil asked Keith Richards.

He nodded and ripped off a dirty blues lick. I felt a jolt in my core and was thrown back against the wall.

"What the fuck?" I said. "Wait…"

Keith pulled off another riff.

"What are you doing?" I said and angled Micawber towards him, protecting myself.

"Jus' playing my git, kid," Keith said and slunk his hands around the fretboard, firing another gritty melody into the room and knocking me off my feet.

"You really should fight back," The Devil said. "Or else you'll lose to this—what did you call him? Chump?"

I picked off a riff, but Keith shot it right back. "What are you doing?" I pleaded, trying to get up. I didn't know what was happening. Betrayal mixed with confusion penetrated whatever magic armor the jacket offered.

"Stop. We don't have to fight each other. Keith…"

Another melody fell off the fretboard and another and another. I fell and was thrown across the floor, crashing into the drum kit. Keith stood over me. His eyes were liquid, swirling lava. He chuckled. He played on and began singing with a voice that wasn't his. *I can tell the wind is risin', leaves tremblin' on the tree.*

My vision went black and I was helpless as I fell into a void, spinning out. The Devil was laughing, and I could hear someone howling and howling…*And the blues fell mama's child, tore me all upside down…Blues fallin' down like hail…There's a hellhound on my trail, hellhound on my trail…*

I was back in the café without the jacket. Without Micawber. Without the pick. I had lost. Keith Richards' soul was now on me and my failure.

"Did you win? Where's Keith?" Bollocks said and ran over to me.

Maybelline and Tanner looked up from the table.

I shook my head. "Let's get out of here. I need to be away from here."

49. SOMEWHERE IN THE BETWEEN

Keith Richards sat on the floor, leaning against the bar. He lit a cigarette and stared out at the glimmering windows. He felt thin, as if layers had been peeled off—something irreplaceable had been removed. He reached out for his old nylon string guitar and held it close to his chest. He slumped his head over it, the cigarette hanging out of his mouth.

"Feeling sorry for yourself?" the Devil said.

Keith didn't respond. He sat there, the smoke from his cigarette enshrouding him.

"You're free to go. Well, I mean from here. Your boy lost, and you're still mine."

"What'd you do to me?"

"Just borrowed a little of that cocky rock swagger to put a boy in his place. It'll come back, don't worry. I'll hold up my end of the bargain."

Keith didn't say anything. He stood up slowly using the bar stool for support. He walked towards the door at the long end of the bar, past the windows, away from the stage, dragging his feet and guitar across the floor. The scraping of wood against dusty wood sounded through the cold and empty expanse of the room. He reached for the doorknob and stopped. He took a drag of his cigarette and blew out the smoke.

"None of this ain't right," he said without turning around. "It ain't right."

He opened the door and dissolved through the frame.

He opened the door and dissolved through the frame.

50. OUTSIDE OF SUN STUDIO—3 A.M.: BY THE WAY, BY THE WAY

"What do you mean Keith Richards beat you?" Bollocks asked. He threw his hands up, "And your guitar and the jacket? The fucking Pick of Destiny?"

"He came out of nowhere and started throwing riffs at me before I knew what was even happening," Marc said.

"Why would he do that?" Maybelline asked.

"I have no idea."

"Something seems off," Tanner said.

"I'd say."

"Are you sure it was him?"

"It looked just like him. Played just like him."

"I don't understand," Maybelline said. "Did he know you were playing to save his soul?"

"Maybe there was something else at stake we didn't know about. Keith wouldn't treat me like that."

"It wasn't me," a graveled voice said from the street.

Keith Richards was sitting in Legba's Lincoln Continental. He was putting something in his jacket and then closed the glove compartment. He got out slowly and the clunk of the door shutting echoed against the building, aglow in neon signs. He leaned against the car and lit a cigarette.

"Keith!" Marc said and ran over. "What the fuck was that?"

"Wasn't me, kid."

Keith Richards explained about the bar, the windows, the hourglasses. How the Devil stole his essence.

"You're free now, Marc," Keith said. "He's not after you anymore."

"I lost Micawber," Marc said. "I'm so sorry."

Keith sighed and then nodded. "He would have never stopped coming for you until you relented if you continued to use her. She came from him and drew you towards him. Called him to you."

"If someone else gets Micawber and makes a deal than you're…" Marc said and then lowered his head. "I thought I could beat him." Marc wiped his eyes. "He made me think of…"

"I know kid," Keith said and put his hand on Marc's shoulder. "I know."

"These tricky motherfuckers," Bollocks said. He shook his head. "This is Legba's car, right?"

"Yeah," Tanner said.

"Cool, cool," Bollocks said and hopped up on the trunk. "Maybelline, I wouldn't watch this. In fact, please don't. I don't want to get stage fright." Bollocks was unbuttoning his pants. "Tanner, tell Alexa to play 'Sludge Factory' by Alice in Chains."

"What are you going to do?" Maybelline asked.

"I'm lactose intolerant and I just had three milkshakes. I'm doing the only thing I know how to right now." He looked to Keith. "I'd move if I were you."

"Oh god," Maybelline said and turned around.

"What are you doing?" Tanner asked.

"I'm going to Philly Tailgate this sonuvabitch," Bollocks said.

"What's a Philly Tailgate?" Tanner asked, holding up his phone, letting the first chords of the song blare out.

"It's when you take a shit in the flatbed of a pickup truck," Maybelline said.

"Or," Marc added, "on the trunk of a car of a deserving individual." "Or," Bollocks yelled down. He grunted, "In the backseat of a convertible." A sound like wet noodles being dumped on marble flooring came from the car.

Tanner looked over Marc's shoulder towards Bollocks. "Oh no." He gagged and turned around. He dug in his pocket for a mint.

"Yo, can someone get me some napkins or something?" Bollocks said.

Marc ran to the van and grabbed a roll of paper towels and tossed them up to Bollocks. Marc jumped on the back of the trunk. He undid his zipper.

"What are you doing?" Bollocks asked, pulling up his pants.

"It wouldn't be a true Philly Tailgate without the whiz." A torrent of piss streamed down onto the leather backseat slick with excrement.

"You two better sanitize your hands before you touch the steering wheel," Maybelline yelled over, shaking her head.

"I apologize for our sex," Keith Richards said to her.

"You guys earned this one." Maybelline's phone rang. "Hello?…It's OK. I'm still awake…In Memphis…we'll be there tomorrow afternoon-ish…really?…now?…I'll be there."

Maybelline put her phone away. Marc hopped down from the back of the car.

"Marc, I have to go to Austin," she said. She bit her lip.

"That's where we're all headed."

"I have to go there now. I'm getting a cover story."

Marc looked confused. "Really? When?"

"Now. They want the story to roll out next issue. Rolling Stone is sending me an Uber to the airport."

"Now?" Marc said. "You're leaving us?"

"I'm not *leaving* leaving," Maybelline said. "I'm meeting up with you tomorrow."

"I know. I didn't mean it like that. It's just…I don't know."

"I'm still going to help. I promise." Maybelline said. "I've got to be on assignment in the morning. Then I'll be at your show."

"I get it."

"We'll figure it all out tomorrow." Maybelline looked at Keith. "We're still going to save you."

Keith nodded to her. "Take care of yourself, kid."

A car pulled up behind their van. Maybelline's phone pinged.

"Fuck, that was fast," she said. She looked at Marc. "I'm sorry. I've got to go. We'll sort this all out tomorrow."

"It's OK," Marc said. "We did our best."

She hugged him and gave him a kiss. She moved from him, holding his hand, and then his fingers, as long as she could. She went to the van and grabbed her backpack and suitcase. The driver of the car put her bags in the trunk. She waved to them as they drove off.

Keith lit another cigarette. He blew the smoke upwards. "She ain't gone, kid. Not yet anyway. Enjoy your time. There's still plenty of it."

"I know. I know."

"About Austin," Keith said. "I've got to make a detour."

51. BACKSTAGE AT A CLUB IN AUSTIN

Brad uploaded a clip from the night's performance to his socials. He closed the lid of his guitar case.

"Brilliant," a man said from over his shoulder.

"Is that my friend from the isle?" Brad said to Paul, closing the clasps. He turned around, grinning wide and opening his arms. The two men embraced.

"So, you ready to play with me tomorrow?" Brad said and patted Paul on his arms at the shoulders.

"I guess we're coming out together now, aren't we?"

"Seems that way."

"Our mutual friend told me ya made the deal with me celestial paps?"

"With," Brad rocked his head back and forth a little, "conditions."

"Yeah?"

"Wish you didn't. Be careful, mate."

"I've got a built-in get out of jail clause."

"Hmm," Paul said. "Be careful, still."

52. HIGHWAY 61 REVISITED

I insisted on driving. I needed to clear my mind. Tanner and Bollocks were asleep in the back. Keith Richards rode shotgun. He hadn't spoken since we started driving about a half an hour ago. Keith told me he had business in Clarksdale to take care of and then closed his eyes once we hit U.S. 61 south.

The silence and unknowing was killing me. "Keith?"

Keith grunted.

"What are you going to do?"

Keith took a deep breath and opened his eyes.

"You're free, kid. I'm gonna do what I gotta."

"I know I'm free, but that doesn't absolve me of your contract."

Keith sat up straight and looked at me. "You're absolved. I made my bed a hundred years before you were born."

"No, I..."

"I know you feel responsible," Keith said. "But this doesn't have anything to do with you anymore."

"The hell it doesn't."

"Marc, it doesn't. I dragged you into this mess, and you freed yourself. I'm damn proud of you, kid."

"You helped me. I have to help you. I need to help you."

"You already did."

"No I didn't. I failed. If I can get Micawber back, and the jacket, and pick, I think I can beat him. No tricks this time."

"The house always wins, kid." Keith looked out the window.

"Then why do you need me to take you to Clarksdale? Can't you just go there?"

"My home is the road. I wanted to spend one last leg of it with you before I head down to Rosedale and meet my fate."

"Why now? Can't you just wait until you're stronger?" I pleaded. "Can't you wait until we get some other help?"

"I was tied to this plane by Micawber—my spirit was intertwined. But now, the horizon is coming. I can feel it. Been feeling it getting closer a while now. There ain't no turning away this time."

"I don't believe it."

"You're gonna have to."

"I can't lose you, too, Keith," I said. My voice cracked and warmth, wet and sudden, filled my eyes.

Keith reached across and I felt a soft weight on my shoulder. "Nobody's ever really gone, kid."

"You know that's not true."

Keith didn't say anything. His hand lingered on me. He gave a light squeeze again and took out a cigarette and lit it. He opened the window. We were still a little while away from sunrise. I could see the slimmest breach of light over the horizon in the rearview mirror.

I drove on through the darkness—the old highway illuminated by headlights alone. There were no other cars on the road. The quiet hours when the whole world is asleep were torturing me. I remembered the days after my parents. I didn't sleep well and I'd wake up in the middle of the night and forget they were gone for the briefest moment, and then the realization would creep over me. So heavy and final. It wasn't fair. It wasn't fair.

I needed noise. Something, anything to disrupt my own thoughts. I turned the radio on and scanned through the channels. A Rolling Stones song came in. I turned the dial quickly.

"Leave that one," Keith said. "Go back."

"OK," I said weakly.

Time is on my side, yes it is

Time is on my side, yes it is

You're searching for good times but just wait and see…

***

"Pull over there, across the road," Keith said.

I crossed the highway and turned into the parking lot of Abe's BBQ. Three pig statues stood in the lawn in front of a series of picnic benches. The building sat just beyond.

I killed the engine. "It doesn't look like they're open."

"Just reminiscing," Keith said. "Many have had their last meal here."

"Before making a deal?"

Keith nodded.

"Did you?"

"I was way up North during the Stones first US tour." He opened the door and got out of the van. He motioned for me to follow. Keith pointed to the building. "Legend says while Robert Johnson was selling his soul to the Devil, old Abe over here was talking to Jesus and coming up with his barbecue sauce."

"Keith…" I said.

"You've got to try it sometime."

"What's going to happen?"

"I'll head to Rosedale. Meet my reckoning."

"How are you going to win without Micawber?"

Keith lit a cigarette and took a long drag. He exhaled. The sun was beginning to edge over the horizon. "I'm like ol' Damocles, kid. Time has caught up." The cresting sun began to burn behind Keith, casting his silhouette in relief. "Keep your nose clean. And remember, the music don't come from magic. Most of us had it way before we got greedy. You got it. Had it before I came in to your life, and you'll have it after."

Keith flicked his cigarette to the ground. "Come here, Marc."

Keith's body hummed. He focused and put his arms out and pulled me in.

His arms wrapped around me—truly solid, no longer ethereal. I hugged him back hard. I squeezed him tight. He was alive. Warm. I believed for a split second that if I held him tight enough and didn't let go, he couldn't leave me.

But then he evaporated, and I was alone. I let out a sob, stifled at first, but I couldn't fight the torrent.

Just down the road, right under the monument of guitars shooting into the sky, I saw the form of Keith Richards walking away. He appeared to be shuffling with something inside his jacket. I yelled out.

He waved back to me, and then he faded away.

"Marc," a voice said behind him. Bollocks. "He's gone?"

I couldn't speak. I couldn't say it because then it would be true.

"Fuck, man. I'm sorry."

"Me too."

53. FLIGHT FROM MEMPHIS TO AUSTIN: SORRY I'M NOT HOME RIGHT NOW

Maybelline boarded a private jet after being driven to a small airport just outside of Memphis. She climbed the stairs to the plane and the flight attendant took her luggage and stowed it in a closet in the front of the cabin. Maybelline was led to a seat, easily twice as big and with more cushioning and leg room than any seat she had ever sat in on a plane or train. The flight attendant brought her a hot towel and offered her a drink. Maybelline took the towel and declined the drink.

"I think I'd like to rest," she said and buckled her seatbelt.

The flight attendant brought her an eye mask and a blanket. Maybelline put it on and reclined her chair. The events of the past few days swirled through her mind. A week ago she was a reporter for a local radio station. Now she was flying on a private jet for a cover story for Rolling Stone. She had met the Devil's surrogate and had her soul wrapped up in possible damnation. She was finally free and about to embark on a blossoming career. Journalists twice her age would kill to be in her position. Journalists who also worked their asses off. *What made me so special?* she thought. She let the idea fade from her mind. She was good at her job and she knew it. So what if she had some connections? That's what paying your dues gets you and she had paid a lot, the past few days notwithstanding. She fell asleep under the weighted blanket before the plane even began to move.

***

She woke up as the plane was landing. The wheels touching the ground sent a small nudge, and then tremors through the aircraft. She slipped off the eye mask and yawned and stretched. She brought her chair into its upright position. The captain came over the intercom.

We'll have you out of here in a few minutes. There's a delay at the hangar, but we're next. Hang tight.

"Morning, young lady," a voice said from beside her. A very familiar voice.

"What the fuck are you doing here?" Maybelline asked, jumping. "How are you here?"

"I can be lots of places," the man said and shrugged. "You know. It's not very nice what your friends did to my car."

"I thought I was free of you?"

"You are. But you're still tangled up with Him because of others. I'm just making sure you'll be ok."

"What? Who? Making sure I'll be ok?" Maybelline said. "What are you talking about?"

"How'd you get the Rolling Stone gig?"

"I'm good at my job and my boss put in a good word for me."

"Brad Johnson?"

Maybelline sat up straight and skewered her eyes at Legba. "What about him?"

"Have you heard from him recently?"

"Not in a couple of days. Why?"

"Hmm," Legba said. Almost a laugh. Curious.

"What?"

"Seems like you're surrounded by those who would be involved with my employer. Well, not really my employer, but we have mutual aspirations."

"The Devil?"

"If that's what you prefer to call him. He's not after you. But, he's not not after you still."

"Why the fuck is he not not after me because of Brad Johnson?"

"Things are contingent. You're in an unintentional orbit. Think of it as an ecosystem. A bee that gets stuck in a spider's web didn't set out to get stuck in a web. It followed what was attractive to it—food, survival, pollination. The spider is part of the garden. It helps keep the balance. Sometimes bees get stuck in the web. Sometimes they get out. Lots of times they don't."

"I'm the bee?"

"That's up to you."

"I don't want anything to do with any of this."

"It's not your choice. It's all incidental. You seem really bright and capable and I just wanted to make sure you know your position since others have been making decisions for you."

"Incidental?" Maybelline shook her head, confused. "Who has been making decisions for me?"

"Where to begin? Brad asked the Devil. The Devil asked Tom. Tom asked Dick. Dick asked Harry. Now you have a job with Rolling Stone and a major assignment."

Maybelline didn't say anything. Brad too? How many people was she getting involved with that were having their lives upended by the Devil? The plane rolled into a hangar. The morning sun was eclipsed by the high metal walls and ceiling of the structure. Shadows fell through the windows of the plane, throwing Maybelline into darkness.

"Do you know who you're covering in Austin?" Legba asked.

"A major artist going solo. It's all a secret."

"Don't you think *you* should know who it is before you get there?"

Again, she didn't say anything. The interior lights of the plane lit up. The flight attendant walked up from the back of the cabin. "We'll be ready to disembark in a minute," she said to Maybelline and opened the closet. She took Maybelline's bag and suitcase out and set them on the ground.

"I think…" Maybelline said and turned to where Legba was sitting. There was only an empty chair.

***

On the car ride to the studio, Maybelline's phone pinged. A text from Brad Johnson.

How was your flight?

"Good," she wrote back. She was going to play it cool. Not let him know she knew about his deal. She didn't want anything to do with the Devil, and right now, until this was all behind her, Brad Johnson, either. "How'd you know?"

lol. I'm here.

"Really?! Why didn't you say anything?"

It's a surprise. I was hoping for a favor.

"Sure. What's up?"

I know who you are covering…

"And?"

I have BIG news…

"???"

Brad Johnson sent her a link to a track he recorded with his band.

Listen to this and tell me what you think.

Maybelline listened to the track. It wasn't her favorite type of music, but objectively listening, it was good. The voice emoted. It sounded familiar, but she couldn't place it. It was a voice she had heard before, but all the greats had that type of voice—they possessed an unbridled newness that also spoke to something familiar, like it had always been there. All the great songs were that way. She wasn't sure if this was a great song yet. It was very good though.

She responded. "That's pretty great at first listen." And then, "Is this who I'm covering? Who is it?"

I'm not telling ;) and then, *but it's definitely NOT the major act you're covering.*

"Ok…"

The favor and then *I want you to write about them too.*

"I'll need more info"

Soon. I'll see you when you get here.

Maybelline put her phone away and leaned back in the seat and closed her eyes again. What was she getting herself into? "Fuck," she said to herself. She opened her eyes and took her phone out. She sent a message to Marc.

54. ON THE ROAD FROM CLARKSDALE TO AUSTIN: YOU'RE SEARCHING FOR GOOD TIMES

The sun was low in the sky as they made their way down 278. Tanner woke up and began thumbing away at his phone in the backseat. Marc was driving and Bollocks rode shotgun.

"Marc," Tanner said. "I think there's still time to save Keith."

"How?" Marc asked.

"If I'm correct, which I'm almost certain I am, he has until tomorrow."

"He's gone, man," Marc said. The words dropped from his mouth.

"Today is the 15th. The more I think about it, the more I think we were right about the 16th. Why else would Keith say he had to leave? Why else would the Devil be so eager to get Micawber, the jacket, and the pick away from you? If you had them, Keith could use them and free himself. I'm not saying this is perfect, but it lines up."

Marc shook his head. "But what can we do? I lost everything."

"But Keith didn't yet. There's gotta be a way. We can't give up right now."

Bollocks sighed. "What do you want us to do?"

"Go to Rosedale," Tanner said. "I have an idea."

Marc pulled over to the side of the road. He turned around to face Tanner. "And what are we going to do when we're there?"

"I think there's one last way we can help if we can get to him. But we need to find a record player first." Tanner held up a record player cartridge.

Mark squinted. "Where's the needle?"

Tanner held up the record the Devil gave Marc. He took it out of the sleeve and turned the B-side to Marc and Bollocks. "Where are the grooves?" he said. "You told us he said it had a hidden track. What if he wasn't fucking with you?"

"How's that cartridge matter?"

"I think there's a connection to Sun Studio, besides the obvious one," Tanner said. "I think the message on the back side is going to tell us something. There's definitely something otherworldly coming from the record. I can feel it like I did with the bottle. But it feels different this time. Like it wants to be played."

"What if it sucks all of our souls into eternal damnation?" Bollocks asked.

"I feel like it sends a message. Elvis' first record sent a message out when it was first played. I think there's something on here that will call the Devil. We can try to help Keith."

"You mean like how the Secret Chord called him?" Marc said.

"Something like that," Tanner said. "Look."

Tanner whispered to the record and golden images sparked off the record like a hologram. An image of a portal was opening.

"Great Scott," Bollocks said. "What in the Shire is that?"

"My hunch is that he included this to keep you in his orbit. Like an AirTag or tracking device or something. But with this," Tanner held the cartridge up again, "we can hack the record and use the spell as a backdoor to get to him without having to make any deal."

"Is that what you went back for?" Bollocks said to Tanner, pointing to the cartridge.

"Yes, sir."

"My man," Bollocks said and gave him a fist bump. "Good shit, Tanner."

"Guess what?" Tanner said.

"What?"

"You called me 'Tanner.'"

Bollocks laughed to himself. "Well, we all make mistakes, Inspector Gadget."

"Ok. If it means I have another shot at saving Keith, let's go," Marc said. "I need to try. Let's play that record."

"Reroute the GPS to Rosedale. There's a pawn shop on the way," Tanner said looking at his phone. "Just keep heading there and I'll direct you."

"Ok," Marc said. His phone buzzed in the cradle. A text alert. Maybelline. He swiped it away and pulled back onto the highway.

***

Two miles south of Gunnison, off of MS-1, Tanner directed Marc to take Waxhaw Road. The asphalt gave way to old, crumbled ground which badly needed repaving. About 200 hundred yards down Waxhaw the road split into two.

"Which way?" Marc said.

"Shit. My reception crapped out," Tanner said.

Marc and Bollocks both checked their phones. Neither had service.

"I think the left," Tanner said.

"Ok," Marc said, shaking his head. "There's nothing out here." He drove on slowly. "This is a dirt road now. You sure you're right?"

"Pretty sure."

Trees and bushes closed in on the road which narrowed down to fit one vehicle. Branches and weeds scratched the sides of their van.

"Oh, oh, I've got service again. It's right up at the intersection," Tanner said. "Shit, it went out again."

"There's literally nothing out here," Bollocks said. "It's just a bunch of fields. Who would have a shop out here?"

"Yeah man," Marc said. "This seems weird."

The van hit a pothole, hard, sending a shock through the frame.

"My gonads," Bollocks said. "Easy, now."

"Sorry, sorry. This road sucks." The van began to rattle, the front passenger side rocked with a *flubbuda-flubbuda-fwipp-fwipp-fwipp-fwipp.*

Bollocks leaned his head out of the window. "Shit. Pull over. We've got a flat," Bollocks said. "My poor girl."

"Goddamnit," Marc said. "Do you have a spare?"

"Under the floor of the trunk."

They all got out of the van. A few yards away, set among the trees was an old two pump gas station with a rusted overhang attached to a general store. A cigar store Indian stood sentry by the door next to a massive Coca-Cola machine.

Bollocks hit Tanner on the arm, "Yo. Is that the shop?"

"Where'd that come from?" Marc said. "I swear it wasn't there a minute ago."

"Spruce's?" Tanner said, looking at the general store and then back at his phone. "Uh, I think so, but I've got nothing still. It's got to be it."

"But am I making shit up? That wasn't there a minute ago, right?" Marc said.

"I don't know," Bollocks said. "I wasn't looking."

Tanner shrugged. "I couldn't see from the back."

"But you said it was a pawn shop. This doesn't look like a pawn shop."

"I was just going by Google. Maybe it used to be a pawn shop?"

"Dude, look at that place. That never used to be anything except what it is," Bollocks said.

"We can check it out after we fix this flat," Marc said. "Let's get the gear out so we can put the spare on."

They unloaded their bags, Bollocks' drums, and Marc's amp and backup guitar on the side of the road in the knee-high grass.

"You brought this thing?" Bollocks asked while picking up the guitar.

"Yeah. I guess it's a good thing, too," Marc said. "I'm counting on it in Austin."

They lifted the trunk floor to get to the subfloor that housed the spare tire. They removed the spare tire, lug wrench, and old scissor jack from the van. Marc loosened the lugs on the flat tire while Bollocks slid under the van and positioned the jack under the jacking point. Bollocks cranked the van into the air. They swapped out the tire, put the lugs back on, and lowered the van. The spare flattened out to the ground under the weight of the van.

"You've got to be fucking kidding me," Marc said.

"Did you check the spare's tire pressure before you packed up for the tour?" Tanner asked.

"Is that a thing people have to do?"

"I'll go see if the gas station can fill us up with air," Tanner said.

"I'll go with you," Marc said. "Bollocks, stay here and watch our gear."

"What? I'm going, too. I don't want to be alone out here. It's weird," Bollocks said.

"But our gear?"

Bollocks looked around at the high grass and trees. The road at the intersection and the open field beyond that. "I think we'll be fine," he said.

They walked the few yards to Spruce's. The bell on the door rung when they entered.

The inside was a place that time had forgotten. The walls were decorated with rusty tin signs, and the space behind the counter was lined with wooden shelves full of cans and bottles and sacks. There were wicker and wooden chairs scattered about the place. Bollocks walked over to a wire rack with dusty postcards and spun it, a low moaning squeak creaked out of the hinges.

"This place is weird," he said. "It's creeping me out."

An old man wearing overalls and then a woman in a smock walked out from behind a curtain at the end of the counter. "Hello there, young fellas," the old man said. "What can we do for you?"

"We've got a flat tire," Tanner said. "Two actually. We were hoping you had some air?"

The old man nodded at Tanner and took a handkerchief out of his back pocket and wiped his brow. "Let's have a look and see what we can do." He walked around the counter to the group. He looked out the door. "Where's the vehicle?"

"Just up the road, right there," Tanner said pointing out of the door.

"Ok, let's get you boys back on the road." He put his handkerchief back in his pocket. "Martha can get you something to eat or drink if you'd like while you wait. Shouldn't take long."

The old lady moved down the length of the counter. "Please. Sit, sit," she said.

Marc tapped Tanner on the arm. He leaned in and whispered. "Do you think this is Legba again? Like in disguise?"

"I don't know," Tanner said. "I'll run a spell and check his teeth."

"What, like a dog?" Bollocks asked.

Tanner shook his head and followed the old man out of the store.

"What can I get you boys?" Martha said.

"I'd love a cup coffee," Marc said. "As long as it's not instant."

"Just put on a pot. Cream, sugar?"

"Please," Marc said. "Um, do you have a record player here? The internet said this was a pawn shop."

"Oh, we've been called many things," Martha said and then laughed. She pointed over into the corner. "All we've got is that old jukebox Ray bought in '55. Still works, too."

Bollocks and Marc looked over to the corner. A jukebox that looked like a cross between a diner's cake display case and a Cadillac sat humming. "Woah, is that a Wurlitzer?" Bollocks said. "That's cool." He went over to it and looked at the record choices. "You never swapped out the 45s?"

"Why would we?" Martha asked. "You boys want anything to eat, or is the coffee fine?"

Bollocks approached the counter. "This is going to sound weird, but things have been very weird for us lately. And you have to answer, like how the cops have to tell you if they're a cop." Bollocks put his hands on the counter and looked Martha right in the eyes. "Are you a witch? You have to tell us if you are."

Martha laughed loud, a quick blurt. "You city boys sure are crazy. Don't know what they're teaching you in those schools about us folks out here, but no. I'm not a witch." Martha half smiled at Bollocks. "But if I was, I'd be a good witch." She winked at him.

Bollocks raised his eyes. "Ok, Glinda. You're cool." He motioned to the door. "What about…"

"No. Ray, isn't either."

Marc laughed and put his hands on Bollocks' shoulders. "I'm sorry. Don't mind my friend. It's somehow been a long day already," he said to Martha. "Just the coffee will be ok. Thank you."

Martha disappeared behind the curtain. They could hear the clink of dishes and the sound of the coffee being poured.

"Dude," Marc said.

"I had to ask. I don't want to accidentally get all tangled up in that shit again."

"That's fair." Marc looked to the door. "Hopefully we can fix both tires quickly. We need to figure out what we're going to do about Austin."

"I'll send an email to the promoter. Tell him we broke down and might not be able to make it. It's not a lie."

Marc frowned. He stared at the floor.

"It's just one gig," Bollocks said. "The Devil or not, we've been on a roll. This won't set us back."

"We also had Keith coaching me." Marc took a deep breath, steadying himself, and then shook his head. "I just miss him, man. He was always there…" He looked away. "Shit wasn't supposed to be this way."

"I know, man. I know," Bollocks said.

"I wish none of this had happened."

"So do all who live to see such times, Mr. Marco. But that is not for them to decide. All we have to decide is what to do with the time that is given to us. There are other forces at work in this world, Marc, besides the will of evil. Keith was meant to find Micawber. In which case, you were also meant to have it. And that is an encouraging thought."

Marc looked at Bollocks and smiled. "Shut up," he said and laughed. "That doesn't even make real sense."

Bollocks punched Marc on the arm. "Things are going to work out."

"I hope so," Marc said. He took his phone out of his pocket. He checked the text Maybelline sent him. "Fuck."

"What?"

Marc showed Bollock's his phone.

Legba was on my plane. Call me as soon as you get this.

Marc tried to call Maybelline but cell service was nonexistent where they were.

"I'm gonna shit in that dude's car again," Bollocks said.

Martha walked back through the curtain with a tray of mugs and a carafe full of steaming coffee.

"Smells good, Glinda," Bollocks said. "Say, do you mind if we play the jukebox? Like if we put one of our own records in it?"

"As long as you're careful. You know how to operate it?"

"Not really, but our friend does."

Marc went to the doorway to see how Tanner was doing. The van was there with its hood open, and the tire was still flat. Just off to the side of the road he saw Tanner's feet on the ground, sticking out of the high grass.

Marc turned around as Bollocks was bringing his cup of coffee to his lips.

"Bollocks, don't drink that," he yelled across the shop. The light coming in from behind him dimmed. He felt the presence of something over his shoulder.

55. A COFFEE SHOP IN AUSTIN: MYSTERIOUS WAYS

Maybelline sat at a table in a semi-private room in the back of Paganini's, an upscale coffeeshop that was decorated like a speakeasy trying too hard to be hip. Dark fabrics and artwork that bordered on kitsch were hung on the walls in between what she thought was an extravagant amount of electric candelabra for a room of its size.

Brad told her to meet him at 8. That didn't leave her with much time to sleep. She took a nap, and the car picked her back up at 7:30. She wasn't sure what the rush was. It seemed weird to her that she was here on a secret assignment, and then another secret cover story emerged. But she'd seen enough over the past week to accept that weird shit is abound, and having a run-in with Legba on the plane put her on alert for a more devious scheme beyond two big profiles to write.

She sat there with an oat milk cortado and checked her phone. Still nothing from Marc. She sent another text. *Are you guys ok?*

"Maybelline," a voice said, booming as the curtain half concealing her booth from the room was pushed aside. Brad was carrying a guitar case. And behind him, a man she recognized. Someone she had met two years prior and formed a casual, though constant relationship with—a friendship even. She hadn't seen him since she managed to snag a backstage pass the last time his band was in town. She tripped on a cable running along the backstage corridor and he caught her as she fell and helped her up. After a minute of being star struck, Maybelline relaxed and they eased into conversation as if they had always known each other. Despite all the chattering that he was a pretentious dick, he was actually a really cool person. They spent a few hours after the show chatting about music and literature. They exchanged numbers and had stayed in touch ever since.

"Maybelline," Brad Johnson said and turned to the man. "This is…"

Maybelline smiled—confused. She stood up. "What are you doing here?"

"Good to see you, too," Paul said. They hugged each other.

"You know each other?" Brad asked.

"Aye. Go way back, this one and I do," Paul said.

"Huh," Brad said. "Well, let's sit." He looked at Maybelline's drink. "The best, right?"

Maybelline looked down. She hadn't actually drunk it yet. "Yeah, not bad," she said.

Brad ordered a coffee and Paul ordered a tea. A tray of fresh fruit and baked goods was brought out.

"Eat, please," Brad said picking up a croissant and ripping it in half. "So," he said, his mouth full, "let's talk." He smiled. "This is who your secret assignment is."

Maybelline looked at Paul. "You're going solo? Why didn't you tell me? We could have started already."

Paul shrugged. "Timing has got to be right. We're in a delicate predicament." He looked to Brad.

"That track from last night," Brad said. "You liked it, right?"

"Yeah," Maybelline said. "It was pretty good, I guess."

"You guess," Brad laughed. "That's your cover story."

She nodded—this wasn't new information. Brad was acting strange—he was usually down to earth, but there was an air of arrogance about him now. Not full on dickhead, but there was something different in the way he sat and moved. The way he talked. Whatever link he had with the Devil was surely affecting him. And it worked quickly, too. A few days ago, he was kind and warm and gave off an aura that was almost paternal.

"It's me," Brad said.

"What?" Maybelline said and almost spit out her cortado. "Since when?"

Brad smiled wide. "I'm coming out of my shell."

Something close to disappointment mixed with disgust coursed through Maybelline. She didn't hate him or dislike him. She felt letdown. Ashamed for him. A secondhand embarrassment. She thought he was different, but in the end, he was just like everyone else who was hungry for power and fame.

"Cool," Maybelline said. "So, I've got to write a cover story on you. And then also a profile on you." She nodded towards Paul. "Why me?"

"You know me," Brad said. "And apparently you know this sonuvabitch, too." Brad gripped Paul's shoulder and shook him. Brad took a sip of his coffee and looked over the lip of the cup to Maybelline.

"What?" she asked.

"I was talking to my contacts at Rolling Stone, and they don't want to miss out by covering both stories in separate issues. It's gonna be a double-sided issue. Like a record. You have to flip the magazine over. We both get a cover."

Maybelline sunk back in her chair.

"I thought you'd be excited," Brad said.

"I am. This is…" she took a deep breathe. "Overwhelming."

Brad clapped his hands together and laughed. He put his arms out. "It's our coming out party. All of us. My emergence on the scene. His reemergence. And you, the new fresh voice of rock and roll journalism. It's everyone's dreams come true all at once."

Maybelline managed a smile.

"Come on," Brad said. "Let's get to the studio. We've all got work to do. We can talk on the way." He stood up and flagged down the waitress and gave her his credit card and then picked up his guitar case and walked over to the hostess and began chatting to her.

"It'll be all right. You'll be all right," Paul said to Maybelline. "I'll make sure of it."

"How did you know Brad? He never mentioned you before."

"Oh, I'm in many orbits. I was thrown back into Brad's now with me record coming out and all."

"It's finished?"

"Down to the liner notes."

"Well, I hope the marketing campaign doesn't include forcing everyone to listen to it this time."

Paul chuckled. "Hey, that was out of my control. Come on. I'll let you listen on the way to the studio."

"Wait. Why are you going to the studio?"

"Aye. Laying some backup vocals. A little harmonica. A favor for a favor."

"Let's go and get famous," Brad Johnson said, approaching them. "Well, more famous," he said and punched Paul in the arm. They left the coffee shop and on the way out Brad winked to the hostess and told her he'd see her later. *Eww. Creepo move number 7,* Maybelline thought, but she saw the hostess blush and wave with her fingers. *What the fuck?* That earlier feeling sunk even lower.

56. SOMEWHERE IN THE BETWEEN, BUT ALSO ROSEDALE, MISSISSIPPI: TAKE ME DOWN LITTLE SUSIE, TAKE ME DOWN

Keith trudged on down Highway 61. The dawn was breaking and he stopped and turned east and closed his eyes. He willed himself to be present and feel the warmth from the sun. He wasn't sure what would happen to his mortal body after today—he hoped it wouldn't be too painful. Keith held out hope on one last play—a final gamble. But that was it. After that he was out of tricks. There was nothing left to give. The Devil held all the chips.

Keith had made a lot of mistakes in his life and not all things could be fixed. For some, it was too late. Remorse began to surface and Keith acknowledged it. He wasn't a praying man—he wasn't sure if there was somebody upstairs, or at least if there was, if they even gave a shit about anyone down here. Regardless, Keith sent his forgiveness to all those who had wronged him, and he asked for it in return to all those alive and beyond. He opened his eyes. He thought of Marc.

He knew a long time ago he wouldn't sell Marc down the river. That was the idea at first, the circle of life and all that bullshit, but he came to like the kid. Still, the Devil and shadows prevailed and he felt shame for his weakness in not being able to beat them back. There was a brief, dark window after bandmate Ronnie Wood's cancer scare where Keith contemplated his own mortality. Two years later, Mick Jagger's heart surgery rattled him. He thought of his own brush with death almost two decades earlier when his head was cut open to remove a blood clot after he fell out of a tree. Life was fragile. It all seemed to spiral away. He felt the window closing and panicked. The pull for self-preservation overcame him and he showed Marc the secret chord. He knew what he was doing. With Micawber, the Devil's grip would be impossible to escape. Keith's soul would be free.

And as soon as he showed Marc the chord, he regretted it. He disappeared for days wandering the in between. He eventually resolved to train the kid for that day when the Devil came calling, though he would do his damndest to save them both before that day arrived. But the Devil was stronger and trickier than him.

He lit a cigarette and laughed behind it. Marc beat the Devil where it counted. He was glad that Marc had been able to do that. Keith had prepared him. He spent every day teaching the kid everything he knew and kept a lookout over his shoulder. He felt good about that. Proud even. He betrayed Marc, but earned it back. That catalogue was complete.

As long as Marc didn't do anything stupid, he'd have a long, promising life ahead of him. The kid would be all right. He looked back up 61. Marc would be on his way to Austin by now.

***

Where Highway 8 and 1 meet, the Devil stood. The landscape was flat and barren. The roads were dirt—but a translucence enveloped the space as it did in all of the in between. Time was not current. It wasn't a matter of where or when they were. Keith knew he had come to the right place. A strange warmth cradled him.

"Now why'd you come all the way down here to meet me? I'd have come to you as a courtesy," the Devil said.

"I didn't think you was one for courtesy," Keith Richards said. "Figured I'd come to the source."

"To beg?"

"I ain't the begging kind. You know that."

The Devil appraised Keith much like he did back in '64 on that mid-June Saturday night below Davenport on the banks of the Mississippi. He took a deep breath and let it out slow. He nodded. "Ok, Keith," he said. "Out of respect to your league, I'll bite. Not many of you make it this long. Proud isn't a word I use, but there's something like it I feel for my creations."

Keith laughed to himself.

"You have my attention," the Devil said.

"I'll say it simply. I'd prefer to keep my soul."

The Devil laughed a vociferous boom. He smiled. "Keith. That's it?"

"I have something of yours."

"And I'll be collecting that shortly."

Keith opened his long jacket and pulled out a bottle from the inside pocket.

The air grew denser, and the Devil began to dissolve into a black plume. Electricity charged the air. *Where did you get that?* A voice said, sliding through the atmosphere.

"Oh, things turn up and I notice 'em."

Have you drunk from it?

Keith felt the grip of ropes like wet snakes tightening around his legs, crawling up his thighs and waist. *Answer. Have you drunk from it?*

"I've no interest in taking up arms and starting wars. I just want to be free."

The bottle. Give it to me.

"Free me. Or I'll change my mind." Keith uncorked it and brought the bottle to his lips. "Free and powerful is what I'll be, right?" The grip tightened, pinning Keith's arms to his body. The bottle slipped a little, but Keith held firm. "You know you can't harm me here. This is sacred ground."

Says who?

"Don't be coy. That's beneath you."

The Devil's grip loosened. *The bottle, Keith…or I'll pull the kid back in.*

"He freed himself. You can't."

He can be persuaded to make another deal. He can come freely—you know this.

"Free me and promise to never pursue him ever again," Keith said. He brought the bottle to his lips. "And the bottle is yours. Unless…"

Lower the bottle. That won't be necessary.

The air lightened and the Devil regained human form. He straightened his tie. Keith looked him in the eyes. He lowered the bottle and corked it.

"If I free you and you break your promise, the boy is mine," the Devil said. "And so many more dear to you. I will hound them."

"I'm many things. A liar ain't one of them," Keith said. "Free me and the bottle is yours," he said again.

The Devil waved his hand ever so slightly. An inhale overtook Keith. An exhale consumed him. A deep sense of something leaving and then gaining rippled through him. He stood firm. The Devil held out his hand.

"A promise is a promise," Keith said. He handed the bottle over to the Devil.

"Thank you," the Devil said. His eyes softened. Glimmered. He was bemused. "There aren't many of you. Not many of you at all."

"Ain't none like me." Keith took out a cigarette and lit it.

"Only a few that I actually liked."

"Liked?" Keith shook his head and took a drag from his cigarette. "Well, ol' chap. I'm not one for goodbyes. It's been a helluva ride. How do I get out of here?"

The Devil nodded. "That's fair." He took a step towards Keith. "You're welcome. I mean that."

"Hmmph," Keith said. What good would it do to tell the Devil to fuck off? That he, Keith Richards, had outsmarted him? Had outmaneuvered him at the finish line? The Devil wanted gratitude. If Keith was being honest with himself, he had benefitted despite the cost. A deep one that ran like water through bedrock, far below the surface. A cost that formed him and unsettled his foundation. Still, he had benefitted.

Keith held out his hand. "A helluva ride, bub," he said again. "Mostly a good one. Now it's over."

The Devil took it. "If you feel like you want another few years on the road, you know where to find me."

"I'd like to get back to my body now."

"Walk towards the river. The water will bring you home."

Keith looked towards the river. "Will I remember any of this?"

"There will be times when you feel it. My friend John Keats said of poetry that it 'should strike the reader as a remembrance of their own highest thoughts,' or something close to that. That's what it will be like."

Keith turned away and headed toward the Mississippi. The water was close. He could smell it, and he could feel its coolness in the air. The great river was now calm. Keith felt light. He stepped in the water. One foot. And then another. He closed his eyes as the water pooled around his body. A happiness, joy even, coursed through him. He was going home.

57. SPRUCE'S GENERAL STORE: DON'T BE ALARMED NOW

I felt a hand on my shoulder. I dropped my coffee.

"Watch out," Bollocks said, dropping his coffee too.

I spun out from under the hand and jumped back, huddling with Bollocks.

Martha sucked her teeth.

"Son," Ray said. "Your friend fainted. You'd better come with me."

"Fainted my ass," I said. "He was fine a minute ago."

Ray looked at Martha.

"They think we're witches," Martha said.

Ray let out a loud, roaring laugh. "Their friend is the only witch around here."

"What did you do to him?" I said. The revelation that they knew about Tanner didn't make me question *how* he knew, but *why* he knew.

"Nothing. He was muttering something and then next thing he was on the ground. Good thing he landed in the grass. Could've cracked his skull wide-open like a watermelon."

Martha moved from around the counter with a towel. Bollocks jumped.

"It's for the coffee you spilled," she said.

"Why do you think he's a witch?" I said.

Martha sighed. "Do you boys think you're the first to pass through here?"

"We got lost," I said. "And then we broke down."

Martha smirked. She nodded minutely. "Ok."

"What?"

"Let's get you fixed up and tend to your friend." She handed Bollocks the towel. "Mind cleaning up while I fix you another cup and pour a glass of lemonade for your friend?"

Bollocks took the towel and began wiping up his spilled coffee.

"Let's help your friend," Ray said and took a blanket off a shelf. "It's for his head."

"Ok," I said and followed him outside.

Tanner was still lying in the grass and we went and kneeled next to him. Ray slid the blanket under his head.

"Lift his legs," Ray told Bollocks. Bollocks bent over and lifted both of Tanner's legs straight up like he was wheelbarrow. "Not like that," Ray blurted out. "Just a little. It's basic first aid, son."

"Oh," Bollocks said and sat down cross-legged and put Tanner's feet on his knees.

"Tanner," I said. I smacked his face a little. "Tanner."

He moaned. His eyes fluttered.

Martha came out with a glass of lemonade. "Here," she said, bringing the glass to his lips. He took a small sip.

"What happened?" he asked, his voice thin.

"You tell me, son," Ray said.

Tanner looked to me. "It's ok, I think. They're cool," I said.

Martha gave him another drink of lemonade. "You know how you came to be in this state? And that you trust we're not harmful?"

Tanner nodded. "I had to be sure."

"And it backfired, didn't it?"

Tanner looked around. He raised his hands and dropped them in exasperation. "I guess so."

Tanner sat up. "There you go, son," Ray said.

"Bollocks, can I have my feet?"

"Oh," Bollocks said. "Yeah." He let go of Tanner's ankles.

"What's going on?" I asked.

"I think I know where we are."

"Finish the lemonade, son," Ray said. "Then we'll talk like we could have before you started with your spellin'."

Tanner drank it all down and we went back into the store. Martha set a table in the middle of the room and brought out some biscuits and fresh coffee for all of us.

"So," I said.

"You can always turn back," Martha said. "You just turn around and cut over to 55. All this will be done with."

"I can't."

"Son," Ray said. "You're strong. We can see that. Brave, too. But you've got a long life ahead of you."

Ray spoke with the familiarity of a grandfather. I never knew my grandfather, so it was a strange feeling to feel. I didn't question it. Ray and Martha could see right through me, but they were without judgment.

"My friend…" I began.

"Has made his peace," Martha said. "It's time for you to make yours."

"What if I'm not ready to?"

"A man's heart is going to beat to its own time no matter the schedule," Ray said, more to himself than any of us at the table.

"I have to try. I couldn't live with myself if I didn't."

Bollocks took the record out of my bag. "Let's at least see what this says?" He turned to the corner where the jukebox was. "Where'd it go?"

The jukebox was gone. In its place was a turntable console.

"What the fuck?" I said. "Sorry," I said to Ray and Martha.

"Nothing we haven't heard or said," Martha said.

"Where'd the jukebox go?" I asked.

"You didn't need that, did you?"

"Yeah. I guess the console will work." I looked to Tanner. His face was slack.

"That's the exact thing we need. I literally just thought that's what we would need when Bollocks took out the record," he said.

"Dude," Bollocks said and hit me on the arm. "We're in the Room of Requirement."

"What, Bollocks?" I said.

"If you have to ask, you'll never know. If you know, you need only ask." He furrowed his brows and closed his eyes.

"Son," Ray said, laughing. "It won't get bigger."

"Jesus Christ," I said.

Bollocks shrugged. "Had to try, man."

Tanner held up the turntable cartridge he lifted from Sun Studio. "May I?"

Martha nodded.

We all went over to the console. Tanner went to work swapping out the cartridge.

"Are you prepared to hear what's on that record?" Ray asked me.

"I already know the half of it," I said.

"But that's not what you're after, is it?"

I shook my head. "Do you know what's on it?"

"It's never anything good," Martha said.

"Who are you two?" Bollocks said. "Like why do you know all this stuff and have a magical general store?"

Martha and Ray looked at each other and smiled. "We've been here quite a while," she said.

"Been helping folks for a very long time," Ray said. "A very long time indeed."

He looked at me again. "You know, there's a good possibility, in fact almost an inevitability, that once you hear what's on the record, you won't be able to unhear it."

I nodded again. "I'm ready this time."

"Got it," Tanner yelled over his shoulder. He stood back. "I still can't believe it. This looks exactly like the one in Sun Studio."

Bollocks handed me the record. "You should do the honors. We'll be right here."

I slid the record over the spindle and down on to the platter. I raised the tone arm. The record began to spin. I lowered the needleless cartridge onto the smooth record. Static. A fingerpicked acoustic guitar line loaded with reverb.

"Stairway?" Bollocks said.

"What the fuck," I said.

"At least he's got a sense of humor. I mean dude's a dick, but this is kind of funny."

"I guess."

We listened to the end. Nothing.

I looked to Tanner. "What if we…" he said.

"What are you thinking, man?" I asked.

His hands were already in motion. The tone arm lifted and set down. He began pushing on the record with his fingertips.

"Oh shit," Bollocks said. "Backwards."

Martha stood up and went behind the counter and took a small tin off the shelf.

Ray sighed.

A pinprick of a smokey dot formed in the center of the room. Enlarging as the song progressed. The air became heavy, thick with incense. Tanner sneezed.

"Martha. Ray," Bollocks said looking towards the formation. "I believe there is a bustle in your hedgerow."

58. A STUDIO IN AUSTIN: IT'S JUST A SHOT AWAY

Paul and Brad were huddled around a microphone in the middle of the live room. Brad was cradling his headphones on both sides of his head and over performing like he was Kim Carnes during the We Are the World live video session. The engineer was adjusting dials and faders on the massive mixing console.

Maybelline took out her phone and texted Marc again. She was beginning to worry that something had happened to him after she left.

"It's not my cup of tea, but I can see the mass appeal," a voice said behind them.

Maybelline turned around.

Papa Legba.

The engineer half turned and lifted the left earcup of his headphones off his ear. "Please don't come in or out during a take." He dropped the earcup, it snapping back in place, and shook his head. He massaged a fader.

"Very important work," Legba said and nodded towards the engineer. "So, have you reconsidered now that you're seeing how the sausage gets made?"

Maybelline glanced to the live room. Brad noticed her looking and winked.

"I'm good," she said.

"Had to try."

"Let's take five and then run that back," the engineer said into the talkback microphone. He took off his headphones and placed them on the console. He leaned back in his chair and stretched and cracked his neck while he rubbed his belly. "Coffee," he said through a yawn. He stood up. "This daylight recording is for the birds." He slid behind Maybelline and past Legba.

"You guys want anything?" he asked, but he was opening and through the door before he finished the sentence.

"Why are you bothering me?" Maybelline said.

"You know, I've been around a long time." Legba put his pipe in his mouth. He looked into the live room.

"That's not an answer."

"There's a lot swirling around this little group."

"What do you mean?"

"I'm curious is all. This should be good."

"I don't follow."

"I'm checking up on investments," Legba said, not breaking his line of sight into the studio.

Maybelline looked back towards Brad and Paul. "Wait," she said. "Investments? Are they both…" she turned around to Legba, but he was gone.

Maybelline called Marc again. Nothing. She texted him again. *Are you ok?* She hoped he wasn't ignoring her. She felt bad about leaving, but she had to. And besides, they were going to see each other that evening. She took out her journal and wrote down a few notes. Observations she'd use for one or both stories she had to write.

"What's up with Father Time?" the engineer said behind her.

"Just a pain in my ass," she said.

"Here. You looked like you could use one."

The engineer handed her a coffee.

"Thanks," she said and took the cup.

"What do you know about that dude."

"Which one?"

"Father Time."

Maybelline wasn't sure how to respond. The engineer could sense her hesitation. "I know who he is," he said. "Just to clear the air of pretense."

She raised the coffee to her lips and stopped. "Wait. You didn't make a deal with the Devil did you?"

The engineer shook his head. "The coffee's not that good."

Maybelline didn't say anything. She stared at him.

"You're serious?" He sighed. "Do you think I'd be here if I did? These aren't the Joshua Tree sessions. But, no. And I'm starting to think I'm the only one."

"Same."

"Here," he said and pulled a necklace out from his collar. He held a blue oval with concentric circles of different shades.

"The evil eye?"

"A *nazar* in my language. But, yes. It wards against the evil eye."

"This isn't your first run-in I'm assuming?"

"You hang around this business long enough and you start to see all sorts of weird shit." He nodded with exaggeration towards the studio. "Exhibit A."

"Does that work?" Maybelline asked and pointed to his amulet.

"Yes and no. It helps that I don't believe in their religion."

Maybelline furrowed her brow. "What do you mean? If you know that he's real…"

"I don't make the rules. Like, yeah, he's real. But I don't believe in him. This," he gripped the amulet, "protects me. Like a cross for a vampire." Then quickly added, "so they say. I have no idea about vampires." He waved his free hand in the air as if erasing the thought. "Hold this," he said, handing Maybelline his cup of coffee.

He fished his keys out of his back pocket, attached to his belt loop by a carabiner. He unclipped the hook and slipped off a keychain. A small nazar. He handed it to Maybelline.

"Take this," he said. "You seem like good people."

He took his coffee back and put the keychain in her hand.

"But what if I do believe in him?"

He shrugged. "You're fucked, I guess." He laughed. Maybelline laughed too. She needed to. She was tense. An anxiety was pooling up inside of her and dancing around her feet like electricity before a storm. It felt good to release.

"Thanks," she said. "I needed that."

"For real though, it should help."

"Thanks," she said and stuck out her hand. "I'm Maybelline."

"Kadir."

***

We'll get it right next time

   We'll make it on a low tide

Brad finished laying a vocal harmony on the track while Paul overdubbed a harmonica part.

Kadir came over the talkback. "That was pretty good. Do you have one more in you?"

"Let me get a tea first," Brad said.

"Roger that."

"Aye. Good cover, mate," Paul said, taking off his headphones.

"It's a song I felt like I wrote, you know?" Brad said.

"I do."

"Listen, thanks for doing this again. I know I've said it, but really. Thanks."

"Didn't have much choice in the matter." Paul laughed more to himself than to Brad. "I'm glad the music is good at least. So, thanks for that."

"You didn't have a choice?" Brad deflated a little.

"Me paps commanded me. Kinda hard to resist when we're of the same flesh and blood."

"But he's not flesh and blood."

"Metaphysically speaking." Paul shrugged. "But serious. This could be much worse. It could have been Jagger's solo album or Imagine Dragons."

"Hmmph," Brad said. "Well, I guess it's all part of the deal."

The studio door opened and an intern brought in a cup of tea and handed it to Brad. He blew on the cup.

"Let me know when you're ready," Kadir said.

Brad gave a thumbs up to the control room.

"Man, I gotta know," Brad said. "What was up with the album on every iPod and iPhone?"

"You gonna bust me balls over that?" Paul laughed. "I literally had nothing to do with it. Me Pa set that up with Jobs. Thought it would help."

"You never know what's gonna hit."

"Truth. Hope this does."

"What do you mean 'hope?'"

"As you said, you never know what's gonna hit."

"My deal was a guarantee. I didn't sell my soul for a maybe."

"Nothing's guaranteed, mate. But I think you'll be fine. Otherwise, I wouldn't be here."

"I sure fucking hope so."

Paul blew into his harmonica, blowing off a riff.

"One more?" Brad said and set down his tea.

"Aye."

Kadir came over the talkback mic. "Your photographer is here to shoot some B-roll."

"That's fine," Brad said and unbuttoned another button on his shirt. "Let them in."

59. SPRUCE'S GENERAL STORE: WHEN YOU FIND YOURSELF IN THE THICK OF IT

A smokey black vortex enveloped the middle of the store pushing Marc, Tanner, and Bollocks to the outskirts while Martha and Ray retreated behind their counter.

"What the fuck," Bollocks said.

"Something like this happened after our gig a few days ago," Marc said, approaching the vortex, looking into it. "This is him."

"Careful, son," Ray said. "Once you go in, there ain't no turning back."

"Where's it go?" Bollocks asked.

"The in Between," Tanner said.

Marc picked up his guitar. "I'm going. I have to try to save Keith."

"Not so fast, son," Ray said. "Think this through."

"It's why we came here. To get this," Marc said and pointed to the vortex. "Right, Tanner?"

Tanner nodded.

"I'll go with you," Bollocks said.

"Me too," Tanner said.

Martha sighed. She shook her head.

"What?" Marc said.

"That record was made for you," she said to Marc. "Only you can go."

"Anyone else who tries to enter it forfeits their soul," Ray said. "He claimed lots of unfortunate cases with that caveat."

"Fuck," Bollocks said under his breath.

"You did ok by yourself last time…" Tanner said.

"But?" Marc said.

"But without Micawber and the jacket or pick, I don't know man. Without help…"

"You don't know?" Marc said. "You talked us into coming here."

Tanner looked at the vortex. He looked into its black nothingness. It called to him. Was pulling him in. "That thing," he said and pointed to the large smokey orb, "doesn't seem like back at Sun Studio. This is purely his realm."

Marc stared at it. Visions of greatness began to form in his head. Arising like steam, enveloping his thoughts. They were a variation on the theme of the visions from Sun Studio. Voices called to him. Familiar ones. He peered into the vortex further. His mother. Father. A sense of completeness and happiness like he'd never known coursed through his being and made him gasp for air as if he had just broken the surface after being underwater for a long, long time. It was a new breath. A new beginning. He could start over. He felt an overwhelming love. The voices called to him, sirens on the edge of a crag. They called and they called…

"Marc," Bollocks yelled, pulling hard on Marc's shoulder and arm. They collapsed on the ground. Hard. Marc's cellphone fell out of his pocket and slid across the floor.

"What the fuck," Marc said. "That hurt, man." He rubbed his hip.

"Dude," Bollocks said. "'What the fuck?' What the fuck were you doing?"

"What?"

"You put your guitar down and got all zombie-like and were going into the vortex talking to someone."

"Talking to someone? I was just standing here. With you."

"This is much more powerful than I thought it'd be," Tanner said. "It's playing tricks on you before you even go in it."

"You're right." Marc ran his hands through his hair. "This is different than last time. I don't think I can beat him without Micawber."

Martha walked around the counter and the perimeter of the vortex. "You'll have to let him go," Martha said, her voice kind. She took Marc's hand.

"He was like my last family. And I did let him go."

Martha squeezed his hand. "I know," she said softly.

A loud buzzing and AC⚡DC's "Hell's Bells" belted from somewhere on the floor.

Bollocks looked over to Marc's cellphone a few feet away. "Neat ringtone," he said and picked up the phone. "Full bars? Nice." He took out his own phone. "Damn it. I gotta switch carriers." He handed Marc the phone.

A slew of text messages and missed call alerts and voicemails were pouring in. Maybelline. He checked the messages. His face went slack.

"What?" Tanner asked.

"He's going after Maybelline."

"Why?" Bollocks said.

"Brad Johnson made a deal with the devil and got her involved."

Marc tried to call Maybelline. No answer. Then no bars.

"Do you think it's a trick?" Tanner asked.

"I was going to ask you the same thing."

The rumble of thunder rolled overhead. The lights flickered and the vortex began to grow smaller.

"What's happening?" Marc asked.

"The portal is closing," Ray said.

"Can we open it again?"

The sound of a five-ton whip cracked over their heads. The building trembled. A surge of electricity ran through the walls. Light bulbs popped. The old record console flared up, its lights going dim and then out, smoke gushing out from its every orifice.

The trembling increased. Ray nearly fell over and he gripped the counter. "I'd say that's a no."

Marc closed his eyes. He took a deep breath. "I have to go. This has to end." He picked up his guitar and looked at Bollocks. "I'll be back." He turned to the vortex. It was half its size and shrinking still. Marc moved towards it. He looked at Tanner. Tanner nodded at him.

"Hold on," Martha said from behind him. "You dropped this." She reached into her apron pocket and pulled out a little piece of wood. She handed it to him.

"Where'd you get this?" Marc said.

"No time for that," she said. "Go." She backed away from him. "Go. Save your friends."

The vortex was the size of a hula hoop. Marc jumped through it. His guitar in one hand. The Pick of Destiny in the other.

The vortex snapped shut and the room went dark. Air violently whooshed around them. Light crept in through broken windows and cracks in the wooden walls. The room was dusty and barren except for some old broken furniture and the empty shelving and counter.

"What in the Tom Bombadil?" Bollocks said and looked around the shop and to where the old console was. There was a record on the ground, covered in a layer of dust. He picked it up and blew on it. One side had grooves, the other was burnt. "Martha, my dear. Look what you've done you silly girl," he said.

"Let's get out of here, man," Tanner said. "There's another way we can help Marc."

"How?"

"There's another way I didn't even think about until right now. It's so simple. And we're so close."

"Quit the foreplay salesman. What are you getting at?"

"The original portal. The crossroads."

"Are we going to try and distract the Devil?"

"Hopefully more than that. I need to think."

They exited the building and their van was right where they left it. It was all packed up. The tires were new. The gas tank was full.

"Strange things are afoot at the Circle K," Bollocks said and punched Tanner in the arm. He put the van in drive. "Let's go save our boy." They drove away from the old building. Its wooden sign hanging on one hook, the soda machines rusted over, roof sagging in.

"Make a right up here," Tanner said, looking at his phone.

"You got bars?"

"Like a soap factory."

Bollocks sighed. "This is going to be a long ride." He took a right and then another back out onto the highway. "We're coming, Marc," he said.

60. SOMEWHERE IN THE BETWEEN: HOLD ME THRILL ME KISS ME KILL ME

Marc was pulled into an old bar. Dusty bottles and hourglasses lined the cavernous shelves. Windows of all shapes, sizes, and angles ran along the wall. An enormous floating stage moored to old whiskey barrels took up half the room. A faint pop came from among the bottles on the shelves.

Marc approached the stage. A menagerie of instruments came into focus. Violins. Brass and woodwinds. Guitars from every era. Drums. A theremin. A keytar. All spectral and hanging.

"Take your pick," a voice said.

Marc whipped around. The Devil.

"That was, pardon my pun, record timing," the Devil said.

"You already got one of my friends. I'm not going to let you get the rest of them," Marc said.

"That's noble of you."

"I came."

"To offer your soul to me?"

"I want an ironclad contract. No technicalities. One battle. If I win, Keith is free and you leave me and my friends alone forever. No matter what other entanglements people in our lives get into."

"Marc," the Devil said. "Why would I do that?"

"If you don't," a voice with an Irish accent said behind the bar. "Our little experiment is over."

Marc and The Devil looked over to the bar. A sunglassed man in a leather jacket was wiping dust off himself.

"Bono?" Marc said, incredulous.

"Son," the Devil said.

Bono bowed with a flourish of his hand. "At your service."

Behind him, stumbling out from between a shelf was Maybelline.

61. A STUDIO IN AUSTIN: DON'T LET ME DOWN

Brad was whisked away to a small press junket arranged to drum up interest in his set that night. Kadir went to the mastering room to get a jump on the tracks so they could be leaked after the show. Maybelline and Bono were alone.

"You're schlepping around with Brad Johnson?" Maybelline said. "Why?"

Bono smiled. "The music's not that bad. And, he can help me with my solo album."

"How?"

"He's got connections I don't."

"Come on. You're in one of the biggest rock bands in the world. What connections does he have that you don't?"

"Aye. I should say he has different connections. Trying to get some of that indie clout."

"Well, a Rolling Stone cover story isn't going to help with that." Maybelline laughed.

Bono sighed. "I know."

"Then why are you doing it?"

"I'm compelled."

"What?"

"I wish we didn't have to have this conversation."

Maybelline eyed him, curious. "What conversation?"

"I saw Reynolds talking to you."

"Reynolds?"

Bono frowned. "Legba."

"Oh, no…" Maybelline deflated. "Not you too."

"Aye. Bit more complicated though."

"Goddamnit, Paul. Everywhere I turn it's the Devil this, the Devil that."

Bono leaned against the wall in the control room. "I was hoping to spare you."

Maybelline laughed, short and dismissive.

"Tell me," Bono said.

"Tell you what?"

"All of it. I can help you."

"How?"

Bono sighed. He took his sunglasses off and put them in his jacket pocket. "You'd be surprised," he said.

"Where to start," Maybelline said. "Do you believe in ghosts?"

Bono smiled a sad smile full of empathy. "Aye."

Maybelline told him everything. From the first night with Marc when the stage collapsed. Keith Richards' ghost. The liquor store. The showdown at Sun Studio. Everything Legba said. By the end of her story, she was fidgeting in her chair, thumbing the nazar Kadir gave her.

"You got it bad," Bono said.

"Who you telling?"

Bono looked at the amulet keyring. "Would you mind putting that away?"

Maybelline held it up. "This bothers you?"

"More of a discomfort thing."

"Why?"

"I like you. You know this. We're mates."

"Thanks?"

"It's best I'm fully honest with you if we're going to trust each other."

"I trust you."

"Promise me you won't write about it. Me family couldn't handle it. It's not their fault any more than it's mine for being born."

Maybelline nodded.

"Appreciate that. This is heavy shite and I hope it doesn't change your opinion about me."

"We're friends, right?"

"Aye."

62. INTERLUDE: MARTELLO TOWER, HOWTH, IRELAND, AUGUST 16, 1959

"You could use a shave," Reynolds said.

"Could use a lot of things at this point in my life," Denis Devlin said. He brought his hand to his mouth and exhaled a burp. His chest hurt. Indigestion from too many pints last night at Lincoln's Inn. "I'm sure you didn't call me here to talk about my appearance."

"Fair enough. It's time to collect."

"So soon?" Devlin rubbed his chest.

"32 years is substantially more than most get. You've been careful." Reynolds nodded. "You've reaped many rewards."

"Being a diplomat and poet isn't what I'd call 'reaped rewards.'"

Reynolds took out a pipe and packed it.

"I could use some fresh air," Devlin said.

Reynolds lit his pipe. "Lead the way."

They stepped out of the old stone tower, built in the early 1800s to protect against a Napoleonic invasion that never came. It was a clear, sunny day. Boats were docked in the harbor. Church bells rang the Sabbath. The wind from the Irish Sea whipped the tails of Devlin's jacket. His hair askew. Reynolds was unfazed. His pipe flared and smoked.

"He could use your help," Reynolds said.

"He?"

"You were given a gift and were a good caretaker. You shaped it, nurtured it, let it blossom into something wholly unique."

"Does he want me to write a poem about him?" Devlin scoffed.

"He wants the gift back."

"I turned my back on my faith for this gift." Devlin wiped his brow. Despite the wind, he began sweating. His back hurt.

"He is prepared to dissolve the contract."

The wind picked up, a stronger gust. Down below, folks in their Sunday whites and blacks walked along the pier. A hat blew off—children's laughter. A chase down the pier towards the lighthouse. The hat blown out to sea, dancing in the air like a marionette. Dancing, dancing until it landed in the water. It would float a while before saturation pulled it to the bottom of the harbor.

Devlin turned to Reynolds and began to open his mouth but stopped—struck by a club in the chest. He clutched his left arm. He fell to the ground.

Reynolds knelt over him, his pipe clenched in his teeth. He produced an empty bottle. "Breath into this," he said and placed it against Denis' lips. Devlin's eyes searched around frantically, beams of light across a dusky landscape.

Reynold

s placed his hand on Devlin's head, smoothing his hair back. "I know. I know," he said. Tender even. "It will be yours. Just breathe."

Denis exhaled into the bottle. "Hospital," he managed. Maybe he never said it. He was losing daylight. A darkness crept over his eyes. He reached for Reynolds who was plugging the bottle with a cork and rising. *Hospital.*

Reynolds was gone. The wind blew harder across the channel. Denis lay there for over an hour before someone came by. He would die in Dublin five days later, spending his remaining time on Earth muttering the prayers he learned in seminary school as a young man. The light left his eyes and would not appear again on Earth—he was finally home in an angel-foaming world for what was left of eternity.

63. INTERLUDE: DUBLIN, IRELAND, 10 MONTHS LATER

The mother held her baby boy in her arms. Her second son. She was expecting a visitor. A man from the church who she had met just before she became pregnant. A missionary doctor spending a year in Ireland before making his way to The States. He took special interest in the woman after she became pregnant and used his skills to counsel her and make sure her pregnancy was without difficulty as best as medical science would allow.

She rested in the front room of her family's modest house at No. 10 Cedarwood Road in the Finglas suburb of Dublin, just northwest of the City Centre. Two-story, squat houses lined the curved streets. Hip-high walls enclosed the neatly kept front gardens of every house. It was a peaceful neighborhood where a young person could grow up in relative safety and comfort.

A knock on the door. Iris' older son, now 8, answered the door and let in the visitor who hung his own hat and moved about the house with familiarity.

"Morning, doctor," she said.

"Iris," Dr. Ensloy said. "How's our little Paul today?"

"Grand. My sweet pea." She kissed his head.

"May I?"

Iris extended the sleeping baby to the doctor. Ensloy cradled the boy gently and sat down on a cushioned bench near the window. He whispered to the boy.

"Latin?" Iris asked.

"*Etiam*," he said.

Baby Paul stirred. Dr. Ensloy removed a small bottle from his coat pocket and uncorked it deftly while still holding Paul. He brought the bottle to the baby's lips. "*Respirare in…poeta linguae…vox bono*," he whispered.

"What's in there?" Iris asked.

"Only those blessed vapors which will help the boy grow strong in all regards." Paul breathed in and a sheen flashed across his eyes and receded, sinking below the surface. If one looked at him long enough, especially during times when the moon was waning, that glimmer could be seen. Later, when this boy grew up and came under increasing public scrutiny, he would take to wearing sunglasses at all times to hide this condition.

33 YEARS LATER: AUGUST 23, 1993, DUBLIN: BONO'S PRIVATE DRESSING ROOM

U2 could have quit in the early 90s and would have gone down in history as one of the great rock bands. Now at the height of their fame Bono found himself drawn to retrospection more and more. He had not seen or heard of Reynolds since a meeting in a pub in early 1980.

"I don't understand," Bono said.

"You know Jesus?" Reynolds said.

"Not personally."

"He wasn't only God's son. He was also a part of God."

"Put here for our sins. Yeah, yeah, yeah."

Reynolds packed and lit his pipe. He blew out the match and took a long puff. "He was God's vessel. God wanted to know what it was like to be human—to better understand the suffering of his children. People think Jesus was his own thing. That he's sitting upstairs as part of the 'trinity.'"

Bono looked up from his pint.

"When he died," Reynolds said, "he was absorbed back into God's essence. Ceased to exist. His experiences, memories, suffering—those all became part of God as if he had lived those 33 years on earth himself."

"What? Jesus isn't real?"

"He was. Not anymore."

Bono stared at Reynolds. The two sat in silence for many long moments.

"You," Reynolds eventually said as if reading Bono's mind, "will enjoy a great life."

"Then cease to exist."

"As everyone and everything else."

"And then my experiences, memories, and suffering will all be his."

Reynolds nodded.

"Why?"

"He wanted to be a rock star. It seemed like fun."

Bono laughed. "You feckin' had me fer a minute." He downed the second pint and stood up. "We've got practice, Mr. Mephistopheles. I'll see you later."

Reynolds put his hand on Bono's arm as he was walking past. "You don't have to believe it for it to be true. Just go and live a charmed life."

Bono snapped out of his rumination. Irritated and growing closer to that day when he would cease to exist, he felt the same panic all mortal men feel when faced with eternal life or the lack thereof. He called for Reynolds. Nothing. He called for the Devil. Nothing. If this was the life that would be absorbed, he wanted to stick it to the man.

He created MacPhisto—a parody of the Devil that wore a shiny gold suit, tall gold shoes, lipstick and makeup to make him ghastly and ghostly. Topped off with devil horns. The persona was comical. A down-on-his-luck, washed up performer who pretended to be of the aristocracy. The character was panned. Public opinion towards Bono was swaying—a self-righteous, pompous loudmouth whose philanthropical endeavors were at odds with his rich rock star status. Bono loved it. The Devil perked up—he was not thrilled.

"Happy 33rd," a voice said. A man in a suit appeared standing across from Bono.

"You're a few months late," Bono said, trying his best to play it cool. He surveyed the Devil. "I thought you'd be taller."

"I thought you'd be more grateful," the Devil said.

The Devil walked around the room. Scratched his finger along the table and straightened his tie in the mirror. "You've done good, kid," he said to Bono.

"I'm not your kid."

The Devil smirked. Turned around. "Why are you throwing this away? Or at least trying to. They still love you, you know."

"Why did you pick me?"

"I knew you'd succeed. With my help of course."

"Help?" Bono scoffed.

"Though, what you did with the second album was adorable. It's a good thing your guitarist has better sense."

"You didn't go after him," Bono said and stepped towards the Devil.

The Devil waved his hand and Bono was flung into a chair and held there unable to move. "Relax. That was a freebie. Purely selfish. What's good for the goose is good for me."

"What the feck? Let me out."

"In time."

"I want my soul or else I'll sabotage this life."

"Davey," the Devil said and smiled, "you've already done great. I'll have my satisfaction when I absorb you. I'm here to tell you that it'd just be real nice if you tried to enjoy yourself a little more."

"Why should I?"

"Why would you not want to?"

"Spite," Bono said.

"You ever hear the one about the nose and the face?"

"There's got to be a middle ground. Some way we can both benefit."

"We both are though."

"Listen, man. These are your rules. I had no say. I don't think that's fair."

The Devil burst out laughing. "Fair? You humans are so precious in your feebleness."

"Why're you such a dick?"

"I learned it from watching you."

The Devil stood straight and approached Bono. He knelt down at his feet. "I'll tell you what, Dave. I'm going to help you out even more now. You won't be able to fail. Just keep doing what you're doing and I'll handle the rest. If you don't, I'm going to call on your bandmate to balance the ledger. Maybe your kids. I don't know. I don't know how I'll feel." The Devil smiled. Stood up. "Excuse me. I've got to see a man about an apple." The Devil vanished. Bono was released from the chair.

64. THE PIGGLY WIGGLY IN ROSEDALE: WATCH OUT STRANGE CAT PEOPLE, LITTLE RED ROOSTER'S ON THE PROWL

"Make a left at the crossroads marker," Tanner said and then directed Bollocks to pull into the parking lot of the Piggly Wiggly off of Hwy 8 in Rosedale.

"What are we doing here?" Bollocks asked.

"I thought it was a joke," Tanner said. "But then after meeting Keith Richards and what he said about Clarksdale, I knew that it wasn't. Or at least it wasn't totally a joke."

"Sméags, what are you talking about?"

"Remember about the tree the Fated Four were made from? And the pick? Grohl's drumsticks?"

Bollocks perked up at the mention of the drumsticks.

"Well," Tanner said. "If my calculations are correct, I think they built this Piggly Wiggly right over the spot where the original crossroads were."

"How do you know?"

"Do you know who Alan Lomax was?"

"That Dr. Seuss dude about littering?"

"No. Lomax traveled around in the late '30s and early '40s with his father and recorded, interviewed, and catalogued the blues and folk music for the Library of Congress. He's the reason we know a lot of what we do now."

"Did he write about the crossroads?"

"The people he interviewed talked about it. When I was reviewing archival materials at Sun Studio I came across some old photos of Highways 1 and 8 under construction. They weren't completed until 1932. There was no building right there." Tanner pointed to the Piggly Wiggly.

"Was there a tree?"

"Not in the photos. But there was a deep indentation like a tree had been uprooted."

"That could have been from construction."

"That's what I thought, but people mentioned it in the interviews. One day there was a tree at the crossroads. Then it was gone. Lomax interviewed so many people. The details and facts don't always line up, but they all say the same thing. There was a tree. And then there wasn't."

Tanner looked out at the Piggly Wiggly. "This has got to be it."

"What are we going to do?"

Tanner ignored him. Deep in thought. "If we enter the portal on our own, we can help Marc. No tricks," he mumbled. "I think..."

"Say that again."

"We're not making a deal. We're not calling the devil or anything. We're just wandering through a back door."

"*Cirith Ungol*," Bollocks whispered.

"What?"

"Come," Bollocks said and killed the engine. "We are men of Gondor!"

"We need a plan," Tanner said. "One does not simply walk into Mordor."

Bollocks smiled. He unbuckled his seatbelt and opened the door. "Tanner, if you really wish to be free of him, then you must help me. But you need not go all the way, not beyond the gates of his land."

"Dude. What are you talking about? I'm going with you."

"Yes, to save our precious."

"Sure. Our precious." Tanner shook his head. "We need a plan. I think I have a plan."

Bollocks' eyes widened.

"Don't say 'giant eagles,'" Tanner said.

"I know, I know. I'm just nervous. I joke when I'm nervous."

"Use that energy. If we can get down there I think we'll need it."

***

The Piggly Wiggly had just opened and there weren't many people in the place. They spotted a cashier, a customer service rep, and someone in the deli. Bollocks and Tanner walked up and down the aisles pretend shopping while making their way to the stockroom where they assumed the basement would be. If the place even had a basement.

"Hey," Bollocks whispered.

"Why are you whispering?" Tanner asked.

"Let's find a clipboard. Follow my lead." He whispered, ignoring Tanner.

They found the stationary aisle and each picked up a clipboard. Bollocks opened a package of pens and took one and then removed a calculator from its package and gave it to Tanner.

"What am I going to do with this?" Tanner asked.

"Just pretend like you're adding shit and writing it down. Be cool."

Bollocks led them to the back of the store and began talking loudly.

"And then he said I'd need to send my receipts to corporate. I mean, it's *their* vehicle that we're using."

"There's the stock room," Tanner said quietly and nodded his head.

"They've got us driving all around Mississippi and now I've got to mail my bank statement with gas receipts to them. Like, just give me a company card already for the per diem, right?"

They walked into the back room. There was a guy putting things on a shelf. He had earbuds in. He didn't look at them.

Bollocks pointed to the ceiling. "That's a 69 reading."

"Nice," Tanner said.

The guy looked over when they were pointing and looking at the ceiling. Someone from corporate probably. Or a contractor. Whoever they were, it was above his minimum wage pay grade to care. Besides, they had clipboards. Fuck it. He went back to stocking the shelves.

Bollocks and Tanner moved around the store room in a similar manner. Looking at things, calling out numbers. Writing them down. Just acting like they belonged. Towards the back of the room, behind the paper goods, there was manhole peeking out from under the shelves. Tanner knelt down and placed his hand on the metal covering. He whispered something that Bollocks couldn't make out. He stood and nodded his head.

"This is it," Tanner said. "I can feel it."

"It looks like it's for plumbing though."

"It looks like it's going to take us underground."

"We need to move this shelf."

They looked at the massive shelving unit loaded high with product. Bollocks gave it a nudge. And then another. The shelf rocked a tiny bit.

"We can't move this," Tanner said.

Bollocks turned around and scanned the store room. The shelves were lined up in neat rows. He gave the shelf a little push with his hip again. "Hmm," he said. "We still have that bag of money, right?"

"Yeah," Tanner said.

"Go get it. Maybelline said ill fortune would befall us threefold if we used it for personal gain. Let's do some good with it instead."

"Ok," Tanner said. "I'll be right back."

Bollocks walked up to the guy stocking the shelves they saw earlier.

"Hey, man," Bollocks said. Stock guy didn't hear him. Bollocks tapped him on the shoulder. Stock guy jumped and turned around, taking out his earbuds. "The fuck," he said.

"Sorry," Bollocks said. "Listen. We don't actually work for corporate."

"Ok." Stock guy couldn't give two shits.

"Are they paying you well here?"

Stock guy tongued his back teeth and looked off to the side. "Eh."

"That's a 'no.' I imagine that front of house isn't doing much better."

"What's this about, man? My manager's gonna be on my ass if I don't get this done."

"What if I told you you didn't have to worry about your manager anymore?"

"How?"

"Come with me," Bollocks said and began walking out of the stock room. "Actually, I have no idea where I'm going. Is there an intercom?"

Stock guy pointed over to a phone on the wall. "#27."

Bollocks picked up the phone and punched in the code. The squawk of audio breaking over the speakers echoed through the empty store. "Uh," Bollocks said. "Emergency staff meeting in the stock room. This is coming down from corporate. Please report immediately for an emergency staff meeting in the stock room."

One by one the weary staff made their way to the stock room and circled around Bollocks. "Is this everyone?" he asked. Stock guy nodded. "What's this about, man?"

Tanner walked up to Bollocks and dropped the duffel bag of money at his feet. He looked around at the employees.

"It's come to my attention that the Piggly Wiggly isn't treating you as well as they could."

There were nods and murmurs of agreement.

"Who here has been passed over for a promotion?" Bollocks continued. "Who here has busted their ass and not been rewarded? Who here has gone that extra mile just so the man," Bollocks pointed to the ceiling, "can get a bonus from the sweat off your backs?"

More verbal sounds of agreement. Louder this time.

Bollocks was getting fired up and pulled over a box and stood on it. The top flaps fell in and his feet busted straight through to the ground and he almost fell over. He grabbed Tanner for balance. "Who here feels like they deserve better?"

A bit of applause.

"You trying to get us to form a union again?" someone said.

"Even better," Bollocks said. "We're here to get you to quit and take a vacation."

"Man," stock guy said. "I need this job."

"Show them, Tanner."

Tanner unzipped the bag. "There are 4 of you. This is about 60k each."

"Ain't nothing free in this life," stock guy said.

"This is true," Bollocks said and nodded. "We do need something from you. We need to get into the basement, and the only way to do that is to move the massive shelf that's sitting on top of it. I need your help. We can't keep this money and we need to move the shelves. And I'm betting that 60k is more than your salary."

The lady working the register stepped forward. "Say less," she said.

"Is this stolen?" stock guy asked. "I ain't tryin' to fuck with the law."

"Earned fair and square at a casino last week," Tanner said.

"Good enough for me."

More people stepped up. Tanner counted out the money.

Once everybody had their dough and the bag was empty, they lined up at the shelf and gave it a push. It took a couple of efforts, but it tipped and crashed into the next shelf and then the next, the whole stock room floored in a massive game of dominos. Glorious destruction, chaotic and cacophonous, resounded through the storage room.

***

"White people are crazy," Marquise said to Alaysia as they were leaving the Piggly Wiggly. He thumbed through his money. "You know, I woulda moved that shelf with the forklift for like $20." They both laughed. "But that was fun."

"What are you going to do?" Alaysia asked.

"I don't know. Maybe go to trade school. Start my own shop. Get high. You?"

"Take my mom out to breakfast."

"Bet. Imma get some pancakes." He looked into the distance. "And some orange juice. That fresh squeezed shit."

"I feel kinda bad there's no basement. Should we have told them?"

"Nah. Fuck those white dudes. They different. Carpetbagging motherfuckers."

Alaysia laughed. "You different."

"One and only, baby. One and only."

A Lincoln Continental pulled into the parking lot. The man driving was wearing a straw hat. He pulled up to Marquise and Alaysia. He looked at the money in Marquise's hand.

"Did some guy with a mohawk who talks too much give that to you?" the man asked.

"Fuck," Marquise said. "I told you this shit wasn't legit."

"No, no," the man said. "You're good. Are they in there now?" He nodded towards the store.

Marquise squinted. "I ain't saying shit, pa."

The man in the car killed the engine and opened his door. He looked into Marquise's eyes. Legba tipped his hat and walked into the Piggly Wiggly.

***

Tanner and Bollocks pried the lid off the manhole that gave access to the plumbing and sewage pipes. Bollocks got down on his hands and knees and peered into the pitch-black hole. Tanner turned on his phone's flashlight and shone the feeble ray into the void. Bollocks sighed. "Let's do this, Dufresne," he said and swung around and went down feet first. Tanner followed.

"How far down do you think this goes?" Bollocks yelled up to Tanner.

"Can't be too far." Fact was Tanner wasn't sure. All he knew is that they needed to get under the Piggly Wiggly and was hoping the portal would reveal itself.

They hit bottom. Maybe twenty feet down. They felt around the walls. The room was small. Round. A slew of voices came from nowhere. Full of static and abrasiveness that bordered on assault.

…This is AM Lumber with your morning wood.

Cartoon bells and an awooga horn blasted from the walls.

Easy now, boys. Later this hour we'll have a new one from 100 Gecs.

Do you still like Imagine Dragons?

Can't get enough.

A horn again.

Well, imagine draggin' these…

"What the hell is this?" Bollocks said.

"Sounds like a morning radio show," Tanner said.

"The worst form of anything."

A loud clank echoed from above and they were bathed in light. Small, caged bulbs glowed around the perimeter of the room. They looked up the barrel section of the hole, over the metal rungs and saw the silhouette of man with a hat.

"Now what are you boys doing down there?" the figure called out.

"He found us," Bollocks said. "I don't know how, but he found us. Let's run for it, Tanner."

They looked around the room. It was a concrete cylinder, walls smooth except for some meters and small access panels.

"You've got to go lower," the figure yelled down and then disappeared before reappearing feet first, climbing down the steps while holding his cane in one hand. When he reached the bottom, he brushed dust off his suit and adjusted his hat. "You boys are resourceful."

"Listen, pops," Bollocks said. "We don't want any deals. We're through with you."

"You," Papa Legba said and poked Bollocks in the chest with his cane, "owe me for the detailing I had to get done to my car."

"I don't know what you're talking about."

Legba waved his hand in the air and something akin to a hologram appeared showing Bollocks standing on the back of his car, asscheeks exposed.

"Ok, ok, ok," Bollocks conceded. "Have your people call my people. We're pressed for time."

"Do you think I came here just for that?" Legba looked up. He snapped his fingers. The radio voices stopped. "Sorry about that. You're close to his realm—it's all that plays down there."

"Why are you here?" Tanner asked.

Legba sat against the ladder and lit his pipe. He looked at Tanner. "You know all about me. You knew I'd be here."

Tanner furrowed his brow. He nodded.

"You know that I'm not an evil spirit. I want to help you boys. It's why I came."

"You would have had to come if this was the real crossroads," Tanner said. "Only you can grant us passage."

"Wait," Bollocks said. "You knew he was gonna show up?"

"Yeah. I didn't want to spook you just in case this wouldn't work."

"But you knew it would work," Legba said. "You've been right at almost every turn. I'm impressed." He took a drag off his pipe. "I'd like to help you in a more personal manner. No strings."

"You said I know about you," Tanner said. "So you know I know I shouldn't trust you."

"And you also know that I can be benevolent as well."

"Hey," Bollocks said. "This is all great, but we're running out of time. Marc needs us like right now."

"You haven't learned a thing, have you?" Legba said. "Time is immaterial. Better yet, let me explain it in terms you'd understand." Legba put down his pipe and conjured an empty can of Lone Star beer. He held it sideways. "Time," he said and crushed the can in a clapping motion, "is a flat circle." He tossed the can to Bollocks who caught it and inspected it. Legba picked up his pipe and gave it a puff. "If we need to get there before Marc battles the Devil, that's when we'll get there. As soon as you set foot in this place you entered a liminal space. Does that make sense?"

Bollocks held the can up. "I think you meant to demonstrate *Interstellar*, not *True Detective*. But, yeah. I get it."

"What do you want from me?" Tanner asked.

"I'm tired," Legba said. "I've been at this a long time. I need a vacation."

"What does that have to do with me?"

"Let me prove myself to you first. Then we'll talk."

Legba stood up and adjusted his tie. He tapped his cane three times on the floor and muttered an incantation. A portal opened up in the side of the room. "You know what you have to do once you go through, right?"

"We do," Tanner said.

"We do?" Bollocks asked.

"You'll know what to do when the time comes," Tanner said. "Just follow my lead."

"You know we could have done this in the parking lot, or upstairs, right?" Legba said.

"But what about the portal where the tree stood?" Tanner asked.

"There's been a septic tank there since '86. Though, this one over here," Legba looked towards Bollocks, "deserved the bath."

"That doesn't sound very benevolent," Bollocks said.

"Let's do this," Tanner said.

"Remember," Legba said. "Although you're going of your own accord, he can convince you to make a deal. If you wish to help your friend, you must remain true."

"It's all we want."

The three of them walked through the portal and it snapped shut behind them. They were dumped out behind an old bar lined with dusty bottles and glasses. Just over the counter they saw Marc and the Devil. Next to him was Maybelline and a guy wearing a leather jacket and sunglasses. Bollocks hopped over the bar.

"We're here, Marc," he said. The man with the glasses turned around. "Holy Siri," Bollocks said. "We're in an iPhone 6."

Bono held his hands up. "Sorry, mate. I swear it wasn't my doing."

"This is really getting annoying," the Devil said.

65. SOMEWHERE IN THE BETWEEN: WON'T GET FOOLED AGAIN

The last thing I was expecting to see was Bono, yet there he was. With Maybelline.

"You think you're the only one, Marc. You don't have to do this alone," she said.

I stopped whatever dumb reprimand I was forming in my head. "Thank you," I said.

"Marc," Bono said and reached to shake my hand. "Maybelline's caught me up. Told me all about you."

I shook his hand. I was shaking fucking Bono's hand. In the Devil's lair. What the fuck.

"I thought you were making fun of me when you said you were pen pals," I said to Maybelline.

"I was, but it was still true," she said.

"This is real heartwarming," the Devil said. He looked at Bono. "Experiment? What's changed?"

"Let's just say that I've finally found what I've been looking for," Bono said.

"And what would that be?"

"The thread is unraveling."

The Devil cleared his throat. "Go on."

"In '87 I had an idea. I didn't think it would have taken hold, but I now know it did. And you didn't like it. That's why you eventually came to see me after I started making fun of you."

"*Rattle and Hum*?" Maybelline asked. "You recorded that in Sun Studio. We were just there."

"Aye. Not all of it, but enough," Bono said. "I didn't realize it had actually worked. We had a midnight session. Legba was the engineer. He told me if I recorded 'Hound Dog' at the exact tempo as Elvis, using the same mic and all the settings only he knew, I'd be able to break the spell."

The Devil's chest heaved.

Bono continued. "I didn't think anything happened but after public opinion kept shifting and then with the Apple flop you orchestrated," Bono pointed to the Devil, "I knew that whatever hold he had on me was loosening."

"That was a great record," the Devil said.

Bono smiled. "But it didn't bring the satisfaction you wanted, did it?"

"You can never be fully free of me. That was futile."

"So it did work?" Bono said. "I feckin' knew it."

"What do you want?" the Devil asked.

"For you to leave my friends alone."

"Why would I do that? All of you think you can come into my domain and tell me what you want and what I should do. This is my world. I made this. I run the show." His eyes went from black to flames to black again.

"I don't think you understand," Bono said.

"What is it that I don't understand?" the Devil said, his voice laced with venom and a patience that was lost, gone, hopped on a freight train and left days ago.

"We're here, Marc." Bollocks' voice echoed from behind me. I turned around and saw him and Tanner and Legba. Bollocks said something to Bono I couldn't quite make out.

"This is really getting annoying," the Devil said. "Your little group is turning out to be more trouble than it's worth."

"Then leave us alone," I said.

The Devil laughed. "Not in a thousand years."

"But you just said…" Bollocks said.

"I know what I said. I'm just going to have to make it worth it." His form shifted into a satyr, then snapped back to his human shape.

"One battle," I said. "You leave me and my friends alone. You free Keith Richards."

"Again, Marc," he said with a sardonic contempt that would make Professor Snape proud, "you have no leverage."

Bono stepped forward and mumbled something in a language I didn't understand. Ropes formed out of the ether and wrapped around the Devil like oily vines. The Devil's face went slack. He turned to mist and dropped out of the entanglement, then reappeared next to Bono. He glared at Legba.

"You." He shook his head.

"He brought me rum and tobacco," Legba said and shrugged and packed his pipe. "You know I like gifts."

"How long have you two been scheming behind my back?"

"Just before the *Hope for Haiti* concert," Bono said to Legba. "Right?"

"Sounds right," Legba said. He lit his pipe.

"Why are you here?" the Devil said to Legba.

"I like a good show." He pulled over a barstool and sat down. "Don't mind me."

The Devil's chest heaved again. "Enough. Let's get this over with. It's going to be fun capturing all of your souls."

"Capture? You said we'd be in a palace of pleasure," I said. "What happened to that?"

"You will be."

Legba sucked his teeth. "It's a palace of pleasure for *him*," Legba said and pointed his pipe. "You, and all the other souls, are used for his pleasure."

"Ew," Maybelline said.

The Devil glared at Maybelline. His eyes caught the nazar around her neck. He recoiled as if stung, burnt from touching a hot pan. He threw out his hand like tossing an evil frisbee and Maybelline, Bollocks, and Tanner were bound and gagged and sat down on a pew.

"Yo, motherfucker," I said, stepping forward, gripping my guitar, ready to blast off a riff. "Let them go."

"Relax. It's just a formality. Here are the terms," the Devil said. He produced a scroll and let it unfurl from his fingertips. "This is between you and me. Nothing from the peanut gallery."

<u>The New Rules</u>

Marc, herein referred to as "The Marked," will cut heads once.
- ✝ *If The Marked loses, he forfeits his soul when he dies.*
- ✝ *If The Marked loses, his friends, present and otherwise, are fair game.*
- ✝ *If The Marked loses, he becomes my mule.*

"These all assume that I'll lose," I said. "I want terms included for if I win. If I win, all of my friends are free from you forever. Put that on the scroll."

The Devil flicked his hands and my amendment appeared on the parchment.

"Keith Richards," I said. "He's included. You release his soul."

The Devil laughed. "Sure, Keith Richards too," he said with a nonchalance that was unsettling. "Anything else?"

"The Fated Four and everything else made from the tree vanishes forever."

"Now that I can't do. That is beyond my control thanks to a little thing called 'free will' you beings are so good at. I did not make those blessed items."

Legba removed his pipe. "I can hang on to them."

"Like you did the bottle?" The Devil said.

"If people find me and what they seek, they deserve to have them."

The Devil breathed out of his nose. "Considering how lax you are lately, I can live with that. They'll be back in circulation before the century is half up."

"It's a good deal," Legba said to me.

I looked to Tanner. He nodded.

"Add it," I said.

The Devil handed me the scroll with the additions I wanted. He summoned a quill and an inkwell and a small wooden desk with a top that worked on a hinge so it was at an angle. These were all set upon a marble pillar. He signed the scroll and handed me the quill. I took it.

"Careful," he said as I was signing the document. "This was used to write Jefferson's declaration." He looked over my shoulder. "So much blood and suffering because of this simple feather."

I handed it back. "Thanks for the show and tell. What's the pillar from? The Fall of Troy?"

The Devil smirked. "Worse," he said. "It's a set piece from Milli Vanilli's 'Blame it on the Rain' video."

"Funny."

"Satisfied?"

I stared through the Devil. "Let's do this." I slung my guitar over my shoulder and reached into my pocket for the pick Martha gave me at Spruce's. I hoped it was enough. It had to be enough.

666. SOMEWHERE IN THE BETWEEN— AUGUST 16—THE DAY OF MARC'S BATTLE FOR HIS SOUL (AND THAT OF HIS FRIENDS, NO BIG DEAL)

The Devil's Lair. The Room of Reckoning. The Bar of Souls. Time in a Bottle 'Til Eternity Passes Away. Whatever you want to call it. That's where shit was about to go down. You see, Marc fucked up. He wanted glory. Power. Trained for it. It wasn't all his fault though.

In a moment of weakness, Keith Richards' ghost soul pegged him to take over for his own deal with the Devil. But then Keith grew to like the kid. Tried to protect him—took him under his wing just in case. A series of success, failure, honor, friendship, and hubris culminated in this final battle between Marc and the Devil.

Many had come before Marc, and many more will come after. But this moment is special. Never had a deal with the Devil become so convoluted and many armed—the tentacles of the deal with Keith Richards branched far and wide touching many souls in small and devastatingly significant ways alike. Sure, Bono is here. In no way is he a surrogate for Keith Richards. It's not really his story (even though he is kind of the Devil's son). He's got his own shit to sort through, and he's got a friendship with Maybelline. That's why he's really here. If there's a moral to this story—which I'm not positing there is— but if there is, and if Bollocks was to sum it up, it would be something like this: In the immortal words of the ageless sage Dominic Toretto, "Friends is Family."

And that's why when Marc said, "Let's do this," and the Devil transported him to the creaky, musty stage floating out into the bar, moored to old whiskey barrels, and Marc was alone, Bono knew that he had to help. This was his moment. Maybelline was his friend. Marc was her friend. And *friends is family* goddamnit.

Bono released Bollocks, Maybelline, and Tanner from their bondage. They ran to the stage.

The Devil looked over, annoyed. "You only brought your souls closer to me." But Bono wasn't done yet. He was biding his time.

Marc gripped the neck of his guitar and squared up with the Devil. Marc was scared, nervous. He remembered reading something about telling yourself you're excited when you're feeling anxious and nervous. That those feelings present themselves similarly, it was just a matter of framing. Marc told himself he was excited. Really excited to free his soul from the Devil and eternal damnation. His friends' souls too. Bollocks, his best friend since forever. Tanner, who turned out to be all right after all. Maybelline, his girlfriend? Shit, Marc, he told himself. Focus. Focus. Still, he was nervous as hell. He reminded himself that even Freddie Mercury admitted to nerves before going on. It's healthy. A nice healthy excitement. Yeah.

Marc eyed the stage waiting for his opponent to show up. His face must've betrayed his thoughts and telegraphed *well?* The Devil smirked and reached over to the wall of instruments and pulled down a violin. A black violin? No, it was blood maroon and ancient. The body rubbed ruby red at the shoulders and heel—the upper and lower bout. The scroll of the instrument seemed to wriggle. Serpents' heads moving the tuning pegs.

"He's going to 432," Tanner called out. Marc was a step ahead and already plucking his A string and tuning down to match the Devil's pitch.

"What's that mean?" Bollocks asked Tanner.

"Hertz," Tanner said quickly. "440 is concert pitch. 432 is supposedly in tune with the golden ratio—with nature and the universe."

"You know that's bullshit," Marc said to the Devil while adjusting the rest of his guitar's tuning to match.

"I prefer it anyway."

"You going down to Georgia with…" And before Marc could finish his sentence, the Devil ran 2 bars of "Toxic" by Britney Spears. A jolt shot through Marc, but he was already in position and countered with a variation on the theme, pounding out an imitation of the bass movement with his palm while running the guitar riff from the chorus and then creating a screeching violin effect with the whammy bar. A thick and shimmery substance flared off Marc's fretboard and the Devil recoiled ever so slightly. Bollocks, Tanner, and Maybelline cheered.

Bollocks called out, "You better work, bitch. That's my boy!"

The Devil smirked. "Just warming up."

The Devil riffed off some Paganini, Vivaldi, Charlie Parker.

Marc's early training with Old Man Coval came back to him. The unending hours spent sight reading scales, etudes, and increasingly demanding repertoire revealed itself just under his fingertips and pick—Marc switched to hybrid picking, using his pick and fingers of his right hand to add harmonies and complexity to the riffs and passages the Devil threw at him. A piece of cake.

The lights on the stage were hot and bright. Marc began to sweat. Nothing new for a performance. It made him feel loose and ready for whatever was next.

"Not bad," the Devil said. "Let's turn it up a notch."

The Devil played something that sounded like Stéphane Grappelli powered by lightning and battlefields. Marc comped for him chunking out the chords on the beat and then took over the lick, stole it from under the Devil's bow and fingers, slender as eels. He invoked all that he could of Stéphane's band partner, Django Reinhardt—a guitar virtuoso and the father of a wholly new and unique style of jazz. Mark aped the Devil's explosive version of "Sweet Georgia Brown" and turned it into a ballad, really leaning into the bends, double-stops, and sustaining the notes. Bringing the melody onto his playing field. Keith Richards' voice echoed in his ears *come on, kid. It's never how many or fast the notes are. You know that.*

Marc used to watch footage of Stevie Ray Vaughan playing with Albert King. Stevie, one of the greats, no doubt about it, was riffing all over the place, just fucking killing it, and then Albert King took up residence on one note, bent that fucker and let it sing and it was better than anything that Stevie could have done. Marc did just that. The Devil was knocked over, but not down.

Marc seized the opportunity. He could end this right now. He ripped off another lick. And then another. The Devil deflected again and again, an animal backed into a corner baring its teeth. His form began to alter—horns, hooves, hatred incarnate. He sprouted fangs and coarse hair, looking like a fucked up half human, half prickly javelina clinging to a violin. The Devil screamed—a howl—and stood, outraged, regained his human form and played a frightening line full of rancor that sent Marc soaring backwards and off the stage. Bollocks, Tanner, and Maybelline rushed forward to hold him up and keep him from landing on the ground.

"I can't battle for you, but I can carry you, Mr. Marco," Bollocks said, giving Marc a final push up onto the stage. "Fuck this motherfucker up."

Tanner clapped and cheered for Marc. "He needs our support," he said to Bollocks and Maybelline. "That's what we can give him— adoration. It's what the Devil doesn't have."

The Devil rolled his shoulders as he returned to his human form. He ran his tongue over his teeth and adjusted the violin under his chin. He began Bach's famous Chaconne, screeching out the impossible chords on the violin—he didn't play the ghost notes, but rather bowed all the triads and four note chords, his bow curved by some broken supernatural law fitting all four strings under the hairs of his bow at the same time. The stage shook, and Marc was knocked unsteady. Almost fell. He gripped his pick and strummed out a raucous D minor chord and then stole the melody from the Devil and turned it into an Amy Winehouse number.

"You went back to Bach," Marc said as he worked the bassline with the pick between his thumb and index finger, and comped the harmony and melody above with his middle and third finger of his right hand. He held a chord with his left hand, let it ring out, reached over with his right and detuned the last string from E to D, gave the chord another strum, all six strings this time, and then pulled away and wrangled out a cutting melody, embellishing the hell out of Winehouse's vocal line while the D note droned and resonated. He turned toward the amp and caught the feedback like a sail finding the wind. He manipulated the noise into a controlled frequency that sent a ping of electricity across the stage and zapped the Devil right in the dick. Marc smirked, "I went 'Back to Black.'" The Devil fell to one knee.

Bollocks threw his fist in the air. "Fuck yeah, man." Maybelline hooted and covered her mouth with her hands, making a cone to amplify her voice. "Get him." Marc looked down to them just as Tanner yelled, "Watch out."

The Devil collapsed into a snake and slinked across the stage holding the violin in its mouth. The snake wrapped itself around Marc and the top half of the serpent turned back into a man. Marc's arms were pinned as the besuited bad version of a Medusa brought the violin back up under his chin.

"Foul! Foul!" Bollocks yelled and hit his hands against the stage like a boxing coach in the corner. The upper half of the Devil hissed at him and shot its tail out like a scorpion and knocked Bollocks backwards on to the ground. Maybelline and Tanner picked him up, each on either side gripping under his arms.

"Whip crack went his whippy tail," Bollocks muttered to himself and rubbed his chest. "Come on, Marc," he yelled. Maybelline and Tanner joined the chorus of encouragement. Marc felt a surge roll through his body. He managed to reach his right hand to his guitar and flicked his wrist to create a percussive groove against the muted strings. It was a simple rhythm. His friends picked up the cue. *Stomp, stomp, clap. Stomp, stomp, clap.* The Devil's grip lessened, and Marc managed to riff off the solo which caused the Devil's serpent form to uncoil and shoot away as if Marc's body was acid. But the Devil was not done, and Marc was not free.

The Devil doubled back before Marc could segue into another counterattack and began playing a trill heavy piece that sounded incredibly close to Tartini's "Devil Trill" sonata—a piece that Tartini wrote after the Devil visited him in a dream. The Devil grew larger and hovered over Marc, his shadow enshrouding him in darkness. All the joy left his body—the seeds of anything that could be happiness were shriveling. He fell to one knee. The pick left his hand and bounced across the stage. His eyes searched for it frantically, panic seizing his brain. He reached for the fretboard but the Devil lunged and shot off another string of notes, each somehow more menacing than the last. Marc winced.

"The fucking pick! I can't beat him without it."

"You can do it, Marc," Maybelline yelled. "You don't need any of that stuff."

Tanner started clapping and hooting. The Devil glanced sideways at the trio but did not let up.

"We have to cheer for him," Tanner reiterated. "Believe in him! We have to believe in him."

"Fuck him up, Tinkerbell!" Bollocks added.

The three of them began screaming encouragement for Marc. It wasn't enough. Maybelline turned to Bono, who was in a meditative state. Eyes closed. "Help us," she said and grabbed his arm. Bono's chest rose and fell, rose and fell. He raised both hands, palms up. A swirl of electricity cycloned around the quartet. It bloomed and spread, expanded and broadened across the whole room. Lights of every sort formed—backlighting, front lighting, lasers. Massive columns of speakers like monoliths burst through the ground. The cheering of Tanner and Bollocks doubled and tripled. Maybelline joined and the crowd cheer quadrupled, octupled, sexdecupled, and grew exponentially over numberless, oncoming intervals. There were hundreds and then thousands, and then hundreds of thousands of clones. A sea of Tanners, Bollocks, and Maybellines stretched beyond what the eye could see, rising up and cresting over—a universe sized stadium filled with Marc's friends buoyed him while booing the Devil.

The Devil hissed violence and scorn at the crowd—the screeching of a wounded banshee. His face and form changed and morphed and twisted. A perversion of many hideous and forgotten icons and idols. Broken horns and fangs. Claws shriveled. Eyes raining blood. There was terror and fear. His grip loosened and Marc stood and wrapped his left hand around the neck of his guitar and dug another pick out of his pocket. He played the opening line of "Tribute" and stepped on a loop pedal that he hadn't realized was there—he thought it and it showed up. He riffed over the groove he played. The Devil was stunned and deafened. The audience roared and the Devil shot fire out of his formless mouth into the crowd. Bono was glowing, hovering like the Buddha—the fire deflected back at the shapeless demon on the stage.

Marc killed the loop and reached for the synth he knew would be there. He held a diminished fifth—a tritone, the Devil's interval—in his right hand. The Devil's face came back and Marc resolved the interval creating a perfect harmony. The Devil evaporated, but wasn't gone. A thick mist hovered over the stage as if they were in a gooey cloud. The audience of friends cheered—it was thunder and pandemonium. Marc began playing "Hallelujah." He sang the verse. The Devil shrieked—beaten, defeated, irritated. Marc sang on. *The minor fall and the major lift…* The Devil regained human form, naked, lying in a fetal position. *The baffled King composing Hallelujah.* The Devil shivered and bellowed. A banshee dying in the wind. Marc sang the chorus. The audience of friends joined, an endless troupe of *Hallelujah*. Marc stood taller, closed his eyes, and sang into the microphone, his voice resonating endlessly through the realm. He began Leonard Cohen's verses. One of the many Cohen wrote that nobody performs.

I did my best, it wasn't much / I couldn't feel, so I tried to touch / I've told the truth, I didn't come to fool you / And even though it all went wrong / I'll stand before the Lord of Song / With nothing on my tongue but Hallelujah…

"Please," the Devil said. "Stop. Stop."

Millions of voices sang the chorus. Marc approached the Devil.

"Please," the Devil said. "No more. I hate it so much…" he whimpered.

Marc unslung his guitar. He knelt down. "It's over."

The Devil nodded. His form was shrinking. Growing wings. He cried to himself, "I hate it. I hate it. I hate it."

"It's over," Marc said, affirmed once more.

"Yes, it's over," the Devil said. "Make it stop."

Marc stood and raised his hand to the audience. The singing faded away. A wave rushed through Marc and over the room like the first drop on a rollercoaster leveling out. Marc looked out to Maybelline, Bollocks, and Tanner. He wasn't alone. Their souls were saved. Somewhere Keith Richards was free. Marc's heart was full—he was glowing. He realized this feeling was comfort. A sense of home. Family.

The room returned to its normal form—a bar filled with dusty bottles and hourglasses. Walls askew and littered with windows and mirrors. The Devil vanished and another sensation rolled through the room like pressure returning. Legba stood up from his chair and put his pipe in his mouth. He clapped his hands a few times and approached Marc who was hopping off the stage. Legba took a contract out of his pocket and ripped it in half and then again and again.

"You did good, kid," he said to Marc and smiled. He reached across the stage with his cane and tapped it one the floor. "You dropped this."

Marc looked over and saw the pick he dropped—the one Martha gave him from Spruce's. The one he got from Johnny Newman. Marc picked up the small wooden plectrum and held it in his open palm.

"I thought these were all supposed to disappear? Back into your lair thing?"

"They did," Legba said. "This one was never magical." He tipped his hat to the group. "I'll see you around," he said to Bono. He winked at Tanner and then walked away, vanishing behind the bar.

Maybelline went to Marc. "You know," she said. "This has been a helluva first couple of dates."

"Kiss her, you fool," Bollocks said. But he didn't need to. They were already in each other's arms and making everyone uncomfortable.

"So, Bono," Bollocks said. "How do we get out of here?"

"How do you want to get out of here?"

Bollocks looked to Tanner, his eyes growing wide with excitement. Tanner nodded and smiled. "Giant eagles," they both said in unison.

Maybelline and Marc disengaged from their embrace. "Uh, we'll take the stairs," Maybelline said.

"I'll join you," Bono said. Light poured in the room as the ceiling cracked open showing sunlight and sky. A distant caw echoed.

67. BACKSTAGE AT A VENUE IN AUSTIN AND THE "WHERE ARE THEY NOW" SEGMENT BEFORE THE CREDITS BUT BEFORE THE STORY IS OVER

"You ready?" the stage manager asked Brad Johnson.

"Fuck yeah," Brad said.

"Excellent. The house is full. All the people you invited are here."

Brad rolled his shoulders and jumped in place a couple of times.

His backup band was walking on the stage. He could hear the audience applauding. He went to his guitar and opened the case. It was empty.

Brad used one of his back-up band member's guitars. The show went well. Not amazing. The duet with Bono was the big crowd pleaser, and it was a cover song. That stung. Brad's performance was like a star athlete's after they've passed their prime but could still pull out a little razzle dazzle from time to time, an echo of the greatness that had been theirs, once. Starting a career on a perceived downhill slope was not how Brad wanted to do it. He would be all right, though. He'd go on tour and open for Eddie Vedder. He'd get a modest following. A cult following they'd call it. A "singer-songwriter's singer-songwriter" is what they'd call him—he'd know what that meant: not popular. He'd hold up his end of the bargain and help Bono's solo record get airplay, street cred. The sonuvabitch actually won the fucking Grammy for the same category he was nominated.

But nothing could take away the deal he had with the Devil. After Bono's solo album was a success, the Devil came calling. The contract absolved. But Brad wanted more—he signed back on.

The fact that he had unwittingly had one of the Fated Four was never part of the deal. Just pure coincidence. The guitar acted as a lightning rod, pulling the Devil to him. Very few people who sell their souls ever have one of the instruments. But Brad was bitter. He ranted and rampaged after that gig in Austin. His guitar went missing. The security footage proved useless—no one in, no one out with the guitar. *Did you leave it at the studio? Was it unattended in the car? During load-in?* A thousand plausible and possible explanations that drove him insane. He put it in the case. Clasped it secure. Never left it out of his sight or under his hand. He wasn't sure where to place the blame and it ate at him.

He played on with a bitterness in his heart. He had touched glory, perfection, nirvana— whatever you want to call it—for an incredibly short moment and he'd chase it for the rest of his career. Instead of the harem of starlets he had envisioned, he ended up being a second rate pimp for the Devil, an addict bringing souls for another boost, another hit, another tour, one more, one more, one more...

68. THE PARKING LOT OF THE PIGGLY WIGGLY IN ROSEDALE

Marc, Bollocks, Maybelline, Tanner, Bono, and Legba stood around the van. Legba's car was idling.

"Well," Bollocks said, his Mohawk pushed back, windswept, "that was a lot of fun."

Tanner was still catching his breath. "I've never been so scared and thrilled at the same time."

"And you weren't even the one's battling the Devil for your souls," Marc said.

Bollocks and Tanner looked at each other. "Oh," Bollocks said. "Yeah. That happened too."

They all laughed.

"You're an ass," Maybelline said. She turned to Bono and Legba. "So, what next?"

"I've got some appointments," Legba said. He looked at the group. He smiled. And fuck if it wasn't genuine. "You did good. This has been fun." He tipped his hat and put his pipe in his mouth. Tanner cleared his throat. Legba pulled long and hard on his pipe. Blew out the smoke in a great pillowy billow. "You know how to find me."

"You said you needed to talk to me?" Tanner said.

"You," Legba said slowly, "have time." He looked at Marc, Maybelline, and Bollocks. "You all have time." Then to Bono, "I'll reach out soon."

He opened the car door and got in. He reached into the glove box and took out a piece of paper. "Son," he said to Bollocks. "Come here." He held out the paper to Bollocks.

"Whenever you get the chance," Legba said.

Bollocks took the paper. "Eight hundred dollars? After all we've been through?"

Legba put his car into gear. He laughed and pulled off, dust and dirt kicking up behind him.

"I don't think we'll be making that Austin gig tonight," Marc said.

"Always got that eye on the ball," Bollocks said.

"Yeah," Maybelline said, "it's not like you just defeated the Devil five minutes ago."

Bono was thumbing away on his phone. "Lads," he said. "Turns out I've got a gig in Austin as well." He smiled. "I hate to make you play déjà vu," he said to Maybelline, "but I think it's back to the airfield for us. Me jet will be there in a half hour. What do you say lads?"

"I will follow," Bollocks said.

***

Bollocks and Tanner were in the back of the jet playing video games. Turns out Bono was a huge gamer and a massive fan of strong, fast Wi-Fi. Maybelline, Marc, and Bono were sitting around a small table having a tea.

"Seems those two are best friends now," Maybelline said to Marc.

Marc laughed. "An unlikely duo."

She took Marc's hand and gave it a squeeze.

"Mr. Bono," Marc said.

"Just Bono, or Paul if you'd like, is fine," Bono said.

"Bono." Marc damn near giggled. "I don't how to thank you. Or even begin to repay you."

"Aye, Marc. Put those thoughts out of your mind. We're all put here to help each other. I truly believe that."

"But your dad…"

"Spiritually, I suppose. I'm still sorting that out, but I'm closer than ever."

"But, I feel like I should…"

"Just say 'thank you,'" Maybelline said. "Trust me. It's useless." She laughed.

"Listen to her," Bono said.

"Thank you," Marc said. He reached across and shook Bono's hand. "Seriously. Thank you."

Bono smiled. "Maybelline told me about your band."

"Yeah?"

"You have a sound. Could use a little more miles, but you two have something."

"That means a lot coming from you."

"I'd like to help if you're willing to accept."

"No offense, Mr. I mean, Bono. I know you're not the Devil, but you're not not either."

Bono laughed. "I understand your apprehension, but I'm trying to get meself untangled the same as you were. I've got no otherworldly designs for souls. Only one I'm concerned with in the afterlife is me own."

Marc looked to Maybelline. She nodded.

"Ok. What do you have in mind?"

"I can't make any promises until some phone calls are made, but we're playing a few dates with the Stones this fall. Could use an opener." He looked to Maybelline. "Be real neat if you covered it."

"I'll run it by my editor."

"Aye."

She looked at Bono, serious, concerned. "What's next for you?"

"Legba and I have some work to do. He's bored. Likes gifts. I've got plenty to do and give and would prefer to have me soul back. It's a good match. The thread *is* unraveling. Just gotta find a way to accelerate that before long. I'm not getting any younger."

"Let us know if we can help," Marc said.

"That's very kind of you. But I think you've had your fair share of dealings." Bono paused. "Though, that witch back there could be useful. I might have to get his number."

The captain came over of the intercom. *We'll be approaching Austin momentarily. Cabin crew and passengers, please take your seats and prepare for landing. As always, thank you for choosing Bono's private jet.*

69. 3 MONTHS LATER—BACKSTAGE AT THE 3ARENA IN DUBLIN: WHO'S THAT FUNKY DUDE?

I couldn't believe the string of luck we'd had after defeating the Devil and playing that gig in Austin. Radio stations across the country picked up our EP and put it in heavy rotation. We enlisted Tanner on bass for our live show. It was tough keeping up with Maybelline on this endless tour—our own, opening for bigger acts, and now this, these dates with U2 and The Rolling Stones. But there was no animosity between us. Rolling Stone had her writing around the clock. We were both following our dreams and we couldn't be upset with each other for that even if we didn't see each other in person very often.

"You ready, or do you need to poop again?" Bollocks said to me poking his head out of the bathroom of the biggest dressing room we'd been in to date.

"I'm good on the bathroom," I said. "Other than being on the verge of a panic attack, I've never felt better." This was the first string of dates we'd play over here. Bono was cool as shit and really took us under his wing making sure we didn't get fucked over. He set us up with his manager. It was all too surreal—happening so fast. We still had to prove ourselves, but the buzz and touring were shaping us.

Tanner walked into the dressing room. "Yo, I just saw Mick Jagger. Or at least I think I did."

Bollocks stepped into the room. I felt him looking at me. We hadn't mentioned Keith Richards since Rosedale. We avoided the topic, willfully it seemed. A minefield we were uncertain of how to navigate. I had made peace that I'd never see him again—that the Keith I knew was free. Happy.

"Do you think we'll meet them?" Tanner said, edging around the topic.

I didn't say anything.

"Let's get ready for the gig, yeah?" Bollocks said. He pulled out the setlist from his pocket. "You good for the key change in 'Golden Child' and your tuning time during my super-mini-mind-blowing drum solo?"

"Oh, yeah. Totally," Tanner said, picking up the cue. "Locked and loaded, boss."

A stagehand came in the room. "You're on in five." She nodded her head indicating that we should follow her. I picked up my guitar—a custom Telecaster Shitblaster I had DiPinto guitars make me. Brand new. I wasn't taking any chances with vintage gear. We walked down the long corridor. Bollocks twirled his drumsticks and did tuck jumps at intervals bringing his knees to his chest. "I'm so fucking pumped," he said. Bono turned the corner. He was holding a package in one hand.

"Lads," he boomed. "Glad I caught you." He looked to Tanner and held up the package. "I knew I could count on you."

Tanner smiled. "It was nothing."

"What's up?" I asked Bono.

"About 13,000 screaming fans," he said and laughed.

"Is that supposed to calm us down?" Bollocks said.

"Don't worry," Bono said. "Most of them are here for the Stones."

"Thanks," I said. "That makes me feel so much better."

"I jest, I jest. Half of 'em are for us."

"You're really not helping."

"You'll be grand. I know it. The monitors are your friends. Don't stray and don't be too afraid to ask for more or less of something up there."

"Fuck," Bollocks said. "I forgot to give the sound guy twenty bucks."

"I knew there was a reason I liked you," Bono said. "That's that working class grit and refinement right there. But no worries. The sound engineers are top notch here. You'll be grand," he reiterated. "But, the pep talk isn't why I wanted to see you. I wanted to introduce you to someone."

Cigarettes, whiskey, chains. A wave of emotion washed over me, under me. The floor fell out. Bollocks put his hand on my shoulder. Keith Richards turned the corner. The two rock stars embraced. Bono handed him the package. "I picked this up for you back in the States." He winked. "I took a swig and it seems to be working."

Keith held the package. Appraised it. "Mick'll like this. It'll pair nicely with my shepherd's pie later on."

"Keith," Bono said and looked to me. "Marc. Marc, Keith."

"This the kid everyone says plays like me but better?" Keith Richards said and laughed.

"Hey," Bono said to Bollocks and Tanner. "Let's leave them for a few."

Bollocks and Tanner shook Keith's hand and mumbled their glee in meeting him.

Keith looked at me. I looked right back. "Well," he said. "Let's have it."

"Sir?" I managed.

He laughed. "The guitar. I've been coveting it since I saw it."

I handed the guitar to him. He ran off a few licks. "She'll do. She'll do all right, won't she?" He handed it back to me. Stared at me. "Hmm. There's something familiar about you."

I looked away. He didn't remember me. I wasn't sure if that was a good or bad thing. I couldn't help feeling let down. But what did I want? What did I expect?

"Maybe I just see myself in you a little," he said. "Hopefully not too much." He laughed. "What do you say you join us for a jam?"

My eyes grew three sizes too big.

"One bluesman to another."

"That would be the honor of a lifetime," I said.

He put his arm around me and walked me the last twenty yards to the wings of the stage. "Give 'em hell, kid," he said and winked. "I'll be right here learning your tricks."

He gripped my shoulder and then gave me an encouraging push on to the stage where Bollocks and Tanner were already taking their place. I walked out, the audience roared, deafening. I looked back for a second to Keith—I felt a letting go and a grounding. Something new. I can't explain it. There was a happiness that was too happy it felt like sadness. I saw him take a bottle out of the package and inspect it. It looked old. Had I seen it before? Then darkness. The roar of the audience.

The house system's music was quieting. Bollocks yelled out to me and shifted in his stool, doing a little dance. "Time to shake some booties and make some sweet love tonight." Tanner and I formed a triangle around him—our gear and his kit set up in front of U2s and the Stones'. "Boys," he said. "I think it's time we got back to the good life."

"That's not how it…" Tanner said.

"Shh," Bollocks said and reached over and put his sticks across Tanner's mouth. The house system went silent. The lights clanked on. The audience appeared out of blackness, no longer a formless body. "It's time we got back," he said again and clicked four. I turned around. I caught a glimpse of Keith. He nodded. He was smiling. And we were off.

ACKNOWLEDGEMENTS

First off, YOU! Slap your name right here: ____. Thank you for trusting me with your time. If you regret it, kindly remember no one made you read it. You only have yourself to blame. If this is your second time around the ol' DiFranco-verse, a heartfelt and humble double thanks. Long live Drix!

An immeasurable well of gratitude goes to Michelle Webber who read an early draft of this and Zorro'd her way across each page with a red pen. This novel is blisteringly slick because of her. Any faults are my own.

Thanks to: Evan Miller, who read this in serial via email; Early readers: Dave Housley, Kevin Smythe, John Penn, William Newman; Everyone at Volo Coffeehouse who continue to let me live the cliché, notably Baristas of Cortados Past: Danielle Polletti, Amanda Burrs, and Kelly Monahan; Frances Daulerio, Nick Mehalick, Matt Boyarsky, Beau Kegler, Lacey Cat and Milo-buddy (rip), Annabel my nugget, Keith Richards and The Rolling Stones. Hail Satan.

Finally, special thanks to everyone at Unsolicited Press for believing in my work. And most importantly, my wife Ellie Miller for giving me the space, time, and support to create.

No thanks to: Big Dairy, the short lives of pets, and people who pronounce it "gif."

LAND AND HISTORY ACKNOWLEDGMENT

This book borrows from African American history, and to a lesser degree, Native American lore. I encourage everyone to acknowledge and make retributions in the awareness that we, as Americans, are living on stolen land that was then built upon the backs of slave labor. The music that we call American comes from *their* history—from the fields, to the churches, to the juke joints, to the countless, nameless session musicians and performers who were instrumental in developing an American sound and continue to do so still. I implore you to go beyond acknowledgment: donate, volunteer, provide space to the best of your ability and in ways that make sense for your community. In this effort, I'll be there with you.

ABOUT THE AUTHOR

Daniel DiFranco is a writer/musician/teacher from Philadelphia. He is the author of the novel Panic Years (Tailwinds Press, 2018). His short stories can be found in Smokelong Quarterly, Monkeybicycle, Fractured Lit, and others. Full list of publications and miscellany can be found at danieldifranco.com.

ABOUT THE PRESS

Unsolicited Press is based out of Portland, Oregon and focuses on the works of the unsung and underrepresented. As a womxn-owned, all-volunteer small publisher that doesn't worry about profits as much as championing exceptional literature, we have the privilege of partnering with authors skirting the fringes of the lit world. We've worked with emerging and award-winning authors such as Shann Ray, Amy Shimshon-Santo, Brook Bhagat, Kris Amos, and John W. Bateman.

Learn more at unsolicitedpress.com. Find us on twitter and instagram.

9 781963 115307